A
Country
Escape

Katie Fforde

A
Country
Escape

CENTURY

1 3 5 7 9 10 8 6 4 2

Century
20 Vauxhall Bridge Road
London SW1V 2SA

Century is part of the Penguin Random House group of companies
whose addresses can be found at global.penguinrandomhouse.com.

Penguin
Random House
UK

First published by Century in 2018

www.penguin.co.uk

A CIP catalogue record for this book is available
from the British Library.

Hardback ISBN 9781780890890

Trade paperback ISBN 9781780890906

Typeset in India by Integra Software Services Pvt. Ltd, Pondicherry

Printed and bound in Australia by Griffin Press

penguin.com.au
penguin.co.nz

Penguin Random House is committed to a sustainable future
for our business, our readers and our planet. This book is made
from Forest Stewardship Council® certified paper.

For Georgina Hawtrey-Woore
3 December 1966 – 27 February 2017

Much loved and missed friend and editor.
It seems wrong to write a book you won't read,
but I did run the idea past you.

Acknowledgements

Ideas for books often come from more than one place, but the notion for this book came from the wonderful Jonathan Crump, farmer, cheese maker and inspiration to many. He suggested to my daughter (who had gone to his farm to borrow a ram) that I should write about farming and she reported back.

I liked the idea but didn't completely latch onto it until I came upon a wonderful television programme called *This Farming Year*. Following the farmers go through the seasons, seeing how much they loved their animals and their land, was inspiring and humbling. While no writer ever wants to make mistakes, the thing I want to get right most is this passion. They work such long hours and days, for very little financial gain, for the love of their farms.

I was inspired to write about cheese many years ago, when I was writing another book and came across Liz Godsell of Godsells Cheese. I knew then that one day I would have to write a book entirely about cheese rather than it just have a walk-on part. I don't think I thanked her enough at the time!

I have also known Ken Stevens of Hania Cheeses from when I worked in Mother Nature, whole food shop and café, a very long time ago. He has been known as Ken the Cheese locally for ever and he knows more about cheese than anyone.

And while he remained elusive and never answered emails, Owen Bailey of Neal's Yard Cheese is owed a thank you. He and I talked a lot about cheese when he lived on our barge in London and he was new to Neal's Yard. That was also a long time ago.

Massive gratitude is owed to my wonderful team at Penguin Random House. Starting with Selina Walker and Cassandra Di Bello for editorial input; Francesca Russell for the wonderful publicity she generates; thank you also to the sales team, including Aslan Byrne, Claire Simmonds, Laura Garrod, Sasha Cox, Natasha Photiou and Kelly Webster; to the entire marketing team, with a special thank you to Celeste Ward-Best; thank you to Jacqueline Bissett and Viki Ottowell, who designed this glorious cover; and thank you to the production team, Linda Hodgson and Helen Wynn-Smith, for ensuring my books make it out into the world on time!

As ever, and may it be for ever, thanks are due to my wonderful copy-editor Richenda Todd who, by her huge efforts, manages to prevent me making a complete fool of myself.

Also always at my side being a Rottweiler in polite, Labrador clothing, is the wonderful Bill Hamilton of A. M. Heath. I would be lost without you – almost literally.

Chapter One

The farm gate clanged shut behind her as Fran steered her little car up the steep track. Now she and Issi had found Hill Top Farm for certain – the name was written (not very clearly) on the post box – she felt a mixture of excitement and nervousness. This was either going to be a wonderful adventure or a humiliating mistake. She decided not to mention her feelings to her best friend. Issi probably guessed how she felt already.

'I always wanted to be a farmer when I was a little girl,' Fran said instead.

Issi, who'd just got back in the car having helped deal with the gate, seemed surprised. 'Really? I never knew that and we've been friends for years. I thought you'd always wanted to run your own restaurant.'

'That came later. I'd forgotten myself,' said Fran, 'but Mum reminded me at Christmas.'

'Do your parents think you're mad to do this?'

'Yup. But they're being supportive. My stepdad thinks I'll be back with them before the end of the month, but I'm in it for the long haul.' She paused. 'Which may only be a year, if I don't make it.'

'Come on,' said Issi, 'let's go and find this farmhouse you might inherit.'

'It's not just the farmhouse, remember? It's the whole darn farm.'

Fran rounded a steep corner and tried to push her nerves to the back of her mind. Now she was finally here she realised no sane person would leave their comfortable life in London and move to a farm in Gloucestershire that they might not even inherit. No *sane* person, obviously, but maybe someone like her whose normal life had stalled rather, and who relished a challenge.

A couple of minutes later, they arrived, having bumped their way to the top avoiding as many potholes as they could. 'I'm not sure a Ka is the right vehicle for this track,' Issi said.

Ignoring her friend, Fran got out of the car. 'But look at the view!'

The farmhouse was on a plateau at the top of a hill that overlooked hills and wooded valleys. Beyond them lay the Severn, a silver snake in the far distance, and beyond the river was Wales.

'I think I remember this landscape!' Fran went on. 'We came here once when I was a little girl. I'd

2

forgotten all about it until we were discussing the farm over Christmas, and Mum reminded me. Mum said we'd all been here when Dad was alive, but I must have been tiny – after all I was only five when he died. But this feels faintly familiar.'

'It is stunning,' Issi agreed.

'Come on,' said Fran, 'let's look at the house while it's still light. It'll be dark by about four, so we'll need to turn the leccy on. I've got a torch.' She paused. 'January's probably not a good time to move on to a farm.'

Issi laughed. 'It is what it is. Let's get in.'

After failing to open the front door, they went round the back. 'I don't think people use front doors in the country,' said Fran as they made their way round the building. 'Here we are.' She fitted the key into the lock and turned. Seconds later they were in.

'Wow! It is dark,' said Issi.

'Hang on. I think I've found the fuse box. I'll just get my torch out. There! We have light!'

They were in a fairly big farmhouse kitchen. The friends looked around in silence for a few seconds, taking it all in.

'An open fire!' said Issi excitedly. 'How lovely to have an open fire in a kitchen.'

'As long as it's not all I have to cook on,' agreed Fran, looking round. Although the central light was on, it wasn't very bright and created shadow-filled corners. 'Oh, look,' she went on, relieved. 'There's a Rayburn. Probably a prototype it's so ancient. I do hope it's not run on solid fuel.'

'But you're a chef. You can cook on anything!' said Issi, laughing at her friend.

'I'm fine with the cooking,' Fran agreed, 'but I have no experience of lighting fires. Oh phew, it seems to run on oil.'

'And look, there's an electric cooker as well. You're in culinary clover.' Issi seemed to find Fran's dismay over the cooking arrangements highly amusing.

'I'll be OK,' said Fran, more to herself than Issi. 'I'm here to farm, not to cook, after all. And I really like all the freestanding cupboards and things. And the sink has a lovely view of...' She lifted the net curtain and peered through the window. 'Ah, the farmyard. But it's lovely beyond that. Come on!' Suddenly she was more excited than dubious. 'Let's go and explore some more.'

The sitting room, which was at the front of the house, was a good size, and the windowsill was covered in pot plants. Some had died, but the geraniums seemed to have survived. There was a three-piece suite draped in crocheted blankets, and a profusion of tables and whatnots covered in photographs. Fran picked a photo up. 'A woman and a cow, or maybe a bull. There's a rosette. How sweet!'

Issi joined her. 'They all seem to be of cows or bulls. There's nothing to tell you anything about the old lady who owned them.'

'Except that she was really into cows,' said Fran, putting down the photo she was holding. 'Oh, look at the fireplace!'

'It's tiny. You'll need something else if you're going to warm this room up.'

'I know it's tiny, but look at the beam above it. I bet there's a wonderful original fireplace behind this little coal-burning thing. I long to take a sledgehammer to it.'

'I'd wait until you're sure you're staying put, but I understand what you mean,' said Issi, looking around her. 'It's not exactly shabby chic, but I do like it. This room could actually have been two or maybe even three rooms.' She looked up at the ceiling, which had large beams at intervals.

'It's "old-lady chic", that's what it is,' Fran decided. 'And I like it too. Although I wish I could investigate the fireplace. I bet there's something amazing behind all this thirties stuff.'

'An old bread oven or something to cook on? You said yourself, you're here to farm not to cook,' said Issi. 'If you thought you were going to miss cheffing, you should have stayed in London, cooking for the pub.'

'No,' said Fran determinedly. 'This time I'm going to work for myself and make my own decisions. But I suppose you're right, I can't knock the house around, not if I haven't actually inherited it yet.'

'So tomorrow you're seeing your aunt – cousin – what is she?'

'I can't remember exactly how we're related but she's some sort of connection to my read dad. I'm Amy's – I suppose I'd call her Aunt Amy – I'm the only relation she could trace. She's been running Hill Top on her own since her husband died. Now she's had to go into a care home she thought she should try and leave it to one of her relations. I think she got in touch with another one but, according to the solicitor, he never replied.'

'Which is why you're here.,' said Issi, who then paused. 'Shall we investigate the bedrooms? They may be damp and we've got to sleep in a couple of them tonight.'

'Thank you so much for coming with me,' said Fran as they made their way up the stairs. 'This would all be a bit daunting on my own.'

'I'm just sorry I can't stay longer. It's such an adventure!' Issi paused. 'Would you have preferred Alex to come with you?'

Fran shook her head. 'No way. One of the reasons we broke up was that he wasn't up for adventure. He seems very happy being an intern for his uncle in New York…Although going on the fact there are supposedly very few straight men in NYC I suspect he has another motive.' She sighed. 'No, I really don't miss him, apart from as a friend, sort of.'

Was she over Alex? Fran knew that Issi was still concerned about this, but she definitely was. He was a kind and lovely man but, when it came down to it, too safe and a bit dull. They'd broken up a few weeks ago after a couple of years together.

Fran knew they'd been going through the motions for a while but the catalyst had been this opportunity – challenge, even. If Alex could have hacked the countryside (unlikely) he couldn't cope with the uncertainty. A straightforward inheritance might have been different – but probably not. Fran, on the other hand, although terrified, was very excited by it all.

A few minutes later, Fran and Issi were making up beds, helping themselves to soft, old flannel sheets they found in the airing cupboard. Then they found hot-water bottles and filled them, although they agreed they didn't think the house was damp. Then it was time for supper.

'So,' said Issi when they'd eaten most of the moussaka that Fran had made and brought with her, and heated up in the electric oven. 'You're seeing Amy tomorrow?'

'Yup. After my meeting with the lawyer. He said in his letter he's arranged for me to have a bit of money to run things with but I don't expect it's very much.' She sighed. 'It is quite daunting when I think about it. I know nothing about farming – and yet here I am. I could have said no when I first heard from Amy's solicitor but...' She paused. 'I wanted to challenge myself.'

'See if you can run the farm for a year and make it pay?'

Fran nodded. 'Of course I don't have to look after the cows myself. There's a herdsman. Amy would never let her precious cows be looked after by an ignoramus, which is what I am as far as farming is concerned.'

'And cows are quite big, aren't they?' said Issi.

'Are you afraid of cows?'

'More to the point, are you?'

Fran swallowed. 'I really hope not but actually – I think I am!'

Issi laughed. 'Let's finish the wine and then get an early night. You have to be up with the lark tomorrow. Better set your alarm for six. Get used to your new life.'

Although Fran knew Issi was joking, she also knew what she said was true. As for being afraid of cows, she'd just have to find out when she met them.

The next morning they were standing in the kitchen, shrouded in layers of woollen jumpers and clutching steaming mugs of tea. Fran's long bob had not been straightened that morning, and her blue-grey eyes had no trace of make-up. Nor were her freckles toned down with make up. She felt she looked like a scruffy ten-year-old but had more important things to think about than her appearance. Issi was looking pretty natural as well.

'It's the lawyer first? Then your Aunt Amy.'

Fran nodded. 'I'm not sure how long it will all take. Will you be OK here on your own?'

Issi nodded. 'I'm going to sort out the pot plants, and maybe do a bit of exploring. I might even move the furniture around a bit and clear out the odd cupboard. Would you mind?'

'Not at all. I'm so grateful you're here. I wouldn't grudge you a bit of entertainment. In fact I think you're going to have a better time than I am.'

'In other words, Mrs Flowers is a distant cousin, a couple of times removed.'

To Fran's huge relief, Mr Addison, the solicitor, a kind, tired man in his fifties, finally summed up the complex relationship that involved different generations and marriages.

'What do you think I should call her when we meet?' asked Fran, who was getting nervous at the thought of meeting a woman who, although very elderly now, had apparently been formidable in her time.

'She'll let you know, don't you worry about that,' said Mr Addison. 'Now let's go through the finances a bit. Mrs Flowers has arranged six months of care in her home. She has set up an account with a thousand pounds in it for your use. There is a bit more money but I'd honestly prefer you didn't encroach on it. Although Mrs Flowers is very well looked after and frail, she may need more than six months' care, which is going to be expensive.'

'But in an emergency?'

'You can apply to me.'

'And what about wages for the herdsman, and other people who work for her?'

'There are a couple of relief milkers employed as and when they're needed, and their wages are all arranged too. For six months.'

'But she wants me to stay for a year? What happens after the first six months? In July?'

He shrugged. 'I think she hopes the farm will be earning money by then.'

Fran noted his careful choice of words. 'You mean, it's not making money at the moment?'

Mr Addison sighed. 'Mrs Flowers has been slowing down for a while. Things have been let slip.'

'So I'm not taking on a going concern. Things are in a bad way?'

'I wouldn't say a bad way; just not a desperately profitable way.'

When she'd first heard about it Fran had thought it was a romantic, dramatic idea to have been brought in to look after the family farm, but she was no longer quite so sure.

'Is that you being tactful?' said Fran. 'You would tell me the truth, wouldn't you?'

Mr Addison's expression closed down. 'I have to act in my client's best interest. I'm sure you're going to do a good job.' He stood up. Fran realised he'd explained everything to the best of his ability but he obviously felt he could do no more.

'What happens if it turns out I'm afraid of cows?'

He shook his head and smiled. He obviously thought Fran was making a joke. 'I'm sure we don't need to worry about that.'

*

When Fran arrived at the care home, she'd anticipated it taking her a while to explain why she had come. But no, everyone knew exactly who she was. And for the first time that day she wondered if she was dressed right. When she'd got up, after a night disturbed by an uncomfy mattress and strange noises, she'd just put on the clothes she'd worn the previous day, more concerned with getting down the drive, finding the solicitor and then the care home than how she looked. Now she wondered if leggings, boots and a tunic that revealed quite a lot of leg was acceptable.

Still, it was too late to worry about it now. She was following a care worker down a carpeted corridor, her boots scuffing against the pile.

The nurse stopped and opened a door. 'Mrs Flowers? It's your young relative.'

The room wasn't huge but it was bright and sunny. There were pictures on the walls and the furniture would have fitted into the décor of the farmhouse. Fran went into the room, not sure what to say.

'Hello – Aunt – Cousin – Mrs Flowers…' She paused. The old lady was sitting on a chair, looking very neat and upright.

'Better make it "Amy", dear,' she said crisply. 'Otherwise I might die before you decide what my name is. And sit down, do.'

Fran sat and inspected her companion. Her eyes were bright and blue and shone out from a pink, slightly weathered complexion. Her thin grey hair was twisted into a knot on top of her head. She wore a long tweed skirt and a neatly ironed white blouse with a lace collar. She seemed bright, cheerful and well cared for. She had obviously chosen her care home well.

'Hello, Amy, it's lovely to meet you finally,' Fran said, sensing it was important that she appeared confident, even if she was anything but. The meeting with the solicitor had turned a year learning about farming and a bit of an adventure into a huge under-taking loaded with responsibility and concern.

Amy nodded, possibly with approval. 'Well, dear, I'm very glad you came. I didn't want my farm to go to rack and ruin while I'm in here.'

'But you realise I don't know very much about farming, don't you?' Amy obviously wasn't the sort of person who appreciated 'how are you' conversations, so Fran got on with what was on her mind.

'Yes, and – please don't take offence – believe me, if there'd been anyone else I would never have got in touch with you. But we are related. I'd have preferred one of my husband's relations – it was his farm – but although I tracked one down, they never replied to my letter. So you're all I could find.' She paused. 'I was eighteen when I married and I lived on the farm ever since, until I came here.'

'Goodness.' Amy seemed to need to tell her story and Fran hoped she'd sounded encouraging.

Amy nodded and carried on. 'The farm had been in his family for many generations. We never had children and it was a great sadness to us both to think it would all end with us. My husband died twenty years ago and I've been on my own since then. I've been worrying about who to pass it on to all that time.'

Fran was touched. 'I can understand that.'

'It's the herd, you see. They're Dairy Shorthorns and quite rare. The cows on the farm now – and I've known them all personally – are related to the original herd. That's very unusual.' She gave a little smile. 'Cows can live to be quite old, you know, if they're looked after. If I don't leave the farm to someone who'll carry on with it, it'll be sold. The herd will go and all that unbroken pedigree will be lost. That would be a tragedy. So it's for the cows, the farm, that I tracked you down and now here you are.' Amy smiled as if this was a satisfactory conclusion.

'I do hope I don't let you down.'

Amy shook her head. 'You won't. I remember you as a little girl. You liked the cows. You liked their red and white colouring.' This had obviously stuck in her memory. 'It's the herd that's important,' she repeated. 'The bloodline. It must be kept going.'

Amy obviously felt extremely strongly about her cows, even given old people's tendency to repeat themselves.

'I see.' Fran offered a little prayer that she still liked cows herself.

'And you have Tig, my herdsman. I would never have left you my herd without someone to look after them. But you have to look after everything else – the office work, feed ordering, looking after the buildings: things like that – so he can look after the cows. I've paid him six months in advance so he won't leave.'

Fran wanted to ask why Amy hadn't just left all of her farm to Tig, but realised this too was to do with bloodlines. Tig was not related to Amy, and she was.

'And there's a bit of money to keep you going, but you have to run the farm for a year and then I'll decide whether you should inherit.' Amy's expression emphasised what a massive reward she thought this was. 'So you will try, won't you, Francesca?'

No one ever called Fran 'Francesca', not even her mother when she was cross. She realised she liked it. 'About the house—'

Amy interrupted her. 'I really don't care about the house. Do what you like with it. But don't let anything happen to the herd.'

Fran nodded, instantly thinking about the fireplace she could now investigate.

'Oh, and don't let that scoundrel who lives next door have anything to do with you. He's always wanted my farm and it's your job to make sure he doesn't get it! Vineyards, indeed!'

'Tell me—' Fran began.

But Amy had closed her eyes and had apparently gone to sleep.

'She does that,' explained the nurse who appeared in the doorway at that moment. 'Bright as a button one minute, fast asleep the next.'

'When is she likely to wake up again?' asked Fran, who felt she really should find out about the scoundrel-neighbour as soon as possible.

The nurse shook her head. 'Not for a while. You'd do better to come back tomorrow, or as soon as it's convenient.'

'OK,' said Fran. She got up from her seat. 'I'll come back. I haven't learnt nearly enough about things.' She went to the door, stopped and addressed the nurse. 'But – are you allowed to tell me? She's generally well, isn't she?'

'Oh yes. She's very good for her age. I suppose she's always led a healthy outdoor life. Never smoked, never drank alcohol.'

'And nothing's likely to happen to her within the next six months?'

'I can't see into the future, but she seems well enough at the moment – although with the elderly you can never really be sure.' She frowned slightly. 'She has got a weak heart but she's managing fine at the moment.'

'That's good enough for me.' Fran smiled. 'Thank you so much for looking after her. I'm looking forward to getting to know her better.'

The nurse returned the smile. 'She's a great favourite with us all here.'

By the time Fran got back to Hill Top Farm it was early evening and nearly dark, she was freezing cold and wanting to open the wine even though it was really only teatime. After her visits, she'd spent a little time investigating the town, then she had got lost trying to get home and so most of the day had melted away. She pulled up in front of the house and saw lights peeping out from behind the curtains, which made the house seem welcoming. As she collected her handbag from the back seat of the car she realised how bright the stars were here, miles away from any light pollution.

Minutes later, Fran was in the sitting room, looking around it. The room, which had been cluttered and a bit claustrophobic, was now far more sparsely furnished. And every suitable surface supported a teacup with a flickering candle in it. It was welcoming and restful, just what Fran needed after her day.

'Wow! You've done some good stuff here – and lit the fire. And candles!'

'Tea lights,' corrected Issi. 'Knowing what a fussy-knickers you are about lighting, I put some in my bag. When I found all the teacups in a cupboard, I put them together. Good day?'

'It's gorgeous! So cosy and pretty. Daunting day – got lost coming home but I'll tell you later. But I can knock the fireplace out! Although not now, obviously.'

'You asked Aunt Amy?' Issi was surprised.

'Not specifically but she said I could do anything to the house as long as I looked after her cows.' Fran collapsed in one of the armchairs drawn up next to the fire and started tugging at the heel of a boot. 'I am so tired. I think it was meeting people and having so much information fired at me.' She looked around. 'It looks far better in here now. Thank you.' Then she frowned. 'Oh, why did you keep that dreadful painting up?'

'Because it hides a patch of wall that really needs redecorating and if you do one bit you'd have to do the whole lot.'

Fran nodded. 'Fair enough. Apart from that, you've made it looked great.'

'Well, I needed something to do and you gave me permission to play.' Issi paused. 'Although the changes haven't been approved by everyone.'

'What do you mean?' Fran pulled off the other boot. 'Who else has seen them?'

'You've had a caller. Mrs Brown. She's coming back tomorrow morning. She used to look after Aunt Amy a bit before she had to go into the home. She seems to know everything about the farm. She looked around with one eyebrow raised, obviously disapproving like mad. I reassured her that every-thing is still safe. I haven't burnt the nests of tables and whatnots and all the other clutter, but she seemed a bit put out.'

'Where have you put all the stuff?'

'There's a little room at the end of the house. It had quite a lot of things in it already so I just stacked more bits on top. I don't think you'll need that room. It's quite a big house, really.'

'Amazing. Is there wine?' The extent of her potential inheritance wasn't a top priority just at that moment.

Issi nodded, very pleased with herself. 'There's wine and there's dinner. I asked your visitor how to light the range and she showed me. Then I put in the lasagne you brought.'

'Sorry,' said Fran. 'Lasagne is a bit like moussaka but I wanted to bring food that was easy to heat up and didn't need saucepans.'

'I can't believe you haven't brought your pans and things.'

'I brought my knives but I didn't want to bring everything I owned. I've left a lot of stuff in my parents' garage.' Fran closed her eyes. 'I've got a lot to tell you but not until I've had something strong to drink.'

'It's still teatime really,' Issi objected.

Fran shook her head. 'No. It's dark. Winetime. At least, today it is.'

'I'll get it. Do you want your dinner early, too?'

'Yes please, Mummy...'

Fran felt revived when she had eaten and was ready to elaborate on how she had got on. 'I feel a bit confused. Both the solicitor, and Amy – she asked me to call her that – told me a lot but left out a lot too. The solicitor said there's a thousand pounds for me to use and although there is more money, it has to be kept for Amy's care.'

'I know care homes can be expensive,' said Issi.

'But I don't need to worry about that for six months because Amy's paid for that long. She's thought it all out. And there's the herdsman, who looks after the scary cows. She's paid him, too – and his relief milkers.'

'And if they're not scary?'

'It should all be fine!'

But Fran knew their cheerfulness was a little false. She may not be able to do this at all.

'I really want this to work,' she said. 'I've left my job and packed up my life to come here, and although I could go back I'd always wonder if I could have made a go of it. Very few people get chances like this. I can't waste the opportunity. It's my chance to make something of my life.'

Chapter Two

Fran awoke early, aware that it was raining. Not a good beginning for her first proper day as a farmer but then she remembered that Mrs Brown was due to call, giving Fran the perfect excuse not to go out and meet the cows. She had to bake if she had a visitor.

'So no cows this morning, Is,' said Fran, crunching toast. 'I'll have to bake instead. Do you think Mrs Brown likes flapjack?'

'How would I be able to tell?' asked Issi, amused.

'I'll do flapjack and shortbread,' Fran decided. 'Then there's a choice. And I'm sure the herdsman would appreciate whichever one Mrs Brown refuses.'

Issi had gone for a walk, in spite of the rain, but promised to make sure she was back to help Fran entertain Mrs Brown, leaving Fran to prepare for their guest. As Fran mixed butter into flour and sugar she looked out of the kitchen window to the farmyard beyond.

It had a cobbled courtyard and was surrounded by outbuildings, but not, she realised as she peered through the gloom, the one that housed the cows. These buildings were too small for that, although she knew the herd was not large. None of these buildings seemed to be in use so the cows must be somewhere else. This was a bit disappointing. Fran had hoped she could observe them from the safety of the kitchen.

However, it was potentially a pretty yard, and she could picture it with stone sinks filled with flowers, hanging baskets and possibly some charming though defunct farm implements decorating the walls.

Then she laughed at herself – and made Issi laugh when she appeared sometime later and Fran told her of her mad plans to civilise the yard. 'Like it's ever going to be pretty! When am I going to have time to put in bedding plants and find old ploughs to hang on the walls?'

'Well, you're probably not going to have time for ages but you might do one day. But I saw your cows while I was walking. They're all in a fairly new building. I saw the cowherd feeding them.'

'Oh? What's he like?'

Issi frowned. 'I couldn't really tell but he's not chatty, that's for sure.

Fran's heart sank a bit. 'He's going to resent me terribly for not being Amy. I just know it.'

'Give him a chance!' said Issi. 'He was a bit younger than I'd imagined. I could just about see him under his hat.'

Mrs Brown, although not old, seemed suspicious as she came in through the back door and into the kitchen. She was wearing a drover's coat, a brimmed hat pulled well down and big wellington boots. It was an outfit Fran instantly envied for its protective qualities.

Mrs Brown took off her boots immediately, and was wearing thick grey socks underneath. She appeared to be a woman who didn't give anything away until she wanted to and although she'd divested herself of her boots right away, she was a bit reluctant to give Fran her dripping coat and hat.

'Really,' Fran insisted. 'They're soaking. It is such terrible weather today. Let me hang these over the range so they can dry off a bit.'

'Very well,' said Mrs Brown and unbuttoned her coat and handed Fran her hat.

'Now let's go through to the sitting room,' said Fran, trying to behave as a hostess, as if she hadn't arrived just two days before.

Fran suspected Mrs Brown considered it too early in the day for a fire. Fran personally thought it added brightness to the January morning.

'Sit where it's warm,' said Fran, 'and would you like tea or coffee?'

Once it was established that tea was the preferred beverage, Fran left Issi to make polite conversation while she made it. Issi did offer but the thought of Issi doing it made Fran feel a bit awkward, as if Issi were a servant, not a friend.

At last, tea was poured and shortbread handed round.

'Oh, this is very nice!' said Mrs Brown, surprised.

'I was a chef in London,' explained Fran, 'and although many chefs don't bake, I started baking with my mother at home and I still enjoy it.'

'So not really a suitable person to take on a farm, then?' said Mrs Brown.

'Not at all suitable,' Fran agreed – it couldn't be denied. 'But as I expect you know, I was the only blood relation of Amy who could be traced and I did come here as a little girl. Amy told me I liked the cows.' She put the rose-patterned cup back in its saucer. 'I am determined to make a go of it. Especially now I know how important it is that the farm carries on after Amy dies.' She frowned. 'Although I'm sure that won't happen for years and years.' Fran couldn't help wondering how on earth the care home could be paid for without the farm being sold.

Mrs Brown seemed to read her mind. 'And that care home won't be cheap.'

'Amy has paid upfront for six months,' said Fran, hoping this information wasn't secret. 'So with luck I'll have got a grip on things by then.'

Mrs Brown looked doubtful. 'It'll take more than luck and it won't be easy for you, you being a townie. But you've got a very good herdsman.'

'Oh? What do you know about him?'

'Quite a lot. He's my son.'

'Goodness me!' said Fran, thinking that Mrs Brown really was a woman who kept things close to her chest.

'Amy thinks the world of him,' the herdsman's mother went on.

Fran took a sip of tea. 'I don't know her well but I'm willing to bet she's a very good judge of character.'

Mrs Brown relaxed just a little. 'She is.'

'And you'll be around? I can ask your advice?' Fran's life experience told her that people were more likely to be kind if you asked their advice. People liked that.

'Not as much as I used to be for Amy. I made a point of it for her or she wouldn't have managed at all. But I've got my sister to think of and she's not local.'

'Oh. Maybe I'd better ask you everything I need to know now!' Fran sounded and felt a bit desperate.

'Go on then.'

Although Mrs Brown's expression was not encouraging Fran felt fairly sure she'd know the answer to the question uppermost in her mind. 'Can you tell me about my neighbour? What is so wrong with him? Amy was just about to tell me when she fell asleep.'

Issi refilled Mrs Brown's cup and Fran proffered the shortbread. Mrs Brown took a sip, a bite and then a breath. 'Well…it all goes back to his father. No, his grandfather.'

There was a frisson of excitement at the knowledge that good gossip was going to be shared.

'Amy's never told me in so many words but I got the strong impression – when she was talking about him – that there was an understanding between her and old Mr Arlingham.' Seeing Fran and Issi looking confused she explained: 'You know, romantically?'

'Ah!' said Fran, in the picture now.

'Anyway, it came to nothing.' She paused for dramatic effect, possibly enjoying the rapt attention of the two younger women. 'Now, I don't know what happened but it was something to do with the land. Maybe she suspected that old Mr Arlingham only wanted her so he could get his hands on the farm. I don't know if you've seen it on a map but Hill Top Farm cuts into the Park House Farm land – that's owned by the Arlinghams – like a thumbnail. I reckon it's always irked the Arlinghams that they don't own all this bit of the valley.'

Fran refilled Mrs Brown's teacup, anxious lest this outpouring of very useful information should dry up.

Mrs Brown accepted another bit of shortbread and carried on.

'I do know that young Mr Arlingham – Antony – came to see Amy a couple of years ago. I happened to be here working in the kitchen. She let him in with a welcome but he went out again looking like thunder. She had her feathers ruffled too. She didn't go into details but I gather he wanted to buy the farm.'

Fran bit her lip for a second before speaking. 'But really, she had no one to leave the farm to. Why didn't she want to sell it? She may need the money, after all, to keep her in her care home.'

'It's what he wanted to do with the land that so upset her,' Mrs Brown explained.

'And what was that?' said Issi.

'I don't know,' said Mrs Brown. 'Could have been factory farming, or raising birds for a shoot, or maybe a place to ride motorbikes. Amy would never see her precious cows sold to make way for motor-bikes.'

'No, that would be awful,' said Fran, although she wasn't quite as horrified as she thought she ought to be. 'Amy mentioned vineyards.'

'Whatever the thing is,' said Mrs Brown, 'this land has never been ploughed, not during the war, not ever. That makes it very special.'

27

'Oh my goodness!' said Issi. 'That is incredibly rare. No wonder Amy doesn't want it used for anything else. That's an outrageous idea!' She paused and then obviously felt obliged to explain her passion. 'I'm doing a PhD on land conservation. There's less than two per cent of this sort of land left in the country. It must be preserved at all costs.'

'But I thought everyone had to "Dig for victory" in the war,' said Fran.

'These fields are too small to plough and too steep,' said Mrs Brown proudly. 'That's what makes this farm unique. So don't you go having anything to do with Mr Antony Arlingham, not on any account!'

'I won't,' said Fran, feeling much more in the picture.

'Anyone who'd even consider – even for a moment – ploughing up fields that have never been ploughed to turn them into a motorbike track is beyond the pale!' said Issi passionately. 'It would be a desecration.'

'That's the word,' said Mrs Brown, satisfied. 'Desecration.' Then she got up. 'I'll leave my number in case you need any more information about things but I expect you'll manage just fine.'

'I hope so,' said Fran, not convinced.

'That was very nice shortbread, I must say,' said Mrs Brown.

'Oh, I'll just wrap up the rest and you can take it with you,' said Fran, running to the kitchen before Mrs Brown could decline the offer. She felt she needed to keep Mrs Brown on side.

After Mrs Brown's outer garments and boots had been returned to her and she had been ushered out with as much gushing as Fran thought they could all cope with, Fran looked at Issi. 'Let's put on our wellies and inspect the farm. I need to know what I'm facing. Although I know it's still raining.'

'Are you feeling a bit overwhelmed?' asked Issi.

'Mmm. I'm determined to do it but it is a big thing.'

'It's a massive thing,' Issi agreed. 'But if anyone can do it, you can.'

Fran handed Issi her parka. 'Thanks, Is. It would be a lot easier if you didn't have to go home tomorrow, but your faith in me makes it seem possible. Now pass me my boots, there's a love.'

As they went out of the back door Issi said, 'I don't expect this yard has seen Cath Kidston wellies before.'

Fran looked at her feet. 'Maybe I'd better get some proper farmer boots.'

'Not until those are worn out,' said Issi.

'True. I've only got that thousand pounds from Amy to live on, and run the farm. Apart from a bit of money of my own that's all there is.'

*

They walked out of the small enclosed yard that Fran had already furnished with flowers and decorative items in her head. Now she could properly inspect the outbuildings. They peered through the dirty windows.

'The buildings seem in fairly good order,' commented Issi. 'But nothing's happened in them for years.'

Fran tried a door and found it opened. 'Absolutely full of stuff,' she said after a few seconds. 'And I bet if I did gussy up the farmyard, I'd find everything I'd want as decorative items right here.'

'What's that?' asked Issi, pointing to something that looked like a press of some kind. 'Do you think it's for cider?'

'If it is it explains why it hasn't been used for years,' said Fran. 'The nurse in the care home told me Amy was a strict teetotaller.'

'Look at those wonderful scales!' said Issi. 'This is fascinating.'

'Let's not get sidetracked,' said Fran. 'I really want to see Tig before he disappears off somewhere.'

'Let's do that,' said Issi. 'This stuff will wait, after all.'

They went through the gate out of the yard and into the short lane that led to the cow byre. Fran looked for Tig, keen to introduce herself, but there was no one about, only the cows.

'We've missed him,' said Fran.

'We might find him later,' said Issi. 'In the mean-time, there are the special, aristocratic cows with the wonderful pedigree.'

Fran looked at them dubiously. They were in a large, chilly barn and they were chewing and looking at her. They were very large and had horns.

'No prizes for guessing what they're thinking,' said Fran. 'That we're two right old townies wearing really silly wellies.'

'They're very handsome though, aren't they?' said Issi. 'I love the way the red and the white mingle. Would you call that that "dappled"?'

'They're Dairy Shorthorns,' said Fran. 'Amy told me. I must google them, when we get back in, see what I can find out.'

'That might be a bit difficult,' said Issi. 'There doesn't seem to be an internet connection at the farm. I tried when you were visiting your old lady.'

The thought of being without an internet connection gave Fran a nasty pang. 'Oh God, well, I'll have to sort that out. But let's carry on round. I think the rain is easing off a bit.'

'Really?' said Issi, obviously not convinced.

They had walked for half an hour and were standing at the top of a field that swept down to a stream. Beyond the field was a row of trees, more trees and hills past that, and then the river, and beyond that the mountains of Wales.

'I know I'm sounding boring now,' said Issi, 'but I think this is the most beautiful spot on earth. The view is great from the farmhouse but up here, it's even better.'

'We've both said it a few times and we're right,' Fran agreed. 'It is beautiful. And the thought that someone is thinking of spoiling it, turning it into a scrambling course for trail bikes or something, is terrible.' A movement by the farmhouse caught her eye. 'Look! I think that must be Tig. Let's go back down and say hello.'

As they walked down the muddy track to the house and round the back to where the cows were kept, Fran felt nervous. It was terribly important that she got on with Tig. If he despised her for being a townie (and Fran felt it was inevitable that he would) this farming thing would never work. She was dependent on him, just as Amy had been. Although at least Amy had knowledge and experience; she, Fran, had nothing. If this farm fell apart he could always get another job.

'Hello!' said Fran, hoping fervently that she didn't sound like an overenthusiastic Labrador greeting a friend. 'I'm Fran, Amy's – Mrs Flowers' – um – relation.'

Tig nodded. He was younger that she'd imagined him, well dressed up against the weather. He wore a hat the same as his mother, with a wide brim. A cracked old Barbour jacket was done up closely and his waterproof-trouser-covered legs ended in muddy boots. He looked the part.

'I've just met your mother, and I'm really pleased to meet you.' She offered her hand. 'This is my friend Issi who's staying for a couple of days to help me settle in.' Now she was near she noticed that he had very bright blue eyes as if he spent a long time looking at the sky.

Tig nodded again.

'I'd love you to tell me all about the cows,' said Fran. 'They're so – so pretty.' She knew this wasn't the word she was looking for but desperately wanted Tig to like her. No – she *needed* him to, but, although she had plenty of charm and confidence with people, he wasn't like anyone she'd ever met before.

Unexpectedly, she saw the weather-beaten face move and the blue eyes crinkle at the corners and she realised he was smiling. He nodded. 'They are pretty. So, what do you want to know about them?'

Issi shivered beside her; they were both freezing to death in their townie clothes and Fran wished she knew the right questions. She smiled.

'What do you think is the most important thing about them?'

Tig inclined his head. 'This herd goes back a long way, longer than most herds. That's important. They give good rich milk and they're good mothers.'

He went on to tell her about milk yields, how much they ate and the different temperaments of individuals.

As Fran stood there listening, her feet turning to ice, she realised he loved his cows, the herd, with a passion. He didn't actually say as much but it was obvious in the way he looked at them, told them the names and personal characteristics, described how they were related and who their mothers and grandmothers were. None of them would suffer as much as an insect bite without Tig noticing, and doing something about it.

Fran asked a question she hoped was intelligent. 'Do you – we – they have large vet's bills?'

Tig shook his head. 'Not if I can help it.'

Which didn't really answer Fran's question.

'I must go in now,' she said. 'I need to make a phone call. I'll see you tomorrow.'

Tig nodded and turned back to his cows.

It was hard saying goodbye to Issi at the station the next day. She was going back to London to continue her studies. It was raining and quite cold and it made the parting seem more poignant, somehow.

Although they'd had a very positive conversation on the drive, Issi saying that with Tig Fran could learn about it all slowly, get to know what he did and why. Fran realised this was true, and that Amy would never have left the farm in her hands if she felt Fran's ignorance was in any way a problem. But having Issi there had made it an adventure. Knowing she was going to be alone in the farm, with no internet, and only a landline as a method of communication, was a bit daunting. Still, she'd found a whole bookcase full of old novels, and Fran knew, if things got too tough, a book was a wonderful place to escape to.

'And of course I'll be down as often as I can,' insisted Issi, having given Fran an enormous hug. 'I love it down here. And now I know how unique the pasture is, I could even call it work! I won't be the only one of your friends who comes either. You'll be the weekend spot of choice.'

'Hmm, not sure I want a lot of townies coming down here expecting me to cook for them while they lie about looking at the view. I'm a working farmer, you know.'

Issi laughed. 'You're also a chef, and quite sociable. You'll need to get friendly with the locals or get your mates down here.'

Fran imagined her London friends in this rural, old-fashioned setting and decided she'd invite them later, when she'd brought the farmhouse up-to-date.

'I think I'll do a supper club,' she said as if that was a plan and not an idea that had suddenly popped into her head. 'I bet people would be curious to see Amy's house.'

'If they can get up the lane, that is,' said Issi. 'But I suppose the locals all drive farm vehicles that can go anywhere.'

'And there's somewhere to park halfway up. I'm getting quite keen on the idea now.'

After another long hug, Fran left Issi, got into her car and set off home. As she drove she tried to think of the important questions to ask Amy when she next saw her. She wanted to make some notes before she went again, so if Amy was awake, she could get some information. Did the farm actually make money seemed the most important one. And by the time Tig had had wages and the cattle had been fed, was there any left over?

Preoccupied, Fran missed the turning to the farm and found herself driving up the hill and along a road that took her quite a way from Hill Top Farm. Confident that she'd be able to find her way back as long as she got home before dark, she allowed herself to carry on driving. She fancied a little local exploration, in spite of the rain. And she might find a bit of coverage for her phone.

The high hedges suddenly turned into beautiful stone walls and Fran realised she was driving past a very valuable property. Although it was raining harder now, she was curious and wanted to see if a mansion would suddenly reveal itself. It didn't, but a gateway with a large pair of electric gates did. The name of the property, Park House Farm, was etched on to a piece of stone. It all looked new and prosperous.

Fran decided to use the gateway to turn in and pulled into the side of the road to see if there was any coverage. She'd just opened the window so she'd hear any traffic before getting her phone out when a car sped up the road towards her. It shot past, far too fast in Fran's opinion and obviously went through a puddle because water jetted in through her window, soaking her and the car.

Fran shook herself like a dog and growled like one too. She then swore loudly and impotently at the driver who was probably miles away by now. She hadn't seen the car in detail but knew that it was large and flashy. She was certain he – she'd glimpsed that the driver was male – belonged in the property with the Cotswold stone walls and equally certain she hated him. And by the time she'd got home and her dripping self inside, she was almost as certain that this was her neighbour whom Amy hated so much and had warned her against.

Righteous indignation warmed her as much as her cursory bath did. (Installing a shower was a priority, she decided, just as soon as she knew if she could afford it.)

She made herself hot chocolate and lit the fire, all the while planning a hideous end for the driver of the car who wanted to turn Hill Top into a motorbike scrambling centre or whatever. Somehow she would make a fortune and buy his farm and turn it into grazing for rare cattle. That would serve him right!

She had just made herself a plate of pasta with chilli oil and garlic and was about to sit in front of the fire with it when she heard a knock on the door. More significantly, it was the front door. She may be pretty much 100 per cent townie but by now she had confirmed no one used the front door in the country.

She put her plate of pasta down and got up from the sofa. Should she open the door? Who would be calling at this time of night?

Rather wishing she had a dog to protect her, she opened the door. There was a tall man wearing a rain-spattered Barbour jacket and wellington boots. But although they were both items that Tig wore they were totally unlike Tig's, in the same way that this man and Tig were both male, but totally unlike each other.

Instinct told Fran who he was. It didn't make her like him though. And no one really wanted to meet a kind-of attractive man while wearing PJs and fluffy slippers, even if she was perfectly decent.

'Yes?' she said.

'Ah – I've come to apologise. For drenching you. My name is Antony Arlingham.'

Chapter Three

A million thoughts went through Fran's head as she stood, holding the door, looking at the man on her doorstep. The most important one being, was she safe? Having worked in London, in pubs, and in private homes as a chef, and on food-market stalls she felt she had a lot of experience of people. This, and, again, her instinct, told her she was. But it didn't stop her being indignant.

'How on earth did you know where I lived?'

'Partly guesswork, I admit. But a strange car, turning in my driveway is unlikely to be local. Everyone knows that Mrs Flowers had a young relation moving into her house.' He paused and Fran noticed that the rain was much harder now. 'And I knew it was you when you opened the door because you're wearing pyjamas quite early in the day so it means you must have had a shower for some reason. I hope it was hot this time,' he added ruefully.

'It was a bath. My – er – cousin hasn't got a shower.'

'Oh.' He hesitated. Fran got the impression he was used to saying what he meant and being listened to and that the current situation put him out of his comfort zone. Which made two of them.

'Your track is in a bad way,' he said.

Fran sighed. She could hardly have overlooked it. 'I know.'

'Look – could I come in so we can have a proper talk? I've got things I could tell you that might be really useful.' Another pause. 'I brought a bottle of wine.'

'I was just about to eat—'

'I could watch you and you could have wine with it.'

Reluctantly, Fran opened the door wider. 'OK.' As he passed her she said, 'Go on through. I'm sure you know your way. I'll find some glasses.'

Fran decided not to waste time hunting in cupboards and but to settle for the tumblers she and Issi had used. While she was looking for a corkscrew and failing to find one she spotted the pasta pan. She had a chef's tendency to over cater – there was easily another portion in it. She couldn't possibly eat with him watching her without offering him a chance to eat too.

She went into the sitting room. 'I hope the wine is in a screw-top bottle. I can't find a corkscrew. And have you eaten yet?'

'I made up the fire. I hope you don't mind. And I've got a corkscrew on my knife.'

'And would you like some pasta? I can make mine do for two easily.'

'Well, I haven't eaten actually. And it smells delicious, so it would be a shame to turn down your kind offer.'

Fran wished she hadn't been quite so kind now but, like a smile given to someone you thought was someone else, it couldn't be taken back. 'You deal with the wine then. I'll be back shortly.'

She retrieved her full plate and went back into the kitchen cursing herself for not just taking the wine and sending him away. But she was proud of her cooking skills and she wanted him to stop thinking of her as the girl who was living in Mrs Flowers' house, the girl whom he'd drenched by driving past her too fast, the girl who would prob-ably roll over and do exactly what he said when it came to the farm. No, she wanted him to realise she was a force to be reckoned with. Having tipped her uneaten meal back in the pan, she added another drop or two of chilli oil. 'Take that if you think you're hard enough,' she muttered.

Fifteen minutes later she and Antony Arlingham were sitting at the little round table in Amy's sitting room, hastily cleared of framed photographs, mostly of ancient cattle, eating pasta with chilli oil. Fran was pleased with the result. It had been worth bringing a few special ingredients with her. There was a lot about the farmhouse that was less than perfect, but being able to produce a good meal made it all a lot better.

'Well,' said Antony, raising his tumbler. 'Here's to you being very happy here.'

'I'll drink to that,' said Fran, clinking her tumbler against his. 'Now, do tuck in. I hope it's not too spicy for you.'

When she had finished her first mouthful, she said quickly, before he could start questioning her, 'You're my neighbour, obviously. Tell me a bit about yourself. Is there a Mrs Antony Arlingham?'

He shook his head. 'There was but our ways parted. It was for the best. We didn't have children so it could have been worse.' He looked at her and she noticed he had interesting eyes. They were hazel with a flash of gold in them and were unusual with his very dark hair. 'What about you? Have you a husband and children?'

Fran raised an eyebrow. 'I'm sure local gossip would have told you that I haven't.'

'I admit we do all know that you're very young and single and come from London. No one expects you to last more than a month at the most.'

'Oh really? We London girls are made of sugar, are we? We melt in the rain?'

'In the rain and cold and snow, yes, you do melt.' He looked at her and once again she noticed his unusual eyes. 'But before that, your track is going to be impassable without a four-wheel drive very soon.'

She wished she could say that she had one but she knew he knew exactly what sort of vehicle she drove. 'I will need to change my car, I think.' She took up another forkful of pasta to stop him saying anything else for just a minute.

'This is really good,' he said, sounding surprised.

She shrugged. 'I'm a chef, it should be good.' Inside she was pleased. 'The wine is really nice, too.'

'Among other things, I'm a wine importer, it should be good.' He quirked his eyebrow back at her.

Fran took a breath. 'Amy – Mrs Flowers – warned me about you. She said I shouldn't have anything to do with you and that you were bad, through and through.' Amy may not have gone quite this far but Fran felt she needed emphasis.

'Mrs Flowers has got quite the wrong end of the stick about me and my intentions,' Antony said, obviously glad to have moved on from small talk too.

'Has she?' Fran said this as if she doubted it. Amy was a frail old woman now but she hadn't run a farm on her own for years without learning a thing or two, and if Amy suspected Antony's motives she, Fran, would suspect them too.

'Yes. She has very romantic notions about farming.'

'Really? Yet she did it successfully for years and years.'

'Did she? How successfully?'

Fran paused. She'd assumed Amy had been successful once, though she'd let things go recently.

Antony put down his fork. 'I think you'll find, when you've had a chance to look into things, that this farm has been losing money for years and years. I suspect it's held together by a huge overdraft and the bank won't stand for it for too much longer.' He paused so Fran could take this in. 'I offered to buy the farm from Amy, to clear the debt, so she could go on living here as long as she wanted. She rejected the offer. As things have turned out she's had to go into a home. But I'll make you the same offer.'

'This farm is not mine to sell.'

'You're due to inherit it. You could live here, have a go at farming a bit, until Amy dies, and then come away with a handsome sum of money you could do something with.'

Briefly Fran thought about the dream she'd had of running her own restaurant and then put it aside. The farm would never be worth enough to fund a little London culinary gold mine. But even if it was, she'd started this project now, she wasn't ready to give up until she'd given it her absolute best shot. 'I'm not due to inherit. Only if I make a go of it.'

'I could help you make a go of it.'

Fran realised she was beginning to like this man. He was attractive, polite and probably quite kind, but she was not ready to throw in the towel before she'd even started.

'I'm sure you could and I'm sure you mean well, but I've been brought from London to this farm by a woman who went to a lot of trouble to find me. I can't let her down without giving it a proper go. Of course it will be difficult. I know nothing about farming but I can't just cave in before I've been here a week.'

Antony didn't speak for what seemed a long time. 'I respect that. I think it will be heartbreakingly hard for you, trying to make a go of a business you know nothing about – one that bankrupts men who've been in the business for generations – when you're not even starting from a level playing field. That said, I do think you're very brave.' He smiled. 'And I'm still willing to help you.'

In spite of the smile, which was effective, she wasn't won over. 'Why? Why would you help me?'

'Because I don't think this farm is viable as it is. Even with my help it's not going to work. But if you have a better time trying because of what I can do, I'll be happy.'

'Well, that's very gracious of you,' Fran said huffily, 'not to say patronising, but I think I'll manage just fine without your help, thank you very much.' She didn't believe it and she knew he didn't either.

He laughed. 'Well done you!'

They found a surprising amount of things to talk about while they finished the pasta and drank half of the wine. But he declined her offer of coffee.

'No thank you, I really must go.' He paused thoughtfully. 'Would you come to a dinner party on Friday? I've been invited and I know if I asked, my hostess would be absolutely delighted to have you too.'

'Why?' said Fran, prickly with suspicion.

'Because this is the country – everyone is desperately interested in anyone new! And Amy Flowers' niece – or whatever you are to her – would be the most fascinating of all.'

'So I'd be there as an object of curiosity?'

'Yup.'

She tossed her head, trying not to show her amusement. 'Sounds delightful.'

'But you'll come? It'll give you a chance to meet some local people.' When she still didn't reply he went on, 'I can't believe a woman who's prepared to take on a farm could be frightened of a few locals wanting to get a look at her.'

It was a challenge Fran had to accept. 'OK, I'll come. What's the dress code?'

'Warm. A bit smart, but warm mostly. It's not the best heated house I've ever visited.'

'Fine.'

'I'll pick you up at seven on Friday then.'

'Super,' said Fran, thinking that was the right Cotswold response.

'Oh, one last thing. How is Amy's internet connection? Get a good signal up here?'

Fran sighed. 'You know perfectly well that Amy isn't, wasn't, and never has been on the internet.'

'Have you got a laptop?'

'Yes. Much good it's doing me.'

'If you give it to me I can see if you're near enough to piggyback on my internet. I have a booster so it reaches all my outbuildings.'

It would have been lovely to say 'no thank you' but the internet would make her life so much easier and happier so Fran fetched her laptop.

Antony opened it up and after a little tapping around said, 'There. We are near enough to each other. I'll just write down my password for you.'

'That is incredibly kind,' she said, swallowing her pride as he wrote on the back of a business card.

'It's going to be even harder for you if you don't let me help because of your loyalty to Amy and because you suspect my motives. If I can help you get online I'd feel better about you being stuck up here on a barely functioning farm.'

Fran didn't reply. She wanted to tell him that the farm was perfectly functioning, thank you, but she didn't know if it was or wasn't. She didn't feel 'stuck up here' because it was a beautiful spot. On the other hand it was a bit bleak on a winter's evening

47

and she did feel a bit cut off and lonely. Although being able to email people, and possibly Skype, would be a huge help.

Fortunately he didn't seem to expect a reply. He handed her the card and put away his pen. 'Of course it's got all my contact details on it. Do get in touch, anytime.'

'I'll give you the landline number. I'd give you my mobile too, but I don't think there's any signal here.'

He smiled. 'Give it to me anyway.' He got out his pen again and found another card.

When she'd written her numbers on the back he slipped it into his top pocket. 'I'm going now. See you Friday.'

Even before Fran had gathered up the plates and glasses she went online and emailed Issi. Having the internet again made everything seem much more possible. She did a little googling about second-hand four-wheel-drive cars, and how much it might cost to repair the track. She concluded it would probably be cheaper to buy a tractor that could go up the track than to have it repaired. Just for a few seconds she considered it and then realised the farm prob-ably had a tractor already and she'd never park one in Sainsbury's car park. She needed a better car but she hoped she could get one without having to ask for a loan from the Bank of Mum and Dad. That would be a last resort.

Thinking about her parents made her feel a bit homesick, so she emailed her mother, saying she would phone soon. Then she made herself a hot-water bottle, for company as much as warmth, and went slowly up to bed.

Chapter Four

Fran awoke the next morning to the sound of dripping, which was never a good way to start the day. She got up, stuffed her feet in her (ridiculously optimistic) fluffy slippers, pulled on her dressing gown and went to search for the source. To her relief she discovered it was from a gutter outside her bedroom. She mentally added 'clear gutters' to her To Do list and went into the kitchen.

She watched the rain pour down outside as she ate her toast. Still, at least she had the internet, and plenty to get on with, really. She shivered and realised it had hardly stopped raining since she'd got here. If she could get through the day without going outside it would be a plus. She needed to find out more about the farm finances anyway. This would be a good day to do it.

However, by the time she'd found Amy's latest account books, which, unlike the years and years' worth of earlier ones, were not neat and accurate, she decided a walk in the pouring rain without proper protective clothing would have been cheerier. At least cold and wetness was fairly temporary. As Antony had warned her, financially, things on Hill Top Farm were not in a good way.

There was a spike with paid bills on it and, in a hardbacked exercise book, similar to the many neatly filed in a ring binder, there were a few entries for milk cheques. The milk cheques didn't nearly cover the feed bills and Fran really hoped there were many cheques not entered, or how was the feed merchant paid? It didn't make sense. There were several scrappy bits of paper with scribbled calculations and one with *Bank, 2.30* written on it, implying Amy had made an appointment with the bank, possibly to ask for a loan. It looked as if bloody Antony Arlingham had been right. The whole place was a financial muddle.

She couldn't find any recent bank statement so she didn't know if there was an overdraft or a huge loan outstanding or not. But how had Amy financed her care for six months without a loan? And sorted out Tig's, and the relief milkers' wages? There were too many mysteries. She made a list of things to ask Amy and resolved to ask them immediately, and not risk Amy falling asleep before she'd said anything important.

She was still going through the list when the telephone rang. It took Fran a couple of seconds to recognise the sound. She hadn't had a landline herself for years. She picked up the old-fashioned receiver, which seemed remarkably heavy.

Ten minutes later she put it down again. It had not been a cheerful conversation. The man from the milk co-operative had told Fran that the milk tanker would not be coming, because the rain made the track impassable. He went on to say that unless the track up to the farm was repaired very soon, the tanker wouldn't even *try* to get up it any more. And while Mrs Flowers had been a member of the co-op for years and they liked and respected her, her contribution was more trouble than it was worth.

After a bit of pleading, Fran had convinced him to give the farm a reprieve if she dealt with the track. The tanker would try and come up the moment the weather let up. Just at the end of the conversation she had asked, 'So, what should I do with the milk? If the tanker can't collect it?'

'Do what the old lady did, pour it away,' was the reply.

Horrified, Fran piled on the waterproof clothing Amy had left behind. When she was fully encased in trousers, coat, hat and her own boots (sadly, Amy's boots were too small) Fran went out into the yard to talk to Tig.

She found him sterilising the milking equipment. She was so concerned, she didn't waste time with small talk about the appalling rain. 'Tig! Is it true that Amy used to throw away the milk if the tanker couldn't collect it?'

He gave a slight nod, indicating he was pleased to see her. 'Yup.'

'It can't come today, by the way.'

He nodded as if she had been stating the obvious. 'So do you want me to drain the tank? Are they coming tomorrow?' He looked concerned but not surprised. He had a kind face, Fran decided.

'I'm not sure when they're coming, to be honest, it depends on the weather. But basically, they said I had to get the track fixed properly.'

'Expensive, that'll be.'

'I know. And I can't bear to keep wasting the milk. Have we got buckets?'

'Yes.'

'Are some of them remotely hygienic? I mean, could I sterilise some? I want to see if I can make cheese or something.'

'There's cheesemaking equipment in one of the outbuildings by the yard.'

Fran realised what she and Issi had thought was a cider press was actually for cheese. She nodded.

'But hard cheese takes a while to make and then you have to let it mature,' Tig went on. 'My mother knows all about it if you want to find out.'

'I think I knew it took ages to mature and I'd love to talk to your mother sometime about making a hard cheese. But for now, there are other sorts of cheese I can make in the kitchen, more quickly.'

She was fairly sure this was true. Cheffing in London, she'd once had to deal with pints and pints of sour milk when the fridge broke down, and she was sure cream cheese wasn't the only one you could make at home. 'So how many buckets might you be able to find me? I probably won't be able to use all the milk so we'll have to waste some, but this farm can't afford to throw away milk. It's the only thing it produces, currently.'

'There's more stuff in the old dairy. That's off the farmyard too. You take a look and tell me what you want sterilizing and I'll do it for you.'

'That would be very kind!'

Tig shrugged off the word. 'Farm's in a bad way, miss. If you can do something to help keep the herd going, that would be good.'

Just for a moment Fran considered asking Tig if he knew any details about loans, or how Amy had got the money to pay her care home, but realised it wouldn't be fair. It was her job to look after the money and it was his to look after the cows.

'You don't have to call me miss,' she said instead. 'Just call me Fran.'

He gave the briefest shake of his head. 'Wouldn't be right, miss. Seeing as you're my boss, like.' But his eyes twinkled.

Fran half laughed. 'Tig! I'm not your boss. I know nothing about cows or anything. We're in this together.'

This time his head movement was more positive. 'True enough.'

'But I really don't mind what you call me,' she said, 'as long as it's not rude.' She smiled at him to make sure he knew she was teasing. 'Now I'd better get to the old dairy. We really need to do something with this milk.'

'If we still had pigs it'd be easier.'

'Pigs? Did we have pigs?'

Tig nodded. 'The old lady gave them up though, but they were useful. Mixed the whey from the cheese with their food, they fattened up well.'

A thought occurred to Fran. 'If you'd like to keep pigs up here they could still have the whey, or any surplus milk. But I don't think the farm could buy them, just yet.

Tig thought about it. 'I'd be happy to buy a couple of pigs, if I could keep them here.'

'Of course you could! You'd have to look after them but you'd do that anyway.'

'I'll see to it then.' He paused for a few seconds and then smiled. 'I'll get back to work then.'

Fran smiled back. 'Thanks, Tig. Having you here is a huge help. I couldn't manage any of it without you, even things that don't involve cows.'

It was hard to tell because Tig was so weather-beaten, but Fran rather thought he blushed.

The dairy was a treasure trove. Although it had obviously been used to dump unused equipment in recent years, the building itself was in good condition. It had whitewashed walls and a level concrete floor.

Everything was dusty, but there were some wonderful old stone crocks, probably used for setting cream, piled up in a corner, a butter churn, and a whole stack of steel buckets that had signs of something purple clinging to them. It could have been blackcurrants or blackberries. Amy had obviously made wine or jam. Fran thought it was probably jam. She'd come across a few jars in the pantry with handwritten labels and had failed to find a corkscrew.

For the first time that day, Fran felt faintly optimistic. If there was cooking involved in this farming lark, here was a contribution she could make.

She gathered together the items she thought would need sterilising and left them for Tig. The stoneware dishes she took into the house, one by one. Then she filled the ancient sink in the scullery with water and started scrubbing.

Later that afternoon Fran had several buckets full of milk. She had also filled a couple of the huge shallow stoneware bowls, hoping to get some cream. She'd spent time on the internet and discovered there was quite a lot she could do with milk without special ingredients and cream was only one of them. While she was longing to start making cheese, common sense told her she should wait until the following day, when the cream would have risen to the top. So she covered all the bowls and buckets with clean tea towels (Amy had an amazing supply of them) and then took her laptop into the sitting room. When she'd lit the fire and settled herself comfortably, she emailed Issi with an update on how things were doing down on the farm, aware she was sounding, and indeed felt, a lot more cheerful than she had the previous evening. Hurray!

Chapter Five

'Hey! You look great!' Antony said when she opened the door to him the following Friday.

Fran hadn't wanted to look too much like a city girl at the dinner party he was taking her to. It was one thing being the object of curiosity, but she didn't want fellow guests saying, the moment she was out of earshot, that she wouldn't last five minutes in the country, especially in the winter. She was wearing her newest jeans, a V-necked sweater that was cut low enough to look like evening wear and a pretty scarf. She was aiming for casual, practical and a bit sexy.

She was depending on Antony to know if it was still the custom to bring bottles of wine but she was fairly confident she should bring something. In preparation she had asked him, via email, if he had a cool box.

'Thank you,' she said briskly. 'Now, did you bring the cool box?'

'Yup. What do you want it for?'

'I have some presents for my hostess.'

'What?'

'Cheese. That I've made myself.'

'Oh!' He was satisfyingly surprised.

'Well, I wanted to bring something home-made as a present. People get fed up with biscuits. I thought I'd bring cheese.' She smiled at him, hoping he wouldn't realise why she had a surplus of milk. She didn't want him to know it was because her track was too bad to be got up by the milk tanker and if she didn't make cheese she'd have to throw away the milk.

The house where the dinner party was to be held wasn't too far away and Fran hoped she'd like the hostess. With Issi in London she was beginning to feel a bit lonely. Although the past few days had been so busy with her cheesemaking project, she needed some local friends.

As they set off up the drive to the house (remarkably smooth, she noted) she said, 'What are Caroline and Julian like? Will I get on with them?'

'I hardly know you well enough to be able to tell but they are fairly relaxed. And it's only going to be a very small dinner. Eight at the most,' Antony said.

'Quite a lot of cars, for eight people,' said Fran as they arrived.

'Hm,' said Antony, finding possibly the last space. 'I didn't think we were late, either. We must be the last to arrive.'

The door was opened by a woman wearing a flour-covered apron and a brave smile. She did not look relaxed at all. Her husband appeared seconds later.

'Hi, Antony,' said the woman, who Fran assumed was Caroline. 'And you must be Fran. Do come in! Let me take your coats. You're safe to take them off – we've had the wood burner going all day.' She embraced them both.

'It's very kind of you to invite me,' said Fran. 'I've brought a little gift – it's in this cool box.'

'It can't be that little then,' said Julian. 'That's a big box.'

'But it's a small present,' said Fran firmly, 'and please don't look at it now. Put it in the kitchen for later. It's edible.'

'Fran was a chef in her previous life,' explained Antony.

'I'm a farmer now,' she said, giving him a dark look.

'Well, come in and have a drink before you die of thirst,' said Julian. 'Here, just sling your coats with the others on that sofa.'

The pile of coats represented far more that eight guests, Fran couldn't help thinking, even if Caroline and Julian kept their coats there too.

They were ushered into a room full of people. Fran's heart sank slightly. Obviously all the locals had persuaded Caroline and Julian to let them have a look at the girl from London who was taking over old Amy Flowers' farm.

'Oh God, Julian, can you do the introductions?' said Caroline, sounding harassed. 'I'll forget everyone's names and I'm needed in the kitchen.'

Fran would have loved to be able to follow Caroline; in the kitchen she could be useful. Here she was just going to be stared at.

Julian did well with the introductions, not forgetting anyone's name, and then said, 'More important than this lot – what would you like to drink?'

'Julian makes a fabulous gin and tonic if you're not driving,' suggested one woman who Fran remembered was called Poppy.

'I'm not driving,' Fran said. 'A G and T would be lovely.'

When she'd been given her drink, which, the first sip told her, was indeed fabulous, and pretty strong, Poppy led the way to a group of women.

'You must think we're all complete ghouls,' said Poppy, 'all desperate to get a look at you, but we're so intrigued to meet you.'

'We don't get much entertainment in the country,' said a woman who was a bit older than Poppy, possibly in her forties. 'I'm Erica, in case you've forgotten. I would have. I think people should wear name badges on all occasions.'

Fran laughed and felt less anxious. 'That would make life easier, but at least the gin is helping.'

'A bit of alcohol does make it all seem less daunting,' agreed Erica. 'I don't think Caroline has let herself have more than a sip of wine though. She's not used to catering for so many. She should have said no to us, when we all begged to be invited to meet the new girl.'

'I feel I should go and help,' said Fran. 'At least I know how to cook, even if I'm very new to farming. I might be quite useful.'

Poppy shook her head. 'She wouldn't want a trained professional seeing the state her kitchen is in. She's not a tidy cook.'

'I completely understand,' said Fran.

'And not only are you an object of interest because you've come from London to live on a derelict farm,' said one woman, a bit younger and noticeably more fashionably dressed than the others, 'but because you've come with Antony, our only Mr Darcy-alike!'

'But, Megan, you are the only one who's single,' said Erica. She sounded a bit irritated. 'So there's not massive competition for him.'

'Unless we've all been misinformed, Fran is single too,' said Megan.

'But Antony only invited me to come with him because I didn't know anyone locally,' said Fran. 'It's not a date or anything.' She was aware of Antony listening to the conversation and saw his wry smile. She took another sip of her drink.

'Well,' said Megan, 'how do you like country life so far? You haven't had the best weather. I must say I would never have moved away from the city if I'd had the choice.'

'But you did have the choice,' said Erica, 'you just didn't want to leave the house and the lifestyle behind.'

Megan shrugged. 'Did you leave a gorgeous flat in the best part of town?' she asked Fran, having a good look at her.

'No,' said Fran. 'I was living above the pub where I worked. Although it was in a good part of town. Quite near Covent Garden.'

'Oh, OK,' said Megan. 'So bit of a step change, coming down here?'

'Well, yes, obviously, but I like a challenge,' said Fran, feeling she was being interviewed and that any moment someone would say, 'Where do you see yourself in five years' time?' She really hoped they wouldn't ask that, because she had no idea.

'And inheriting a rather gorgeous farmhouse would be an incentive,' said Megan.

'I really can't believe you all know about that,' said Fran.

Megan raised her eyebrows. 'But of course! This is the country; everyone knows everything. You stick it out for a year, you get to inherit. Well worth a year of mud, I'd have thought.'

'Actually it's not quite like that—' Fran began as Antony came over.

'I think the Geneva Convention requires that the interrogation stops now,' he said with a worryingly charming smile. 'Why don't you tell Fran all the best places to go around here? Like the best pubs, restaurants, or maybe even places to get a haircut.'

'Actually I'm more into knowing about the restaurants and foodie pubs,' said Fran.

'There are some lovely pubs,' said Erica, 'but no restaurants.'

'So where do you go if you want a romantic night out?' Fran asked.

'To someone else's house where there's an attractive man to flirt with,' said Megan.

Fran laughed, not because she was amused particularly, but she wanted to divert attention away from herself. 'Like here, you mean?'

Megan nodded. 'If you like retro food.'

Caroline came back into the sitting room. 'OK, come and eat everyone. Julian? I'm relying on you for the "placement".'

Fran made sure she finished her drink before she followed the others into the dining room. She was not enjoying herself. Although the evening had been informative in some ways – she knew to avoid Megan if she possibly could – she wasn't feeling at ease, in spite of the enormous gin.

Fran found herself at her host's right hand, which was nice, because Julian was easy to talk to. She noted that Megan was sitting next to Antony and that Megan had her arm on the table so no one else could get to him.

Fran also noted that none of Caroline's friends had offered to help her. There were a lot of people for one person to deal with and although the menu was simple (seventies inspired, possibly – kipper pâté with Melba toast, fish pie) it was only Caroline and Julian who ferried plates.

Thus, when the fish pie had been cleared away, Fran excused herself and followed her hostess. The conversation had drifted towards local schools and how to deal with head lice anyway, so Fran was happy to hunt out Caroline in the kitchen.

'Hi! I really don't want to get in your way,' she said to Caroline, taking in the evidence of an over-faced cook with insufficient worktop space for such a big dinner party. 'But I wanted to explain the cheese. You don't have to feel obliged to serve it if you weren't going to have cheese. Or even then.' She smiled. 'It's various soft cheeses that I made myself.'

'Oh God, who knew you could even do that?' Although Caroline was polite, Fran could see she was very distracted.

'Do let me help!' Fran couldn't help feeling dreadfully sorry for her. 'It was so kind of you to invite me and I gather you wouldn't have had so many people if they didn't all want a look at me!'

'To be honest, I'm past praying for. I've kept it all really simple to make life easier for myself and I've still rotted it up!'

Fran sensed that if Caroline had known her better, she would have used a stronger expression than 'rotted up'. 'Really? How?'

'We're having plum sponge – nursery food, plums out of the freezer – it should be easy-peasy. Only I'd forgotten I'd frozen them with their stones in so it took ages to take them all out – and now I've gone and over-whipped the cream. I've only got children's ice cream to serve with it now.'

'No you haven't!' Fran said. 'I mean – I put some cream in the cool box along with the cheese. If it's not enough, there's mascarpone and ricotta too.'

'You're an angel sent from heaven!' said Caroline after a few stunned seconds. 'Let me see what you've got. Megan brought chocolates that someone gave to her first – you can tell by the overdue sell-by date.'

'First rule of regifting chocolates,' said Fran solemnly. 'Check the sell-by date.'

Caroline laughed.

'So why did you make all this, if you don't mind me asking?' Caroline said a little later, after various containers had been inspected. 'There's masses!'

Fran shrugged. 'I had all this milk. The track to Hill Top Farm is so bad the tanker couldn't fetch it. It was all going to be thrown away so I went on to YouTube and saw what I could make with it.' Somehow Fran felt OK about confessing all this to Caroline. It was because her kitchen was messy and she had a kind heart; she wasn't a critical yummy mummy like most of the others seemed to be.

'You are clever!' Caroline was clearly impressed. 'I would have made a lot of custard and maybe frozen some milk but I never would have thought of making cheese.'

'I had to use it up somehow. There was gallons of the stuff.' Fran was glad to talk to someone about her milk surplus and equally glad that Antony wasn't in earshot.

'You need a market for this,' said Caroline, digging a spoon into the mascarpone, rich and thick. 'How did you make it?'

'Mascarpone is the easiest: it didn't need anything except milk, cream and some lemon juice. I've sent away for what they call grains, so I can make kefir, which I expect you know is fermented milk. Fermented foods are very popular. I bought rennet for some of the other cheese off the internet and luckily it arrived the next day – in time for tonight.'

'But how are you going to sell your cheese? I'd suggest you tried for a stall at the farmers' market but you'd have to wait ages for a space and there are regulations. Mind you, you'd probably qualify if a space came up.'

Fran had spent a lot of time thinking about this. 'I think I might have to take it to London. I've got contacts there – I used to work in quite a few places.'

'As a local girl, that seems a shame,' said Caroline. 'Now, I'd better put this on the table. Would you mind taking the sponge in? I'll take the tray with the cream and stuff.'

Fran didn't have time to ask Caroline to keep quiet about why she'd made cheese. She sighed again. She was used to solving problems, making decisions and forward plans, but she wasn't used to doing them without someone else to discuss them with. So far the only person who would have done that for her was Antony, but while she liked him, he was still classed as the enemy in her heart.

'Hey!' said Caroline, setting down the tray that now carried pretty bowls full of Fran's various products. 'Fran has made all this stuff from Amy's milk. Isn't she clever?'

'Very clever,' said one of the men. 'Are you planning to sell it?'

Clearly she was going to be asked this often. 'I think I'll take it to London. I have contacts there.'

'So you plan to make the cheese regularly?' said Antony.

'It's a good idea to add value to the milk,' said Fran. This sounded businesslike and sensible and better than having to admit that otherwise she'd have to throw the milk away.

'Nothing to do with the tanker not being able to get up Amy's track, is it?' said Antony, who'd obviously guessed the real reason for all the cheesemaking.

'Oh God! I remember Amy's track,' said Megan. 'I had to deliver something to her once. Bloody

68

nightmare.' She paused. 'It was after Amy moved into the care home. I had a little look round while I was there. Fantastic position! Must be worth a fortune, that place,' she added. 'And all that land.'

'Sorting out the track'll be expensive,' said a man in a pale pink cashmere jumper.

'What sort of expensive?' Fran asked.

'Hard to tell. Could be twenty grand, could be five. I could send a man along to do an estimate if you like.'

'It might be cheaper to get a car that can cope with the track,' said Fran.

'I can help you out there,' said another man. Unlike the man in the pink jumper, he accompanied his offer with a leer. Fran couldn't remember – if she'd ever known – which woman was his wife. She felt sorry for her.

'How will you get your cheese up to London if you haven't got a decent car?' asked Megan. 'Though I dare say Antony could lend you one if he trusted you to drive it.'

'My car is fine really,' said Fran quickly. 'I can always park it at the bottom and walk up the track.'

'I must say,' said Antony as he helped himself to cream, 'this does look as if it's worth the heart attack.'

'I could help you out with a decent van,' said the man with the leer again. 'Four-wheel drive, maybe refrigerated.' He reached into his pocket and handed Fran a card. 'Get in touch. I'll do you a good deal.'

Fran took the card, glad that she was wearing jeans and so had a pocket. 'I don't think I'll need a refrigerated van, not yet.'

The man sucked his teeth. 'Expensive to get the wrong thing and have to change it.'

'I'll have a think,' said Fran and was grateful when someone changed the subject.

At last, people started to mutter about babysitters and begin to leave.

When she and Antony were going, the man who wanted to sell Fran a car kissed her rather too affectionately and reminded her to get in touch. 'I'll see you right,' he assured her.

But once outside the house, Antony said, 'Don't buy a car from that man.'

'Oh? Is he untrustworthy then?'

'I wouldn't buy anything from him myself. I'm not saying he's a rogue but he charges over the odds and would try to get you to take out finance for it which is never a good idea if you can avoid it.'

'I may not have much choice. I hate the thought of it but I must be practical.'

'I must say I was very impressed by the cheese. Would you really take it up to London to sell?'

'It's where I know people who'd buy it.'

'It shows initiative that you did something with milk that would have been wasted.'

'Glad you approve,' she said, hoping he couldn't tell how grumpy his approval made her. If she'd made the cheese because she thought it was a good idea it would have been fine. But she'd made it because the track was too bad for the milk to be collected. And although the rain had eased off and the tanker had made it up the previous day, it could all go wrong again at any time.

'I don't know if you're interested, but I go up to London about twice a week. If you wanted a lift I'd be happy to take you,' Antony said.

Amy would turn her shoulder and decline politely, Fran knew, but she was tired and a bit frazzled. 'That might be very useful. Although I do still need a four-wheel-drive car.'

'You do, but don't rush into it. And as for the track – if you like I could lend you the money to fix it.'

This amazingly generous offer took her aback. And she knew Amy would refuse it, under any circumstances. She should too. She took a breath. 'That's very kind but if I'm making cheese with the milk I won't need to fix the track.'

'You will, you know.'

She did know. There was no point in trying to make the farm profitable – if such a thing was possible – if people couldn't get to it.

'So, how about the lift to London?' Antony went on.

This was an offer of help she felt she could accept. 'Which day are you going?'

'I'm going up three days next week. Monday, Wednesday and Friday.'

'Shall we say Friday?' Fran said. This should give her time to see Amy, make more cheese, get herself a bit better organised.

'Friday's fine. I'll pick you up.'

'I'll meet you at the bottom of the lane if you like,' said Fran.

'No need for that,' he said. 'Besides, if you're going try and sell your products you'll have samples. But I will just tell you that I always work on the drive to London. I have a driver.'

'That's all right!' she said, part relieved and part offended. 'It means we don't have to make polite conversation all the way to London.'

'Or indeed any sort of conversation.'

Fran suspected he was laughing at her. 'Did that sound rude?' she asked. 'I hope it didn't.'

'It sounded honest, which is always nice and unusual.'

'Unusual? Do people usually tell you a whole load of lies, then?'

He shrugged. 'Not lies exactly.'

'But what comes out of the back end of cows?'

He laughed audibly this time. 'Exactly.'

Fran sat in silence for a minute or two. 'So are you a multi-millionaire then? Having a chauffeur and all?'

'Certainly not. You could say I was comfortably off, but that doesn't make me the spawn of the devil, you know.'

'Hmm, in Amy's eyes you'd be the spawn of the devil if you didn't have a brass farthing, as I'm sure she'd say.'

'True. Amy thinks I'm the spawn of the devil for all sorts of other reasons.'

Fran suddenly found this rather depressing. Amy's dislike of Antony was always going to be a problem for her.

'I'll tell her how kind you've been to me,' she said.

'Don't. She wouldn't want me to be kind to you. She'd suspect my motives.'

'Would she be right to suspect your motives?' Fran was suddenly suspecting them herself.

'No,' he said firmly. 'I'm just offering you a lift. It's no big deal.' He sounded a bit cross.

Fran couldn't help wondering why.

Chapter Six

Fran didn't take any samples to Amy in the care home. She knew that old people shouldn't have products made from unpasteurised milk and she didn't want to be accused of trying to bump off her elderly relative in order to get her hands on the farm sooner than she might do. She did tell her about it though, at her next visit, a few days later.

'Amy? I made some cheese with the milk.'

Amy was being particularly deaf today so Fran didn't bother with details.

'Cheese?' said Amy. 'Did you find the presses and things in one of the outhouses?'

'No. At least, I think I did, but I'm making soft cheese to begin with.'

'Our milk makes lovely Cheddar,' said Amy. 'It's the grass the cows live on. Full of flavour.'

'Oh, I know! The soft cheeses all taste amazing!'

'You want to age the cheese in the little quarry,' said Amy, ignoring Fran. 'Six months – even a year – in there and you'll have the tangiest, tastiest Cheddar you'll ever eat.'

'Oh? Where is the quarry?' said Fran. This was really useful information.

'It's on the farm!' said Amy, as if Fran was being stupid. 'And now if you don't mind, Francesca, dear, it's time for my nap.'

As Amy frequently fell asleep without it being time for her nap, Fran felt flattered to be warned.

'Just before you nod off, could you just tell me where the quarry is? On the farm?'

But it was too late, Amy's eyes were closed and her chest was gently rising and falling. Fran decided to ask Tig sometime about the quarry. She also resolved to go and see Tig's mother, Mrs Brown, and find out about how to make hard cheese. As she drove home she pondered the quarry. She knew cheese was aged in caves and mineshafts but a quarry? It would have to have some sort of roof, surely? In her mind quarries were open to the skies.

Thanks to Tig finding a number of old milk churns, which he presented to her, sterilised and clean, Fran managed to use all the milk on the days when it wasn't collected. It was hard work, having to make the cheese in such small batches, but she kept on because she knew the milk co-op would like to stop collecting from her altogether. If she had a proper market for her products before that happened, she could get some help and maybe buy some equipment. Currently she was storing it all in the domestic fridge, which was not ideal. She needed a dedicated fridge. Although to be fair, it took a lot of milk to make quite a small amount of cheese.

She would also need a dedicated cheesemaking room that would pass all the health and hygiene requirements, proper sterilising facilities and possibly a refrigerated van. How she'd ever pay for all those things made her head hurt. Perhaps she should start buying lottery tickets.

Fran enjoyed travelling up to London with Antony the following Friday. The fact that he was working meant she could sit in the front with the driver, Seb, who, though pleasant, didn't chat so Fran could look at the scenery. She could also plan what she was going to say to the various people she had arranged to meet. (One of them was Issi, for drinks, which she was greatly looking forward to.) In the boot of the car was a selection of very smart cool boxes, lent by Antony, containing her samples.

As they approached Mayfair, where Antony's offices were, he said, 'Oh, by the way, I won't be needing Seb during the day, if you'd like him to take you from place to place.'

Fran was taken aback. She had been worrying about getting around with her samples but had decided she'd have to cab it. 'Really? But would Seb want to do that?'

'I wouldn't mind,' said Seb.

Fran looked at him properly for the first time. He was the same age as Antony and was casually dressed. He and Antony had also been informal with each other when he'd dropped Antony off. He was more than just a chauffeur, Fran decided.

'I've a few places to visit round here and in Knightsbridge,' she said now, 'but eventually I want to go to Fitzrovia. If you could take me, it would be absolutely brilliant.'

'You could keep the cool boxes with your samples in the car and fetch them as you need them.'

'That would be amazing!' said Fran. 'Like being in *The Apprentice!*'

Antony laughed.

It was, she realised as Seb drove her and her cool boxes to Fitzrovia, exactly like being on *The Apprentice*. You thought you had a brilliant product that everyone would love and yet, although everyone did love it, not a single pub, deli or restaurant wanted to buy any. And worse, her old boss Roger was out of the country and so didn't even get to taste it.

By the time Seb was slowing down outside the most important cheese shop, in Fitzrovia, she was ready to ask him to keep the cheese in the car and hope Issi could meet her for drinks early. What was she thinking of – visiting one of the major cheese retailers with her little cheeses made in her kitchen? She must be mad!

In fact, she opened her mouth to do just that but Seb, who was obviously a mind reader, forestalled her. 'Come on, Fran,' he said. 'I know what you're thinking; no one has wanted the cheese so far, so why would this place? You think you should never have come and should just go home. But think about it! You've come all this way and you're lucky to get a meeting with these people. Don't waste the opportunity. Get in there and sell cheese!'

'If ever you get fed up with being Antony's driver, you should set up as an inspirational speaker,' she said, trying to sound ironic and cool but realising she just sounded frightened.

'The cheese is great; you know it is. Now get in there!'

She had produced a spreadsheet with costings and prices on it. (Antony had kindly printed it out for her) to take in with her and she had her cheese. Mascarpone, ricotta, cream cheese and mozzarella. She also had some cream, as she'd had spare pots and couldn't think of another cheese that she could make.

She had an appointment with the owner of the cheese shop: John Radcliffe, who turned out to be surprisingly young, with a very intense expression and a serious-looking beard. He interrupted her opening spiel. 'Let's start with the nice bit, shall we? Let's taste the cheese.'

'OK, well this is—'

'No, don't tell me. I'll know. Just put a bit of each on a plate.'

It was nerve-racking, waiting in silence while the man scooped off bits of cheese with a knife, not even bothering with a cracker. (She had water biscuits ready in her bag.)

'Mm, yes, well, it's nice cheese and we could be interested. But as I expect you know, provenance is very important to us. When we sell a cheese we want to know everything about it from the pasture, the breed of cows—'

'The "terroir"?' It was probably too soon to make jokes but Fran felt too agitated to be completely sensible.

'Yup. We'd make a site visit, make sure you're producing this in hygienic conditions.'

'OK.' Would she be able to turn the dairy into a cheese room in time? Unlikely.

'But really, we'd like a hard cheese. Unpasteurised. The flavour of these soft ones indicate a properly matured Cheddar-type cheese would be delicious.'

'How long would it take for it to be properly mature, do you reckon?'

'A year really, possibly two. We could taste at six months.'

Fran exhaled. Even if she could make really good Cheddar she'd need to be selling it sooner than a year's time. She could be kicked off the farm way before then if things didn't turn round.

'I'm sorry,' said John Radcliffe, 'I can see that's depressed you a bit. Making cheese isn't a way to make a quick buck, you know.'

'I do know. The thing is, the farm I'm...managing is in a bad way financially. I need it to earn some money, fast.'

'Why don't you try to sell it locally to you? While it's good to come to the top, you'd find it easier if you kept things smaller, and closer to where you're producing the cheese.'

'I don't know anyone locally. I used to work in London, in pubs; I thought I might sell them my soft cheese.' She realised her voice had a tremor in it and really hoped she wasn't going to cry.

'They'll want hard cheese too. Think of the shelf life.'

'I know. I should have thought. I suppose I wanted them to make amazing pizza with my home-made mozzarella.'

'Why don't you make pizza? It might well be an easier sell than cheese.'

'Because I want to make cheese! I know the pasture on the farm is special. It's never been ploughed – even during the war – and the wild flowers are amazing. Not that I've seen them, I haven't been there long enough, but know the cheese would be really special. Anyone could make pizza.'

'You have passion. That's good.'

'The trouble is,' Fran said, getting up, gathering her bits and pieces, 'I have passion, but not very much knowledge and no money at all. I think I'll need all of those things.' She was near tears now. She had to get out before they appeared.

John Radcliffe put out a hand. 'Sit down,' he said. 'Let's have a coffee or some tea.' He got up and went to the door. 'If anyone could send a couple of teas in here I'd be grateful.'

The tea came with some chocolate brownies and very soon Fran found herself telling John Radcliffe everything. She told him how she'd come to be on the farm, and about the milk. 'The trouble is, if I can't sell it as liquid, and I don't think I will be able to, long term or for much money – I'm sure you know how low milk prices can drop to – I have to make some-thing. And there are gallons of it.' She paused for a sip of tea. 'Although I am getting much better at making the cheese, which does use up masses of milk.'

'And is there someone who could teach you to make hard cheese?'

She nodded. 'There's the herdsman's mother.'

'Go to her. Get her to tell you everything. She'll tell you things you'd never find out from a modern cheesemaker, things that will make your cheese unique. Which is what we're looking for.

Cheesemaking isn't entirely scientific, there's a bit of magic involved too. Producers make cheese every day, but sometimes the cheese wins prizes. No one ever knows what they did differently that day to make it prize-winning.'

'Apparently there's a quarry somewhere on the farm that I haven't had time to look for yet that's a good place to age the cheese.'

'It sounds absolutely ideal,' said John Radcliffe, putting the last piece of brownie into his mouth. 'I'm going to come and visit you in the summer. I have a feeling about you; I think you could produce something really special.'

Later, in a cocktail bar with Issi, near to Antony's offices, she related all this.

'So it's good news really,' said Issi, watching her friend take a gulp of her Cosmopolitan.

'Yes, but only in the long term.' Fran put down her glass and realised it was now empty. 'I need money now!'

'Well,' said Issi. 'I could take a few days off from my studies. Why don't I come down and we could do a supper club together? You could give samples of the cheese and perhaps sell it from the back door, so to speak.'

'Is that legal?'

'Well, you'd have to make sure it was all hygien-ically produced and things, wouldn't you? The same as if you sold it at a farmers' market.'

'I'm going to have to convert a building or resurrect the dairy. I need somewhere I can make cheese in hygienic conditions,' said Fran. 'But where there's a problem there's a solution.' She looked at her watch. 'I've got time for another cocktail. Have you?'

Fran and Seb were waiting for Antony who'd been delayed. 'So what is it he does, actually?' Fran asked Seb. She might not have felt brave enough to be so direct if it hadn't been for the cocktails.

'He does a fair few things. The farm is run by a manager, although Ant does know his stuff there. Mostly, he works in the City, but what really floats his boat is his directorship of a wine-importing business. He likes going out to find the small vineyards that no one knows about,' said Seb. 'I like those road trips, they're a lot of fun.'

Fran realised she didn't know Antony well enough to think of him as fun. But she was very glad that Seb did.

'So, how do you come to be Antony's driver? I mean did you just apply for the job in the normal way?'

Seb shook his head. 'Ant and I were at uni together. He happened to mention he needed a driver just when I'd mentioned I needed a job. Works perfectly. I live up above the garages at Park House. Nice little flat and room for me to follow my passion, which is making music.' He grinned. 'Works well for both of us.'

Fran slept most of the way home. She got in the back next to Antony and started by pretending to sleep, so she wouldn't have to tell him that things hadn't gone as swimmingly as she'd planned (given that no one wanted her to supply them with soft cheese), and then, exhausted by the whole process and two strong drinks, the real thing followed.

Although she had sounded upbeat to Issi – and when she was with her she always felt upbeat – finding premises that would meet the hygiene requirements so she could make and sell her cheese wouldn't be easy. Getting the old dairy into shape would take capital, and she didn't have any of that.

She woke up just at the end of the motorway.

'Do you want a drink of water?' said Antony, offering an unopened bottle.

'No thank you,' said Fran. He'd witnessed her sleeping; she didn't want him now to watch her chugging water from a bottle – it seemed an unattractive thing to be seen doing.

'So how did your day go?'

She had been about to say, 'Really well, thank you,' but in the dark of the back of the car she found herself saying, 'Not as well as I'd hoped.'

'Oh?'

'None of the pubs I tried – where I used to work, for example – wanted soft cheese. And the big supplier in Fitzrovia really wants a hard cheese, too. I'm fairly sure I could learn to make that, but where? The buildings on the farm would cost a lot to bring up to hygienic standards. I don't have the capital.'

He didn't answer for a few minutes. Fran watched the hedgerows passing, looking out for signposts to give her clue of how near home she was.

'Look, why don't you come back to mine for some supper? I'll run you back afterwards. We need to talk.'

'Do we? Aren't we talking now?'

'We are, but we need to talk more seriously.'

'OK. I mean, that would be nice. I think.'

'You're not sure?'

'No. When people say "we need to talk" it usually means they're going to sack you or break up with you. Although obviously, not in this case.'

'Then why the doubts?'

'I think you know,' she said quietly. Maybe Antony had somehow forgotten that as far as.she was concerned, he was the enemy. And if she liked him – he was quite kind – it didn't make her hobnobbing with him any more acceptable. Not really.

Seb drove them up the driveway to Antony's house, which Fran had been longing to see, but would have

85

preferred to do it in daylight. Still, there were a number of security lights, which helped.

It was, she had concluded before they'd even stopped in front of the door, not to her taste. If she had the millions she assumed he had, she'd have had a gorgeous period property, not this fifties-style house, which seemed designed to show off wealth rather than taste.

Pleased she could dismiss his house so easily, she got out of the car with a certain amount of grace.

'Was there any cheese left?' asked Seb, retrieving the cool boxes from the boot.

'No. It all went.' Fran was quite pleased about this. No one really wanted to buy her cheese but at least they were happy to eat it.

'Oh, shame,' he said. 'I was hoping to try some.'

Fran felt awful. Seb had been so kind to her. 'Next batch, I'll bring some over. Which kind do you particularly like?'

'Any of them. And when you do get round to making Cheddar, I love that!'

She smiled. 'You'll be the first to have some, if and when I ever manage to make it.'

'Thanks. I'll make sure you don't forget.'

By the time Seb was walking back down the drive to his cottage, Antony had opened the door. 'Come in. Now, would you like a proper drink? I've been overdosing on coffee all day and could do with a little alcohol.'

Fran might have had two strong cocktails with Issi but she didn't think tea would be enough of a prop to take her through a conversation she suspected was going to be awkward. He was going to offer her help and she would have to refuse.

'I'll have what you're having.'

'Good choice. Then let's go through to the sitting room. The wood burner should be going.'

The sitting room wasn't cosy. It had very high ceilings and a lot of panelling. The fireplace was surrounded by small red bricks and reminded Fran of her doll's house, which had been her mother's. It was fine in a doll's house, she concluded, but not so good full-sized.

'Do sit down.' Antony gestured to the huge leather sofas that were pulled up near the wood burner.

'How come your fire is lit when you've been away all day?' she asked.

'Staff,' he said ruefully. 'And the housekeeper will have left supper, too. There will be enough for both of us. I'll heat it up and we can have it in here. The dining room is a bit gloomy and will be cold.' He handed her a tumbler half full of a golden liquid. 'It's my favourite single malt. I hope you like it.'

She waited until he had revved up the fire, put on another log, and sat down before she sipped. 'It's delicious. Smoky. Strong.'

'I know. I think we need it. It's been a long day.'

'Did your day not go well, either?'

'It went fine. I just don't much like being in London. Well, I don't mind it sometimes, but today was all work.'

'Shall we get the "having a word with" over with?' suggested Fran. 'Otherwise it'll be hanging over me.'

'You don't want to eat first? I'm starving myself. Everything seems more daunting if you're hungry.'

'It seems more daunting because you're putting it off!' said Fran.

He chuckled. 'It really isn't. There – that was the microwave. Drink your whisky and I'll bring through our supper.'

Considering they didn't really know each other and eating off one's lap was usually only something you did with close friends, Fran did find herself relaxing. The sofas (they had one each) were very comfortable, if rather unattractive. He handed her a plate of beef stew and mashed potatoes with green beans and set a glass of red wine on the coffee table in front of her.

As she wasn't looking forward to the 'we must talk' part of the evening she decided to hold it off with light conversation, also known as nosy questioning, while she ate.

'Have you lived here long?' she asked.

'All my life, on and off. My grandfather bought the farm and had this house built.'

'It's very – grand.'

He laughed. 'It's the vision of a man who made his money quite quickly and wanted to show it all off. Not really my taste but it's home.'

'You could have it all extensively remodelled,' said Fran, thinking that was what she would do if she had as much money as he seemed to have.

'I could but I can't quite face the upheaval and don't know exactly what I'd do to replace it all.'

'You'd get a good designer to do that,' Fran said, sipping her wine and thinking how delicious it was.

'There's still the upheaval.'

'Yes, well, you'd have to go on an extended holiday to get away from it all.'

'Which I'm not likely to do.'

'But you said you liked it down here? Living in the country, I mean. Why don't you make your living space nicer?'

Antony shrugged. 'It's OK. It's comfortable. Now, enough quizzing about interior-decoration choices, I want to talk about you.'

Just for a second Fran allowed herself to imagine what it would be like if he really wanted to talk about her and not Hill Top Farm. It was a pleasant second, she acknowledged, and then she snapped back into reality.

'OK,' she said cautiously.

'I know you don't want my help. I know that Amy has said I'm a bad person who only wants to get my greedy hands on her little corner of heaven – and some of that is true.'

'Which part?' Fran couldn't help this little dig.

'I really do want to get my hands on your little corner of heaven,' he said smiling, yet serious. 'But I'm not a bad man. I just think you've been given a task that's very hard indeed for anyone who hasn't a huge amount of experience or capital.'

'That's probably true, but I have been given the task. I have accepted it. I have to do my absolute best.'

'That's great! I really admire that. But will you please accept a little help?'

'Help often comes with strings attached,' Fran said. 'If you help me I'll be indebted to you. I won't like that. And nor will Amy.'

Antony didn't answer immediately. 'I get that. I wouldn't like that either if I was you, but I'm finding it really hard watching you struggle when I could help you so easily.'

'We all have our crosses to bear.' She smiled at him.

'You're not helping.'

'Nor are you.'

'I am at least trying to! More wine?' He got up and came back with the bottle and put some in her glass. 'I was going to do Dry January but now I've decided Dry February is better.'

'Oh, me too! Only I might take the weekends off.'

'So we're not going to drink during the week for four weeks at most,' said Antony. 'Not very taxing.'

'And less taxing for me. I haven't got a cellar full of delicious wine to tempt me.'

'I'll leave bottles of it on your doorstep so we're both tempted.'

She laughed. 'I could save the bottles up until Friday night.'

'We're going off the point,' said Antony, suddenly serious. 'If I could think of a way you could pay me back for my help would you let me?'

'What do you want to do to help?'

'I want to have your track done.'

'So, in your mind, when I sell the farm to you there'll be one less job to do.'

'True. I also want to help you have a building converted into somewhere you could make cheese that is hygienic, so you could sell it.' He raised his eyebrow at her. 'You can't say I'd do that so I'd have somewhere to make cheese when I buy the farm.'

'All right, but I expect a nicely done-up building would be useful for something.'

He sighed. 'You are exasperating! If I did those things for you, you'd at least be in with a chance of making that farm profitable.'

'I agree, and it would be really, really kind of you—'

'I promise you I can afford it. I wouldn't have to go without a single new car or foreign holiday or anything else people spend their money on.'

'You could have your house remodelled?'

'Well, I'm not going to. What do you say? Will you let me do that?'

'Only if you can think of some way, or something – or many things – that I could do to pay you back.'

'You won't be able to pay me back financially, even if Amy has an undiscovered insurance policy lying in a drawer.'

As Fran was fairly sure Amy hadn't got an undiscovered anything in that line, she nodded. 'I accept that. So, what can I do? Or do you need time to think about it?'

'Actually, I think I know. Have you finished eating?'

'Yes, but—'

'Come with me for a minute. We'll have some cheese with the rest of the wine later, if you can face it, of course. But I think you could be the one to solve a problem I've had for months.'

She followed him through the kitchen (massive, not her taste at all) into an equally vast integral garage. 'Here,' he said, gesturing to a vast chest freezer.

'What about it? It doesn't look problematic to me.'

He opened it.

'There isn't a body in there you want me to dispose of?' She was joking but as she said the words she wondered. After all, he was suggesting spending thousands on the farm with no hope of return. If a job was going to repay that it would have to be pretty enormous. But although Amy had said how wicked he was, Fran was fairly sure the word 'murderer' had never been used.

'In a manner of speaking. Look.'

She went over and peered into the enormous chest freezer. In it were rows and rows of frozen packages not instantly recognisable.

'What is it?'

'It's pheasants. And some grouse.'

'Where on earth did they come from? Did they fall off the back of a shoot or something?'

Antony looked sheepish. 'It was a bit like that.'

'I think you have to explain further.' Having Antony on the back foot was not a situation to be wasted.

'A friend had them. I felt obliged to help out.'

'You bought them? Why?'

'Because...' He shrugged. 'It's a long story.' He looked at her appealingly. 'Can you get rid of them for me?'

'You could just hire a digger and bury them.'

He made a sound indicating outrage. 'What a waste that would be! You're the woman who can't throw away milk that has hardly any value. No,'

Antony went on, still sounding cross, 'I'm happy to help you with money to fix the track and do up a building but—'

Fran put up a peace-making hand. 'I was joking! You're quite right. I hate waste and I hate to pass up free stuff. What I'll do is make pies.'

'Pies?'

Fran nodded. 'I spent today in pubs who want good home-made food, something a bit different. I was offering them cheese, but they didn't want mozzarella – or at least not much of it – but pies? Oh yes. They'd want pies.' She paused. 'I happen to make rather wonderful puff pastry. Not that I'm one to boast.'

'But boasting anyway!' Antony laughed teasingly. 'I think pies are an excellent idea! It'll give you some form of income when the cows go dry.' He looked at her. 'You did know that cows go dry about three months before they calve?'

She forced a smile. 'Oh yes. Of course I did.' But she knew he knew she was lying.

Chapter Seven

Although she was extremely tired, Fran wrote Issi a quick email as soon as she got back. *We need to do the supper club quite soon I think so we can start to raise some money. Let me know when you could get down here and we can get going on publicity.*

A few minutes later she sent another email. *Any chance you could bring your KitchenAid?*

Not on the train, no, came Issi's reply. *Talk in the morning.*

As she snuggled down to sleep Fran decided she'd have to buy her own food processor, and possibly a printer, too. Unless, the thought crept in just before she drifted off, Antony had one she could use.

She was up and into her unsuitable wellington boots early the next morning. She wanted to talk to Tig.

'Morning!' she said gaily as she found him ushering the herd into the milking parlour. She admired the huge brown- and white-flecked beasts whose coats seemed curly, almost woolly, but she kept out of their way. 'I need to ask you a few things.'

'Can it wait until after milking or won't it take long?' he asked.

'No, it's really quick.'

He nodded, indicating she should say what she wanted. He wasn't a man to waste movements or words. She liked that. He had a good strong nose, she noticed, that set off his eyes and his weathered skin.

'Firstly, I need to know when the cows go dry and for how long.'

'Late March. Three months. Usually.' He seemed about to elaborate but Fran hurried on, conscious she was keeping him from his cows.

'Fine. The second thing is, I'd really love to talk to your mother about making hard cheese. The soft cheese I've made already, while delicious, isn't what the major wholesaler wants. I need to know about proper cheese.'

He nodded again. 'She's your woman for that. I'll let her know you want to talk to her and she'll come up. But she's due to visit her sister soon.'

Fran shook her head. 'I think it would be better if I went to her. Perhaps she could come up later if she's got time, and we can find the equipment that may be here, but I think I'd like to visit her first.'

96

'And the third thing?' he asked.

'How did you know there was a third thing?' She was surprised. He didn't usually initiate conversation, he just replied when she talked to him.

'You're still here, not rushing off.'

Fran laughed. 'OK, well, you're right, there is a third thing. When I last saw Amy she mentioned an old quarry. She said it would be good for ripening the cheese but I haven't found it.'

'Can't help you there. You need to look for it yourself.' He seemed amused. 'You need to walk the land, miss—'

'Fran—'

'Fran. "The best manure on a farm is the sole of the farmer's boot." It's an old saying.'

'Really?

'And talking of boots, you should get yourself a decent pair.'

She looked down at her Cath Kidstons and thought maybe he was right.

'I'll take you, next time I'm going to the supply shop,' said Tig. 'There are one or two things we need.'

'Thank you,' said Fran. 'I have to say, Tig, you're very talkative today. Positively garrulous.'

His face formed an expression that in anyone else would be laughter. 'Getting to know you a bit better.'

This was almost as good as him saying he trusted her to make the farm pay, but as this was a long way off, she couldn't expect that yet. 'So, where does your mother live?'

'Little cottage, down by the bottom of the lane. Turn left at the bottom of the track and you'll see it. Hers is the second one along. Mine is the first one.'

'Thanks. And would now be a good time, do you think?'

'Possibly. Mornings are best for her. She has a nap after lunch and later she watches *Pointless*.'

Fran laughed. 'I like *Pointless* too. I'd rather go now while I can see the potholes in the track.'

'That'll need seeing to soon, I reckon. The track's been bad a long time.'

She sighed. 'I have a plan to get it sorted out, but you know what happens to plans. But if the track's in good condition maybe I won't need to make cheese.'

'You'll need to make cheese,' said Tig firmly. 'Not enough money in liquid milk, not the amount we produce.'

Fran found the pair of cottages quite easily. She realised that if they were part of the farm, they could probably be sold and solve all the financial problems. But she would never do that, she realised, before the thought was fully formed. It would be wrong for so many reasons. It would break up the estate and make Tig and his mother homeless. She rather hoped they owned their cottages and then the thought need never arise again.

Instinct told Fran to walk round to the back door and the speed with which it was opened told her this was the right thing. Mrs Brown seemed less daunting than before when she had made Fran feel judged and wanting. Now she was wearing black trousers and a pretty V-necked jumper. Her hair, though greying, was in soft curls round her face and she had Tig's bright blue eyes. She had his skin too, weathered but firm and attractive.

'Hello, Mrs Brown,' she said immediately. 'Tig thought it would be all right to call.'

'I've just put the kettle on for my second breakfast. Come in.'

'I want to learn about cheese,' said Fran when she was in the spotless and tidy kitchen, sitting at the table. 'I can do soft cheese now, but I need to make a hard cheese. I know you're quite busy with your sister and Tig, but I thought I'd find out as much as possible before you go away.'

Soon both women were seated with tea and a plate of biscuits between them, Fran started on her list of questions. Mrs Brown was calm and easy to talk to. Possibly Fran had passed some sort of test, but now Mrs Brown was an ally, Fran was sure.

'Did you make the cheese at the farm, Mrs Brown? If so, which building?'

'We used to make it in the dairy, but it's been a junk store for a while now. When my sister was ill, I had to go and look after her so Amy didn't have anyone to make the cheese. She said she didn't have time to make it herself.' Mrs Brown frowned. 'She didn't quite have the knack, truth be told. She knew what to do but it never came out quite right.'

Fran remembered what John Radcliffe had said about there being magic involved. Maybe Amy didn't have the right spell. 'She told me about the quarry where you used to ripen it?'

Mrs Brown laughed. 'Oh yes. The quarry. It wasn't just a quarry obviously. It had a roof. But it was a good place for the cheese.'

'So where is it, exactly?'

Mrs Brown shook her head. 'She'll tell you herself when she wants you to know. She's always been very secretive about it. It goes back to the War when I think they hid bits of extra food up there. She only told me where it was when she found getting up there too much for her.' Mrs Brown paused, putting an end to the subject of the quarry. 'So, just how much about cheesemaking do you know?'

'Nothing really. Except what I've learnt from making soft cheese.'

'Well, it's quite simple really. What you'll need to do is find out what sort of state the old equipment is in.'

'You wouldn't make the cheese for me?'

Mrs Brown laughed again. 'No, no. I'll help you, but I won't do it for you. When it comes down to it, cheese is mostly washing up! There's so much equipment that has to be washed and dried, sometimes it seems that's all you do!' She paused and became more serious. 'I have my sister who's not well who I have to visit quite often. Besides, it's important that you do things for yourself, if you're going to take over the farm.'

'I may not. I may not have the opportunity if I don't make a go of it.'

Mrs Brown looked anxious for a second. 'But you want to make a go of it? You're not just here for a little rural holiday?'

Fran laughed. 'Sorry, but the thought of this being anything like a holiday is hilarious. There's no phone signal, no shower, no central heating, the bed is as old as the house and less comfortable to sleep on. This is not a holiday!'

'So why are you still here?'

Fran took a breath. It mattered to her that both Mrs Brown and Tig should understand why she was putting up with all the difficulties, the challenges, the anxieties, for a life that was pretty foreign to her, really. She searched for the words that would make it clear. She took a deep breath. 'I'm not sure,' was what she came out with. 'I can't really explain but although it's so tough here, one way and another, I do love it. It feels right for me. I love the scenery, I love the way of life, I'll get to love the cows – I'm sure I will, when I know a bit more about them. There's no sensible answer, really. I just really want to make a go of it.'

Mrs Brown put her hand on hers. 'Then that's good enough for me.' She cleared her throat. 'One of the reasons Amy doesn't want the farm sold, one of the many reasons, is that it will put Tig out of his home – I own this cottage but Tig is tied to the job. Oh, I suppose the new owner might keep him on, and if him-next-door—'

'Antony Arlingham?'

'Yes. If he bought it he probably would let Tig go on living here even if he sold her herd – but – well, Amy would turn in her grave if Antony bought it!' Mrs Brown suddenly realised what she'd said. 'If she was in it, I mean,' she added, looking embarrassed.

Fran overlooked this faux pas. 'But why would Amy react so badly? Antony seems a really nice guy.'

'As I told you when we first met, it goes back to his grandfather's time and Amy doesn't forget. Or forgive, in this case.'

'But that's ridiculous. None of what happened all those years ago could be Antony's fault.'

'It's not only that, it's what he'd like to do with the farm. Some people say he'd turn it into a vineyard.'

Fran nodded. He had connections with the wine trade, Seb had told her. Wouldn't he have mentioned his plans to her? Apparently not. And while a vineyard would be so much better than a motorbike scrambling centre, which was one of the other suggestions, it would still be wrong.

Mrs Brown nodded. 'It's got the perfect sunny slopes you need.'

Fran realised Mrs Brown was right; it was a possibility. 'It would be dreadful for the land to be ploughed when it never has been, for the structure of the soil to be changed after hundreds of years.' (She'd done a bit of internet searching about ancient pasture since Issi had told her how important it was.)

'Exactly.' They had both finished their tea and Fran felt it was time to go.

Back in her own kitchen, Fran emailed Antony thanking him for his kindness the day before. She went on:

I will come and collect the pheasants and grouse as soon as I can arrange to make the pastry etc. (I may have to buy a food processor.) As I may have mentioned, I do plan to have a supper club (when people invite strangers to dinner in their homes and they pay what they think is appropriate, just in case you're unfamiliar with the concept). I'll get my friend Issi down from London to help me.

Thank you for everything,

Fran

PS You don't have a printer I could use, do you?

Fran had planned to walk the farm sometime, see every corner and find the quarry. It wasn't that she needed it yet, she was just annoyed that she didn't know where it was and equally annoyed that no one would tell her. But as the rain had sleet in it, she concluded that today wasn't the day and decided to check out the dairy to see how easy it would be to turn it into a cheese room. And if that wasn't right for her cheese room, she'd find somewhere that was.

The room she felt was best had whitewashed walls and a stone floor. It was the same size as the dairy, but it had a lot less stuff in it and she thought the walls could be lined with something washable, and the floor tiled. Eventually she'd like to have both rooms. Between this room and the dairy, she found a wooden cheese press, some moulds and something with a screw and a handle that was possibly a mill, for crumbling the cheese before it went into the moulds. This much she felt she knew.

But it would take a lot of work to make it suitable for producing cheese she could sell, she could see that. And she'd have to buy new moulds and probably other things to make sure they were up to standard. And she had better check when she herself had last passed a food hygiene certificate. While she looked at the piles of stuff that would have to be cleared out she allowed herself a few moments of envy for Amy. When she had cheesemaking going on here she probably didn't have to worry about Health and Safety. People had probably eaten quite a lot of germs but, mostly, they had survived. Things were a lot stricter now.

Fran was feeling a bit depressed when she got back into the house. Tomorrow she'd have to make more cheese, she was certain. What with the weather making the track impassable for the tanker, it was inevitable. She decided to get all her kit in order. This cheered her up somewhat as she'd had the culture through the post so she could now make feta. Feta was a good cheese to cook with.

However, checking her emails later that afternoon gave her cause to become even more cheered. It was Issi.

I've been working things out and wonder if I could come down for more than a few days? Would you have me for a month or so? Hill Top would be the perfect place to work on my thesis and I could help you set up a website and with all the online marketing. I've got a good bit saved up so I can contribute to the housekeeping and I could carry on with the online stuff I do already. It would be so great – if you'll have me.

Fran got straight back. *It would be amazing! Come as soon as you can and stay as long as you like. I can't wait for you to be here.*

Chapter Eight

Just before she was properly awake the following morning, Fran was aware of feeling happy. Then she remembered that Issi was coming down. She felt she'd done well in the short time she'd been on the farm – nearly three weeks – but the problems were pretty insurmountable. Having Issi for help and support and pooling their housekeeping money would make it far more doable.

She decided to visit Amy early – she could get a phone signal in town and talk to Issi too. Sundays at the care home were always cheerful. Also, she felt she should tell Amy about Issi. She was sure Amy wouldn't mind her having a friend to stay, but maybe asking her would be politic. And if Fran didn't tell Amy herself, someone else surely would!

To her surprise the farm gate was open when she got back from the care home and there was a contractor's van pulled into the layby before the farm gate. The signwriting on the side told her it belonged to a firm who specialised in 'Track-Repair & Road Services'.

A cheery-looking man in a high-vis jacket and waterproof trousers appeared.

'Hello!' said Fran brightly, trying not to feel unnerved by the prospect of the farm track being attacked by powerful machinery.

'Morning!' said the man. 'Antony sent me over to sort out your track.'

'But it's Sunday!'

'I'm fitting you in specially.'

'Thank you so much!' Antony must be a very important customer.

'It's in a bad way, isn't it?'

'Yes.' There didn't seem anything else she could say.

'It'll take a few days, I'm afraid.'

'I'm sure that's fine.'

'Do you want me to tell you what we're going to do?'

No, Fran didn't. 'I'm sure if Antony hired you to make the track suitable for the milk tanker, that's good enough for me.'

The man grinned. 'That's the plan. He has high standards, has Antony. We've done a lot of work for him. If it's not up to scratch, he makes us do it again.' He paused. 'Pays promptly though.'

'Well, that's good.' Fran smiled. 'I'd best be off up the track. Will I be able to walk on it while you're doing it?'

'Oh yes. Should be fine. But good you're keeping your car down here.'

When Fran reached the back door she was surprised to see a large cardboard box. It couldn't have been left by the postman, he never came up, and nor did any other delivery service. She opened the box. In it was a fairly new-looking food processor and a printer. There was a card with Antony's address printed on it.

I don't use the food processor so you can have this and I also have a newer printer. Enjoy!

'I will, thank you, Antony!' said Fran to herself. 'But how can I ever pay you back for all this? Cooking a few – even a lot of – game birds won't really do it.'

But it was all she could do at the moment. She was determined, however, that something would occur to her. She couldn't be in his debt, and while she couldn't repay him in actual money, there would be more things he needed than having his chest freezer emptied out.

When she had got her new toys into the house and had unpacked the bits and pieces she'd picked up after seeing Amy, she poured the morning's milk into wide bowls so the cream could rise for the following day. What she couldn't fit into the bowls she left in the churns. She'd learnt to be adaptable when it came to her cheesemaking but some better equipment would make her life easier. The food processor was a start.

Three days later, she picked up Issi from the station. The amount of jumping up and down they did as they greeted each other caused a bit of amusement among the less-excited travellers but they were both so happy.

'I felt so jealous of you, having this whole new life to get into,' said Issi, not for the first time.

'And I'm so thrilled you're going to be here to share it with me. It'll be so much more fun with two of us.'

'So, what's our first project?' asked Issi as they walked to where the car was parked, dragging her suitcases.

'Getting home? But when we've had lunch and you've moved in, I'd love to see if we can get rid of the old fireplace.'

'Oh, me too! Maybe we could ask Tig if he could help? Find some mates who could supply some muscle?'

'Good idea. If we can avoid hiring a builder and just pay friends, it could save a lot.' Fran paused. 'God, this case is heavy!' she went on, trying to heave it into the back of the car. 'What have you got in here? Kettle bells?'

'It is mostly text books and kitchen equipment I thought you might need,' said Issi.

'Oh, brilliant! If I have a properly equipped kitchen I feel I can do anything. Although a properly equipped dairy is probably more what I need really.'

'Have you got any sort of dairy?'

'Yes, but it hasn't been used as one for ages and is full of junk and probably won't be considered hygienic by Food Standards.' She paused. 'But there's another building I think would be easier to convert.'

'We need to get on to that then,' said Issi, possibly sensing the dip in Fran's mood.

'Antony said he'd do it for me. But I don't think I can accept, not really.'

'Tell me about this Antony?'

Fran did up her seat belt. 'You know almost as much about him as I do. He's Amy's sworn enemy and, so far, my best friend.'

'Just a friend?'

Fran allowed herself a sigh. 'Well, if things were different, if he wasn't Amy's sworn enemy, if I wasn't so busy trying to keep things together here—'

'So what do you have to do, Fran? Tig does the cows...'

'I'm trying to get the books in order, sort the house out a bit and I've even had to fix bits of farm building. Things are falling apart rather. I quite often have to check on things for Amy, or find things for her. It's hard to pin down what I do, but it takes up a lot of time.'

'Jill of all work, then?'

Fran nodded. 'I don't know where the time goes except I don't even seem to have time to cut my toenails let alone wax my legs.'

'So that means Antony is out of the question? Because you've got hairy legs?'

Fran laughed. It did sound pretty trivial. 'It's not that really. If we didn't lead very different lives, I might be interested in him. I mean, he is quite attractive, but honestly, Issi, he's way out of my league and, after Alex, I am rather off men.'

'You were unlucky last time. Alex was attractive but a bit wet.' Issi had made it clear, after it had all ended, exactly what she'd thought of Fran's previous boyfriend. 'And as for being out of Antony's league, you are a very lovely woman, you know.'

'Thanks for the vote of confidence, honey, but really, you should see his house! Horrible but very expensive. And it's a well-known fact that couples are usually of similar status, financially and looks-wise,' she went on briskly, not giving Issi time to comment. 'Now let me tell you what Amy said about you coming.'

'Well, go on then!'

'She said, "Oh, you can't cope on your own then? That's disappointing."' Fran sighed. 'I think I'm destined to always disappoint Amy. I just can't do what she did for so many years: run the farm on my own.'

'Fran, Amy had years of experience. You have none. Of course it's going to be harder for you.'

'I know all that but I'm not sure Amy does. She thinks the younger generation have things far too easy. Spoilt, I think was the word she used.'

Issi laughed. 'I do hope you're going to take me to see Amy. She sounds a real character.'

Fran snorted rudely and turned into the farm. The gate was already open and there was a generator thumping away. There was also a huge pile of small stones that was obviously due to form the final surface.

'Oh, you're getting the track repaired!' said Issi. 'How are you paying for that?'

'Antony,' said Fran, sounding appalled. 'And what Amy would say if she knew that, I really hate to think. It would probably be enough to send her dicky heart into spasms.'

'Well, don't tell her then,' said Issi, ever practical.

'I won't but someone will, I'm willing to bet.'

'Oh come on, let's get home,' said Issi. 'I'm dying to move in.'

Chapter Nine

'Have you thought about the menu for the supper club?' asked Issi one bright morning a few days later, after the sitting room had finally, after a lot of work, been declared almost dust-free. A couple of days earlier Tig, Seb and the relief milkers had got rid of the fireplace, happy to do it for cash in hand, home-made brownies and beer. Now Fran and Issi were moving all the furniture out so they could see how it could work for the supper club.

'Well, it'll have a large cheese element to it—'

'Obviously.'

'But the main course will be game pies. Antony has a couple of freezerfuls of frozen birds. I've said I'll get rid of them for him. To repay him for doing the drive...I know!'

Issi looked at her friend a bit oddly but didn't pursue it. 'Will you buy the pastry, or make your own? Rough puff or proper puff?'

'I was wondering if I should make the butter for the pastry!' said Fran. 'And proper puff, of course. I love making it. It's soothing.'

'OK, that sounds good. What else?'

'Well, I thought a winter salad with goat's cheese but as that would involve buying cheese...'

Issi waited. 'And hell would freeze over before you did that?'

Fran nodded. 'So I thought I'd try making halloumi.'

'Is that even possible?' Issi obviously felt this was taking 'home-made' a step too far.

'Yup. It's a longer process but perfectly possible. It's all on the internet. The advantage I have is gallons of unpasteurised milk with a good butter-fat content.'

Issi smiled. 'And for pudding? Cheesecake? Followed by a cheese board? Any cheese as long as you can make it in your kitchen?'

Fran accepted this gentle teasing. 'Nearly right. But I am a bit bothered by the food hygiene side. I think for a supper club it may be all right to make cheese in less than perfect conditions but it's not ideal. I'll be feeding the public, and they will be paying.'

'I know this is going to sound like blasphemy,' said Issi, 'but could you do your first supper club without all the cheese? It would give you a bit of time to get a cheesemaking room sorted out.'

Fran sighed deeply. 'I know that would be sensible but it would break my heart. One of the reasons I want to do the supper club so much is to showcase my cheese.'

'Well,' said Issi briskly. 'Go and see Antony in the morning and agree to him lending you the money to make a cheese room.'

Fran made a calculation. 'I think he'll be working from home tomorrow.' She frowned. 'I really don't want to though. I hate asking for favours.'

'Hmm. Hadn't noticed that! You never seem to mind asking me for favours.'

'You're my best friend. It's completely different.'

They had decided they'd probably need to borrow some tables and chairs for the supper club but that it would be nice to use as many of Amy's as possible.

They were seeing how far into the corner a table could go while still letting people actually sit at it when Issi asked, 'So, individual pies, then?'

Fran shook her head. 'No. I'm going to do family-sized ones. Part of the point of food – particularly at a supper club – is the eating together. I'll put big pies, bowls of vegetables, extra gravy, things like that, in between groups of four or six. People will have to serve each other, talk to each other even if they're strangers, and it'll be like joining a large family.'

'Oh!' Issi was impressed.

'Apart from anything else, doing all those individual pies would be hellishly fiddly,' Fran added.

'But do you have enough pie dishes? Should I add it to the list of things we need to buy on eBay?'

'Amy has a very nice line in Pyrex, so we may be OK, but before we go to eBay, which I know is the sensible thing, we could see if there are any sales coming up at the local auction house. I love auctions!'

They concluded they could get twenty people into the sitting room if they divided them up into one table of eight, one of six and three of two.

'What sort of veg are we having?' asked Issi, disentangling the chairs they were using to check all the tables were usable.

'Carrots, probably, and whatever else is in season.'

'What sort of potatoes? Nothing too complicated, I hope.'

'Mash! Obviously! Pie and mash with gravy. People love it. I think we'll have to move that little table further away from the fire or the people sitting there will singe, and we can't have that.'

'If it passes its flue test, will you light the fire?' asked Issi. 'It might get awfully hot in here, with all those people.'

'I'll get Tig to light a fire that looks pretty but doesn't actually push out any heat,' said Fran. 'I bet he can do that.'

'And if it fails its test, we could just fill the fire-place with candles, set well back so they can't set light to anything.'

'Oh, good idea, Is. Now let's have something to eat. I'm starving.'

Later that evening Issi asked Fran three times if she'd emailed Antony to see if he could see her the following day, and so eventually, Fran did it. A reply pinged back saying yes, she could come at ten o'clock.

The next morning, having walked down the now nearly completed track, Fran set off in her car to see Antony. She planned to visit Amy later, and would ring Issi to see if she wanted collecting so they could go into town together. Issi had got up surprisingly early, saying she wanted to see Tig milking the cows.

Fran could not avoid comparing the sleek, well-kept feeling of Antony's property with Hill Top Farm as she drove up the perfectly smooth driveway. She really did prefer Amy's place: more hilly, definitely more scruffy, but also more welcoming and, she was sure Issi would confirm, more environmentally friendly. But there was probably a middle way between ramshackle and show home. She really wished she could be visiting Antony for a different reason, if he'd invited her for supper or something. As it was she was practically begging, and she was someone who found it so much easier to give than to receive. She really didn't like asking for favours – except from Issi – and she was going to be asking Antony for what amounted to the loan of several thousand pounds. The fact he could afford it didn't make it one bit easier. Still, it had to be done. There was more at stake here than her pride.

'Why are you laughing?' Antony asked as he handed Fran a cup of coffee made in a machine the size and value of a reasonably priced family car. They were sitting at the breakfast bar in his enormous kitchen.

She tried to stop giggling. 'It's just so funny – I mean the contrast! You've been up at Hill Top in all it's scruffiness, and you come from all this…' She gestured to the gleaming kitchen, which seemed never to have been sullied by anything as mundane as a chopped onion. 'To – well – a care home for items that will one day be referred to as "kitchenalia".'

'Rustic,' he said firmly. 'Hill Top is rustic.'

'It's sweet of you to give it an appealing name but not only is it rustic, it's probably unhygienic.'

He sipped his coffee thoughtfully. 'You're right,' he said eventually.

'You're not supposed to agree with me! You're supposed to say, "You've got to eat a peck of dirt before you die."'

'Most people agree that it's best not to eat it all at once.'

Fran sighed. Antony was drinking a double espresso, while she had gone for a latte. His taste in coffee made him seem severe, somehow, and hers made her a lightweight.

She put her head in her hands for a minute, resting her elbows on the stainless steel work surface, then straightened up. 'I've come here to say yes please to the cheese room. I need it if I'm going to serve cheese at my supper club and I want to. It's mostly to advertise the cheese that I'm doing it.'

She didn't mention that she'd wanted to do a supper club before she'd dreamt of making cheese, or that she hoped to make a bit of money out of it that she badly needed if she was going to have a chance of paying him back.

'Fran, just how long do you think it would take to get one of the outbuildings at your farm up to scratch as a place to make cheese?'

'I don't know. I'm not exactly sure what would be involved. And I accept that the supper club will have to be postponed while we do this but I thought if we got things going it would be done quicker.'

'If you don't want to sell the cheese per se just at the moment…'

'What do you mean?'

'I mean, if you just want to make cheese to serve at the supper club without giving people salmonella poisoning, you could make it here – and keep it here too, if your fridges are a bit full. I don't suppose

120

this kitchen would pass regulations for making cheese on any kind of scale, but this kitchen has been passed relatively recently as fit to provide food at some big dinners.'

'Really?'

He made a gesture. 'If you look over in that corner you'll see a wash-hand basin, which, as you know, is essential in a commercial kitchen. I know the environmental health officer. I could get this kitchen passed again fairly quickly. Would that help?'

Fran almost couldn't speak. 'That would be amazing! I could bring the milk over here and make all the cheese I needed to for the supper club. Then no one could get funny about it having been made...' She thought of the kitchen back home. 'Well, you know...'

'You could do any other cooking here that you wanted, too. I'm not here most of the time and the kitchen is rarely used for much, except to make coffee.' He smiled, somewhat wistfully, Fran thought.

'That would be really helpful,' said Fran. 'I'm planning to make puff pastry for the game pies and I could do it over here in peace with plenty of space.'

'Sounds good.'

'You will come to the supper club, though, won't you, Antony? As our guest? We wouldn't want you to pay.'

'If I come I'll pay. What do you do about wine?' he added.

'BYO – bring your own. Not a problem for you, of course. Not sure what to do about people who forget. Even if we have wine just in case, we can't sell it without a licence.'

'There is a licence you can get. It lets you have about five events a year. I could supply you good wine and you could make a bit of profit on it.'

'That sounds a good offer but I don't want people to feel they can't bring their own.' She took another sip of her latte. 'But I'll look into it.'

Neither of them spoke for a few moments, and then Antony said, 'I know you don't really like accepting help – it goes against your desire to be independent, but you shouldn't, you know. I like being philanthropic. Seb would say it massages my ego, being nice.'

'I've accepted a lot of help from you already—' Fran began.

'But you haven't wanted to. It's nearly killed you, coming here, asking about the cheese room, hasn't it?'

'Yes.' Her voice was very small.

'Well, you've done it and I think you should feel proud of yourself.' Antony smiled in a way that suddenly made him a thousand times more attractive. And he'd been quite attractive before.

'One day I'd really like to do something for you. Something you'd really appreciate,' she said on a flood of gratitude. Then she remembered – his generosity might not be entirely unselfish. 'Except sell you the farm, if I inherit it,' she finished quickly.

He laughed properly now and she couldn't help noticing how his throat rippled and how good his teeth were. Gratitude is making me susceptible, she decided. 'I'd better go. I'm visiting Amy now.'

'I'd say "give her my love",' Antony said, 'but I don't think she'd appreciate it.'

'I'm sure she'll feel differently when I tell her how helpful you're being.'

'Don't tell her.' He was very definite. 'It will worry her, make her suspicious about my motives.'

'I could explain—'

'No. She's disliked my family for three generations or so. Nothing you could tell her about me is going to make her feel differently.'

Fran regarded him, good-looking, powerful and, to her, extremely kind, and felt a sudden stab of discomfort. Was it wrong of her to take advantage of his kindness when Amy felt like that about him? It probably was. But what alternative did she have?

He sensed her conflict and put his hand on her shoulder. 'Don't worry about it, Fran. Just don't tell Amy. I'm not as wicked as she thinks. Really.'

'But are you wicked at all?' said Fran, aware of his hand which he hadn't taken away.

He laughed. 'Well, no one's perfect!' Now he did remove his hand. 'Go and see your Auntie Amy. I hope she's well.'

*

Amy was in excellent form. Given where she had just come from and what her head was full of, Fran would have preferred it to have been one of her more sleepy days. She decided to give her progress report on the fireplace and broach the subject of the supper club.

'We're waiting for the sweep to give the chimney the all-clear,' she said, after the weather, the state of the food in the care home and whether the local agricultural show would go ahead this year had all been discussed.

'Sweep? Tig's got brushes, he'll sweep the chimney for you.'

'Yes, he has, but I want to make sure the chimney's safe before we use it. We need a man with a camera he can put up there, and check for cracks.'

Amy tutted. 'People make such a fuss these days.' By people she meant Fran.

'It would be a shame if the house burnt down because there was a chimney fire,' said Fran, rattled.

'I've no idea why you felt you had to take the fireplace out in the first place. I paid good money for that fireplace, years ago,' Amy grumbled. 'Very economical on coal.'

'Anyway, moving on from fireplaces, I've decided to have a supper club in the farm.' Amy's look gave Fran permission to continue. 'It's a fairly new idea. People come and eat dinner at your house – or rather supper – and they pay what they think it's worth.'

'Why?' demanded Amy.

'Why would they pay? Because they've had a good meal, I hope.'

'But why would you want to invite people for a meal and then expect them to pay? We never charged people in the old days.'

'No, well, it is a very new concept' – Fran felt that in Amy's eyes anything that happened after the Second World War was new – 'but I want to meet more local people and let them know about the cheese. And then I can sell it. I have a small stock of the various kinds in the fridge.'

'Have you met many local people already?'

Fran could have sworn that Amy was a mind reader and knew what subjects Fran wanted to avoid. 'Not that many. There's Tig of course, and I've met his mother. I've got Issi, my friend staying at the moment.' She was hoping Amy would express a desire to meet Issi, who was in town, scouring the charity shops for vintage pie dishes while Fran was visiting Amy.

'Have you been obliged to have anything to do with the scoundrel next door?'

Fran wished she could lie but couldn't because (*a*) she wasn't good at it and (*b*) Amy would be able to tell instantly that she was lying.

'Actually, Antony has been very helpful—'

'Antony, is it? Christian-name terms! Don't forget that any help he offers while he's pretending to be neighbourly is only to make the property better for him when he fools you into selling it to him!'

'Really, Amy—'

'Mark my words! He's up to something if he's being helpful.'

As Fran hadn't had a chance to tell Amy about the track or his generous offer to make a cheese room, she suspected Amy knew about the track at least. 'He has been brilliant sending good people to repair the track,' she said defiantly. 'The milk tanker couldn't always get up it, you know.'

'It managed perfectly well in my day!' said Amy.

Fran realised that Amy had probably forgotten her last months on the farm and how difficult they had been. 'It's nice to have a good track,' said Fran.

'Are you selling the milk to the co-op?'

Fran wondered who the mole was. Who knew she was making cheese with the milk and not selling it? She sighed. It could be lots of people. 'No, I'm making cheese. I thought I'd told you.' She knew she hadn't told Amy that the co-op had practically sacked her and that she was living off her savings, more or less.

'Then you don't need a fancy new track!'

'About the cheese,' said Fran, feeling it was better to just ignore this remark, given that Amy seemed to have had chilli powder or some anger-producing additive with her breakfast. 'I would like to make a Cheddar-type cheese. Will you tell me where the quarry is? Where you used to mature the cheese when you made it?'

'No,' said Amy. 'If you're so keen on cheese you can find it yourself. I didn't leave you my farm so you could consort with the enemy and let him pay for you to have a new track.'

Amy seemed to be getting angrier and angrier with every word.

Fran swallowed and took a breath. 'Amy, you're still very much alive and so you haven't left me the farm. We agreed that I'd try farming for a year to see if I can make a go of it. Well, I can't make a go of it if I can't get up and down the track.' She realised she was getting angry herself, which would not be helpful. She paused and smiled. 'Now, is there anything you need? Anything I can bring you? You could try my cheese?'

Amy fixed her with a look. 'Are you trying to poison me? Everyone knows that the elderly shouldn't eat soft cheese. I could get listeria or E. coli!'

Fran made her excuses and left as soon as she could. Honestly, Amy was a piece of work! She thought making sure the chimney wasn't going to catch fire was 'making a fuss' but wouldn't try a scrap of cheese in case it gave her food poisoning!

She swept into the coffee shop on a cloud of indignation. 'You'll never believe what she's said now!'

Issi regarded her friend. 'Don't tell me. Have some cake.' She pushed a plate of chocolate gateau across the table. 'Everything is better after cake.'

Chapter Ten

Spring had arrived early at the farm. Fran and Issi were able to dig up primroses and transplant them into small dishes and teacups and use them as table decorations for the supper club. Fran explained to her helpers, Issi, Seb and Tig, that they could remove any primroses that flopped. They were all going to be planted afterwards anyway.

'I think the room looks spectacular!' declared Issi, wiping her earthy hands on her apron after they'd put primroses on every table.

'I am quite pleased,' said Fran, less confident. Although the supper club had quickly booked up, which was wonderful, she had to make sure the food was perfect and every one of their careful plans worked.

'It reminds me of an old-fashioned tea shop,' said Seb, who'd offered to help move furniture – possibly because there were always baked goods as a reward.

'Is that good or bad?' asked Tig, who was there for the same reason.

'It's fine,' said Issi, who'd taken on the role of cheerleader – if anyone was less than cheerful she rallied them. 'After a couple of sips of their complimentary cocktail they'll all think it's wonderful!'

They were going to serve 'Heavenly Dew' for this free drink which, they gathered from the internet, was a feature of supper clubs.

Fran had discovered several bottles of cowslip wine in a dusty cupboard although everyone knew that Amy didn't drink. She had discussed this with Tig who said his employer would have described it as a 'country wine' and therefore somehow non-alcoholic. They had decided to use it for the supper club. Seb had shown a good knowledge of cocktail mixing and combined it with a little brandy for extra kick, topped up with cava from the local supermarket. Everyone was happy with the final result.

This was to be served in Amy's random collection of glasses with a few extra borrowed from Mrs Brown, who had volunteered to be a waitress and to help with the washing up. Fran had worried that some people were getting a better deal than others given the glasses varied quite a lot in size. Issi had said it didn't matter.

Mrs Brown, who'd got well into the spirit of the supper club, had provided extra chairs courtesy of her key to the village hall and also produced her own fairly extensive collection of pretty plates and dishes to add to Amy's, as she hadn't got enough.

'Well, I really like the vintage look,' said Issi. 'It looks perfect in here, with the fireplace and every-thing. Who wants everything matchy-matchy?'

'It does have that "country auction leftovers" vibe,' said Seb. 'But maybe that's OK.'

'It's charming,' said Issi firmly.

Fran worried that he might be right, it did look a bit 'tea shoppe' – with a double 'p' and written in Gothic script.

Along with the Heavenly Dew (which was quite strong) they were serving various canapés, some of them cheese-based, all of them fairly economical. The general favourite were the cheesy-stuffed mush-rooms which Fran had served as supper at least twice.

'It's brilliant that we're fully booked,' said Issi. 'After all, no one really knows us round here.'

'I did go to that dinner party and I think Antony helped spread the word,' said Fran. 'As well as us putting up postcards and things in the local shops. And you've been brilliant with the online marketing.'

'My mum told all her friends,' said Tig, 'but if they come it'll be because no one's been in this place for a while.'

'I expect lots of people will come because they're curious,' said Issi, 'but as long as they pay for the privilege, that's fine!'

'And if they have a good time, they'll come again,' said Tig.

'Plus there aren't many restaurants near here,' said Seb, 'and you're offering something a bit different.'

'Pie and mash, do you mean?' said Fran, suddenly worried that her menu was far too unsophisticated.

'*Game* pie,' said Issi.

'From game shot on very grand shooting estates,' added Seb. 'You could call it Posh Pie and Mash if you wanted.'

Issi and Seb spoke in a way that indicated they'd said similar things before and were getting just a bit fed up with it.

'As long as people pay enough,' said Fran. 'We need to cover our costs and make sure we can pay everyone—'

'I don't need to be paid,' Seb interrupted. 'I have a job.'

'So have I,' said Tig.

Fran felt suddenly tearful. 'Thank you so much! I absolutely insist on paying you, but I really appreciate all the effort you've put in to helping us.'

Issi, possibly guessing her friend was a bit overcome, changed the subject. 'It's a shame it isn't summer. People would pay just to look at the view.'

'Well, we can do another supper club or two,' said Fran. 'If this one goes well.'

'I've got cows to milk, so I'll be off now,' said Tig, who had refused to be a waiter, or to just eat the supper, but had agreed to hang around in the kitchen and wash up if necessary.

'You've been brilliant. Thank you so much, Tig,' said Fran.

'Yes you have,' Issi agreed, and gave him a hug.

'I'd better go too,' said Seb. 'Ant's got a meeting later. What time do you want me tomorrow?'

When the goodbyes and thank yous had been said, and the two women were on their own, Issi said, 'Remind me what we're doing about alcohol? Is it Bring Your Own?'

'Oh, Is! I've been wondering if I should have applied for that licence that lets you do five events per year that Antony told me about but I left it a bit late and ended up not doing it.'

'Well, you have been busy, doing all the cooking over at Ant's and having the cheese room built.'

'I have but I probably should have gone for it. I just didn't think we'd do this five times a year.'

'So people will bring their own?'

'We made it really clear they had to, but Antony has supplied some nice but inexpensive table wine. People will donate to his favourite charity to pay for it.'

'I think you're his favourite charity, Fran,' said Issi, studying her friend.

Fran sighed. 'He has been incredibly kind but he hasn't ever given me any sign he likes me more than just a neighbour. Not that I've actually seen much of him. I know I always seem to be over there recently, but he's never there at the same time.'

Issi laughed. 'You know what Mark Twain said – that there's no such thing as an unselfish act. He likes you.'

'Not like that! And if his generosity to me has an ulterior motive, it's because he wants to buy the farm if I inherit.'

'You will inherit, don't worry. Amy is very fond of you.' Issi had finally been to meet Amy and had since been to visit her with Fran a couple of times. To Fran's relief, they had got on really well.

'Not always. She accused me of trying to poison her with my cheese, don't forget, even though I didn't actually give her any!' Fran fiddled with a loose curl as she thought about it. 'Sometimes she does seem fond, and keen for me to make a success of the farm, but at others, she's all, well – I don't know – argumentative and difficult.'

'She's old, she's allowed to be.'

'I know,' said Fran. 'But it makes it hard for me. For example, she won't tell me...'

'What?'

'Oh, never mind. You know, I'm still not sure that people can actually sit at the chairs. It's one thing being able to squash everything round the table, but they've got to be able to actually use their knives and forks.'

In the end Fran and Issi sat next to each other on the table where space was tightest and mimed eating. It was just about possible.

Fran was encouraged. 'As long as I haven't forgotten how to cook for big numbers, it's going to be fine. At least everyone's having the same thing at the same time, more or less. The publicity material said to ring if you were vegetarian and no one has, but I will make some individual veggies pies, just in case. You know what people are like.'

Although they had started arranging the room in plenty of time, it was late when they were finally satisfied with how it looked.

'I'd come and eat here,' said Issi. 'In fact, you could offer cream teas in the summer, with your own cream, now the track's been done.'

'Farmers do have to diversify to survive these days,' said Fran, 'but I'm hoping I'll be making cheese from my cream. Although I suppose I could keep some back. I'll think about it.' She yawned. 'I am so tired, and we haven't even had the supper club yet.'

'You've done an awful lot of prep and moved an awful lot of furniture. Tomorrow will be easier.'

Issi sounded very reassuring but Fran could tell she wasn't actually convinced.

*

'At least it's not snowing, or even raining,' said Issi the next morning, handing Fran a cup of tea across the kitchen table. It was extremely early, still dark outside, but Issi was an early riser and knew Fran wouldn't want to sleep in today.

'No,' said Fran. 'Think how dreadful if no one could get up the lane because of ice after all the work and expense that's been lavished on it.'

'It would be quite difficult for us, too,' said Issi. 'I'm going to take Tig some coffee. Anything you want me to ask him?'

'I don't think so. I won't need him here until about six this evening. He should have time to shower and change after the afternoon's milking, but then I want him to light the fire, but so it won't actually give out much heat.'

'He can do that,' said Issi and left, carrying two cups of coffee. Fran allowed herself a sentimental sigh at her friend's blossoming relationship before gathering ingredients to make enough puff pastry for at least twenty people and setting off for Antony's house.

That afternoon, Fran consulted her list. She was about as far ahead as she could be. The range was burning well and the small ordinary cooker was also up to temperature. She planned to put the pies in an hour before the guests were due to arrive. That would give her time to swap them around so they were equally brown on all sides.

The veg was all prepared, mountains of potatoes peeled to make mountains of mash. There were carrots, spring greens and peas, which she was going to serve together to look bright and fresh and not cabbagey. The peas were frozen but the carrots and greens were local and organic.

She had roasted beetroot for the starter and was going to serve it with her home-made feta to make a salad. Given the potential heaviness of the main course, she'd felt a light starter was a good idea. For pudding she had a choice of chocolate tart (served, naturally, with home-made clotted cream) or lemon mousse made (surprisingly) without cream, so it was fresh and light and almost diet food.

Then there would be cheese, with home-made crackers, shop-bought crackers and soda bread, made by Mrs Brown.

With the coffee (or a selection of teas) would be home-made tablet, just in case, Issi declared, anyone went home having eaten fewer than two thousand calories. Just to make absolutely sure, Fran was sending them all away with a little bag containing a further selection of her home-made cheeses.

To give herself a breath of air she went outside and looked at the view. She could see blossom starting to highlight the hedgerows and some early lambs in a distant field. She knew Tig's cows would soon stop being milked, to be 'dried off' before calving.

That would give her a reprieve from making cheese but in the future, it would mean her income could dry up as well. She needed to make hard cheese that would keep. Still, no point in worrying about that, she told herself. She might not be here next year. Making a living without milk might not be something she needed to concern herself with.

But the thought made her heart ache. Life wasn't easy but every day brought a challenge, something to be achieved, or overcome. She loved it.

Fran and Issi, who were both in the kitchen putting finishing touches to the canapés, jumped when they heard the first car arrive.

Issi looked out and said, 'It's only Seb and Antony.'

Fran didn't actually feel 'only' about Antony but had convinced herself it was because she hardly ever saw him. He'd become more attractive and sexy in her head because she hadn't had the dose of reality that actually being with him would give. She knew a lot of her feelings for him were because of gratitude. If it hadn't been for Antony she'd have probably had to give up and go back to London weeks ago.

Issi went out to meet them, but Fran stayed where she was, filling mushrooms with a combination of bacon, fried breadcrumbs, fried mushroom stems and a little garlic. When she'd finished, she'd put cheese over the top and put them in the oven. Although her gaze never moved from the task in hand she was alert to the sound of Antony coming into the kitchen.

She didn't have long to wait. Both men came in, talking. 'Hey!' said Seb, giving Fran a casual kiss on the cheek. 'Those look amazing!' He took a mushroom canapé. 'Delicious,' he declared, still chewing.

'They're not finished,' said Fran.

'Sorry,' said Seb, wiping his mouth with his hand.

'How can we help?' said Antony, looking less relaxed than Seb did, and without kissing anyone.

'You could go into the sitting room and see if it looks all right. Make sure that we haven't forgotten anything vital,' said Fran.

'Come with us,' said Antony, taking her elbow.

She allowed herself to be towed into the next room because she knew she ought to make a final check herself.

'It's perfect,' said Issi.

It did look pretty good, Fran thought. The tables were beautifully set with mismatched crockery and knives and forks. It was a look that was much harder to achieve than it should have been, they discovered. While the side plates and glasses were different they had to be put next to china that was complementary. There were a few nearly complete sets, but they had to be kept apart from each other so there were no clumps of colour all together.

They'd removed any of the transplanted primroses that had faded earlier in the day, and Tig had lit the perfect fire, giving light and a bit of flame, but very little heat.

Fairy lights were draped along the windowsills and pinned across the newly exposed beam over the fireplace. Tea lights on the tables and well-placed table lamps gave the room a warm, inviting glow. Yes, there were far too many tables and chairs, yes, people would be a bit cramped, but the atmosphere was delightful.

'Very *gemütlich*,' said Antony.

'What does that mean?' asked Issi.

He gestured. 'Cosy, warm, intimate. What this is, really.'

Fran knew the word and was pleased. It was exactly the effect she and Issi had been aiming for.

Before she could say anything they heard another car and she made for the door. For some reason she didn't want to be caught in the dining room.

'Hey! No need to run away,' said Antony, following her.

She paused. 'I know but I must get my mushrooms into the oven. Is? Do we need Seb to make the aperitif or have you done it?'

'It'll need testing,' said Seb. 'Antony's driving tonight.'

'You do that then, I'll get back to work.'

Fran knew the deal. At a supper club you were not only the chef, but the hostess, you had to put in an appearance. It was annoying there wasn't anywhere for the guests to mingle before taking their seats but there just wasn't. When she took off her grubby apron and replaced it with a clean one, and went to say hello, everyone would be seated. It would be like making a speech rather than going up to groups of people and saying hello.

As there was nothing she could do about it, she took a deep breath and went into sitting room.

She took a moment to admire it. Everything looked even better now the chairs were filled and everyone was chatting. Proximity lent itself to conversation and a lot of people knew each other anyway.

She banished the feeling that she was the head-mistress about to address her school at a mealtime, coughed and waited for people to be quiet.

No one noticed. Antony, who was sitting quite near her, banged his fork on his water glass.

'Ladies and gentlemen, if we could have your attention please!'

Although she was grateful to him, Fran now felt obliged to make a speech. She'd keep it short.

'Welcome, everyone. It's lovely to see so many of you here. I hope you'll bear with us if everything doesn't appear bang on time. We're not a restaurant, and we can't get the staff – so I'm relying on friends to look after you. Please finish the Heavenly Dew and the canapés and then we'll get your beetroot salad with home-made feta out to you. There are menus on the tables but it's not a choice, it's a warning!'

Obligingly, people laughed at her joke and Fran was able to retire to where she felt she knew what she was doing.

Issi came in with empty canapé plates and glasses stacked on a tray. 'I can't believe the washing up has started before the meal is on the table! Where shall I put this?' Every surface appeared to be covered with plates of beetroot salad, including Amy's ironing board.

'We need another tray or five really,' said Fran, mentally cursing herself for forgetting something so basic.

'Tell you what, I'll empty this lot into this cardboard box and then fill up the tray. Tig's here. He'll serve salad if you ask him.'

'Thanks, Issi,' said Fran. 'It's great having you here. You're always so calm.'

Issi made a dismissive noise and started putting plates on the tray. 'We take it in turns. I'm calm for you, and you're calm for me when I need it.'

The hardest part was getting the food to the tables, trays notwithstanding. There was hardly any space to walk between the chairs and there had to be a lot of reaching over and passing. But people didn't seem to mind, Tig and Seb helped with corkscrews, and only a few people had forgotten to 'bring their own' with regard to wine.

When at last the cheese boards (made by Tig with an old oak bough and his lathe) were on the tables, and everyone was tucking in, Issi came back into the kitchen.

'You've got to go out there now,' she said to Fran. 'Everyone wants to congratulate you.'

'OK.' Although she knew this was part of the deal and she wasn't usually shy, now she just wanted to stay in the kitchen and wash up.

She was very pleased with the meal. She'd tasted a crust of pastry and knew it was delicious, as was the rich pie filling which was tasty and not too gamey. The vegetables were mostly perfect, though a few carrots may have been a little too al dente for some.

The chocolate tart had been pretty good, although too late she worried about serving pastry for two courses, and the mousse might have separated on a few of them. But she'd been more than happy with the cheese. A couple were home-made but there was a very fine local blue cheese and a spectacular Cheddar-type she decided was the standard she was aiming for, if ever she made hard cheese herself.

She ducked into the scullery and peeked at herself at the small, spotty mirror that hung there. Her hair was frizzy and she had no make-up left on, but it was too late to redo herself. She'd have to brave it out.

She went through to the sitting room, wishing she'd had time to have a glass of wine or something during the evening, to soften her sudden anxiety.

The moment she appeared, Antony was there, putting his arm round her waist.

'Here she is, our marvellous chef for the evening. I know you all want to show your appreciation.'

Much to Fran's embarrassment, everyone broke into enthusiastic applause. She looked round the tables at the smiling, congratulatory faces. Some she recognised from the dinner party Antony had taken her to: there was Caroline and her husband Julian, Erica, a couple of men she'd seen before and then – standing out among the crowd because she wasn't even remotely smiling – Megan, and she was looking daggers at her.

Antony went on. 'I think you will all agree we have enjoyed restaurant-standard food in a truly original and delightful setting. Fran will kill me for saying this, but can I suggest you are generous in your contributions for the food tonight? Then she might be persuaded to do it all again.'

There was another huge round of applause and then people started the awkward process of getting up from their chairs.

Fran went back to the kitchen. Issi was helping people find their coats and Seb and Tig were on hand to receive the envelopes that had been left on the table for the contributions. Antony had gone to talk to Megan; Fran had seen him make his way through the crowd towards her.

She had hardly had time to start on the washing up when people started visiting her. The first was Erica, the older woman she'd met at Caroline and Julian's.

'That was amazing,' she said without preamble. 'The cheese particularly.'

'I didn't make all the cheese,' said Fran quickly, sorry that she hadn't. 'Only the soft ones.'

'Oh, I know you didn't make the hard cheese, or the blue – I know those makers. But I have a stall in the farmers' market and I'd love it if you'd let me sell your cheese. You'd have to make sure it was being made in properly hygienic conditions, all that annoying but important stuff.' She smiled. 'But you'd want to do that anyway?'

'Of course,' said Fran. 'I'd love to talk to you about it all sometime.'

'Me too. I was going to see if you could come and have coffee or something. Not everyone wants to talk about cheese.' Erica smiled again.

'I know. And I'd love to find out everything you know about it.'

They didn't chat for too much longer because seemingly everyone wanted to congratulate her personally. Fran began to relax. It really had been a success.

Fran thought everyone must have gone and Issi was organising the washing up with Mrs Brown when Megan appeared.

'Hi there,' she said. 'I was just chatting to Antony about Mrs Flowers. I wanted to know how you were related. He thought she was some sort of cousin?'

'Why would you want to know that?' asked Issi, coming through from the kitchen to collect some glasses, possibly aware she was speaking for Fran, too.

'I am fascinated by genealogy,' said Megan swiftly, as if she had been expecting this question. 'Everyone is, these days.'

'Oh,' said Fran, 'well, I don't know exactly. My father *was* a cousin of Amy's but a fairly distant one. Although I'm sure genealogy is fascinating, I haven't had much time for it.'

'Not even when you found out about this farm?'

It did seem a bit odd now, Fran could see. 'Well, I was prepared to take Amy's calculations as to how we were related and my mother agreed with her. It wasn't a complete bolt from the blue.'

Megan shrugged as if not understanding Fran's laissez-faire attitude and changed the subject. 'It was quite a nice meal. Did you mean to serve pastry for two courses or was that a mistake?'

'It was a mistake,' said Fran. 'But no one but you has mentioned it.'

'They probably didn't like to,' said Megan. 'Although the pastry was quite nice.'

'Quite nice?' raged Fran when Megan had gone. 'Quite nice! That pastry – both pastries were fabulous!'

'They were,' said Antony. 'Now come and sit by the fire and have a big drink. We're going to clear up.'

In spite of her protests, Antony led her to the fireside, where someone, presumably him, had cleared away the nearest table and found an armchair. The fire now blazed away.

Seb was there. 'Now, what would you like?' he asked. 'Brandy?'

'We haven't got any.'

'Seb never travels without a flask,' said Antony, laughing.

'That's you, actually, mate,' said Seb, 'but I do happen to have a little drop of cognac that doesn't taste half bad.'

Having been poured a large amount, Fran took a sip and then closed her eyes. It had been quite an evening.

Chapter Eleven

It was March and Fran gazed around happily. The room next to the old dairy had been made into a cheese room and the room next to it an equally hygienic store. It had been an amazing transformation made by a couple of builders well known to Antony and the rooms were both gleaming and sterile.

Now, all the walls were lined with wipeable surfaces. Wash-hand basins and sinks were installed in the dairy. Both floors had been resurfaced and there was a selection of new white wellies and Crocs that had to be worn if anyone entered. Inside was all other equipment a cheesemaker could desire. There were buckets, a cheese mill, cutters, moulds, a pile of vivid blue cloths for wrapping hard cheeses. It all looked amazing.

It had also been passed fit for purpose by the health and hygiene officer. Fran had been half delighted and half appalled to realise he had been at the supper club. As a trained chef with the right certificates she knew about hygiene and how important it was, but it was a bit embarrassing to think she'd been feeding this man unawares. Supposing a stray hair had crept in somewhere and ended up on his plate?

But he was youngish, kind and very interested in cheese, and had declared the cheese room perfect. All Fran needed to do now was work out how to sell the cheese and start paying Antony back – it must have cost him a fortune. And also, she realised less cheerfully, start wearing away at the farm's overdraft, which she had discovered was substantial.

But she was feeling very upbeat and positive about life when she set off on her regular afternoon walk. She told herself the same as she'd told Issi, that she was eager to see if the primroses, replanted after the supper club, had taken. Really she was looking for the quarry. She knew it was on the land, but no one would give her directions to it, or give her a hint where she should look. Maybe only Amy knew? And she wasn't telling. Perhaps it was a test, something she had to find before Amy would really trust her with her beloved farm.

She was on her way back, having failed yet again, but feeling better for the exercise anyway. She had decided to invite Antony for dinner, to thank him for his kindness, with Issy and Tig for support, when she turned the corner and saw a man peering into the sitting-room windows.

Fran bit back a scream of shock, suddenly yearning for a dog who would alert Issi and Tig that there was a stranger about. Who on earth was he and what the hell was he doing?

'Excuse me!' she said loudly, sounding braver than she felt. 'Can I help you?'

The man turned as she arrived by the front door. He was tall and suntanned with a narrow face that just missed being good-looking. 'Are you Fran Duke?'

'Sorry, who are you?' asked Fran.

'I'm Roy Jones. If you're Fran, I'm your long-lost cousin from Australia.'

It took Fran a moment or two to take this in, but then she realised he must be the other distant relation that Amy had tried to contact and who hadn't replied to her letter. It took her aback.

'Oh! Why are you here?'

He gave her a lopsided smile. 'Why do you think? I've come to have a look at the place. I'm going to inherit it, after all.'

Fran didn't know what to say. She never assumed she would inherit although other people seemed to, but for this man to take it all away from her was an outrage. She coughed.

'Aren't you going to invite me in?' said Roy.

Fran managed a smile. 'We'll go round the back. No one uses the front door in the country.' As they walked round the house to the back door, which she had left unlocked and now felt terrible about, she asked, 'Where's your car? I assume you must have hired one?'

'I left it at the bottom. I didn't know what the track was like. Didn't want to get stuck.'

As the track now looked and was in perfectly good order, Fran didn't quite buy this. He'd left his car at the bottom because he wanted to sneak up and look at the farm without anyone knowing. If she hadn't arrived back when she did, he'd have found the back door unlocked and walked straight in. She shuddered.

She opened the door and ushered him into the kitchen. She put the kettle on the range. 'How long are you planning on staying in the area?'

'Well, that rather depends,' he said, looking at her oddly.

'On what?' Fran felt cornered. Was she expected to offer him a bed for the night?

'On how long the old lady takes to die.'

This came like a blow. Surely Roy didn't mean that? It was outrageous! 'You mean, you want to get to know her before she dies?'

'Oh no. I'm just going to make sure she gets the measure of me before she dies. Nice for her to know the man who's going to take up burden of the old farm.'

'I can't believe we're having this conversation,' Fran muttered, finding coffee and spooning it into the cafetière.

'We go in for plain speaking where I come from,' he said. 'We don't pussyfoot around.'

'So where will you stay? Will you rent a cottage or something?'

'Oh, I'm staying here. You're here; I should be here too.'

Fran suddenly needed to sit down, but as she had a boiling kettle in her hand she couldn't. 'But I'm looking after the farm—'

'I probably know more about farming than you do.'

Fran poured water on to the coffee and then found milk, put some into a jug and put it in the microwave. She wasn't going to panic; she was going to take her time, breathe, and give the impression she was in control.

'So why the sudden interest in the farm?' she asked. 'Amy told me you didn't reply to her letter.'

'I didn't know what a nice little property it was. At least the site is good. When I inherit it, I'll knock down this place and put up a few houses in its place.'

'I'm not sure you'd get planning permission to do that, and it would break Amy's heart.'

'She'll be dead by then, sweetheart.'

'She may not leave the property to you.'

'Oh, I think she will. I'm a farmer, and my connection to her is closer than yours is. That'll be important to her.' He smiled. 'I'm a man, you see. And to women of her generation, that counts. And I'm a much better farmer than you will ever be.'

'But Amy ran this farm pretty successfully for years. On her own. And she's a woman.' Fran felt breathless with indignation.

'Did she, though?'

Fran poured coffee and got the milk out which she put it in her own mug before offering it to him. She didn't respond to this question. Instead she asked what she really wanted to know. 'How did you find out it was a "nice little property", as you put it?'

He shrugged and gave a smile which was almost a sneer. 'Let's just say, a little bird told me.'

'Who?'

It was definitely a sneer this time. 'Wouldn't you like to know?'

Fran sensed he wanted to go on teasing her with this so she changed the subject.

'Well, I'm afraid you can't stay here. I have a friend living with me. There isn't the space.'

'A man friend, or a woman friend?'

'Why do you want to know?'

He shrugged. 'It makes a difference. If it's a man friend presumably you share a bedroom. If it's a woman, you'll have to tell her to leave. I'm going to live here and I've as much right to as you have.'

Fran thought rapidly. There were actually a couple of unused bedrooms. But did she really have to have this man in the house?'

'I'm not sure Amy would approve of you living here with me. She's quite old-fashioned.'

'I don't know why you think that. After all, she'd prefer me being here than you running around with the enemy.'

'What do you mean?' Although Fran thought she knew. She was also fairly sure who'd tracked him down and suggested to him it was worth his while to come over.

'The neighbour.'

'Which neighbour?' She wasn't going to help him out here.

'Antony Arlingham.'

Fran took a sip of coffee. It was cold and bitter and perfectly summed up how she felt. Megan had done a very good job with her interest in genealogy.

'You see, I know all your dirty little secrets, Francesca.'

'I don't have any secrets, Roy, dirty or otherwise. I suggest we go and visit Amy together and see what she feels about you moving into Hill Top. She's given me a year to make a go of this farm. If I succeed, she's also said she'll leave it to me. I think you've missed your chance.'

He shook his head slowly. 'No. She'll leave it to me, without me having to do a thing. I'm the closest male descendant of her late husband, and this farm is mine. She only offered it to you because I didn't get back to her. Once she sees me, she'll leave it to me.'

Fran looked at her watch. 'She'll be having her lunch about now and she has a nap afterwards. I suggest you go away and sort yourself out somewhere to stay and then we'll go and see Amy together at about two.'

'That's not going to happen. I'll go and get my car and bring it up, while you get my room ready.'

The moment he was gone, Fran sent Issi a text, hoping she was somewhere where she could receive it. Then she went upstairs slowly, wondering how her life could have gone so wrong in such a short time. This morning she'd been full of hope and optimism, excited about her shiny new cheese room, and now it seemed as if it could all be taken away from her by some man from Australia, who didn't care about the house, who hadn't so far shown any interest in the farm and who was basically going to hang around 'until the old lady dies' so he could inherit, and destroy everything Amy had spent a lifetime building up. She couldn't let it happen!

She realised Issi probably wouldn't get her text until she and Roy were on their way to town, but she might be back in the house before she and Roy returned. That would be comforting. Issi might even bring Tig. Frantically she tried to remember if Tig would be milking and decided that he probably would.

She heard Roy's car and ran downstairs. She would have whisked him into her car and off down the drive to visit Amy but realised she had to give him time to use the bathroom and put his bag in his room.

'Your room is up the stairs, second on the right, at the end of the corridor.' He followed her and she went on with the tour. 'The bathroom's there round the corner. There's a hand-held shower and the hot water is better in the evening.'

'I'd be more comfortable in a double bedroom—' Roy began.

Fran was prepared for this. 'I'm sure you would be, but possession is nine-tenths of the law and I was here first.'

'Fair dinkum.'

'I can't believe you said that!'

'No worries. I only said it to annoy you.'

Fran glared at him. 'While we're annoying each other, can I have proof that you are who you say you are?'

His eyes narrowed, never leaving hers as he reached into his coat and pulled out a letter. The envelope was identical to the one she had received from Amy and she could recognise her writing from where she stood. He handed it to her. 'That good enough for you?'

She didn't need to read it to know what it said. 'OK. Now I know you really are Crocodile Dundee, let's go and see Amy. I'll just get ready.'

She wanted a moment to text Antony. She felt she needed to tell him about this invasion. He couldn't do anything about it but she'd feel better if he knew.

'Right,' she said, having reappeared by the back door. 'We should go. If we don't get our moment right she'll be asleep and we'll have to do all this again tomorrow.'

'Wouldn't bother me. I'm not going anywhere for a while.'

How could she bear it? she thought as she locked up the house and they made their way to the car. This man was going to be living in her house and she couldn't think of a way to get rid of him. There must be a way though. She only had to find it.

'It's pretty round here,' said Roy as they drove along the lanes towards town.

'Are you planning to settle in the area?'

'Oh no. It's pretty, but cramped. Couldn't cope with the little twisty roads and the hills getting in the way of the view all the time. No, I'll be back to Oz when I've made my money.'

'You're very certain you'll inherit.'

'I see that really pisses you off, but yes I am.' Roy paused. 'It makes perfect sense. I've had a good look at both family trees – that girl Megan was really helpful with that – and I'm more closely related. Not by much but the thing is, I'm a man, and someone like Amy will want a man to inherit. And secondly, I'm related to her late husband, as I said before. She'll want the farm to go to me.'

Fran didn't comment. She just concentrated on driving without attempting to kill him in a carefully staged crash. While part of her couldn't believe that even Amy could be so old-fashioned, part of her could. It seemed perfectly feasible.

She heard a beeping on her phone meaning they'd got within reach of a signal. She pulled in at her usual place. 'Excuse me. I've just got to see if anything urgent has cropped up. Most of my friends don't realise they have to use the landline if they want to get me on the phone.'

There was a text from Issi indicating she'd got Fran's frantic one. She was in town with Tig's car, picking up something for him, and would be home as soon as she could. There was an email from her mother, which she planned to read later, and a voice-mail. She listened to it. It was from the bank asking her to make an appointment to go in and see the manager.

Her heart did a somersault. Although she'd suspected there was a loan Amy hadn't told her about she'd never found direct evidence for it, and so she'd managed to put it to the back of her mind.

Well, she couldn't go on doing that. 'I'll have to call in at the bank after we've seen Amy,' she said, feeling sick. 'They want to see me.'

'Don't you mean they want to see both of us?'

'Listen, Roy, you haven't been here long enough to take your coat off! I'm in charge of the farm until Amy says otherwise. Anyway, they only want me to make an appointment.' This was something solid she could rely on: she was in charge, even if that wasn't always a pleasant thing to be.

She put her phone in her bag and set off again.

'So, what will you do when the farm's sold?' asked Roy a minute or two later. 'Go back to London?'

'I don't have a crystal ball,' Fran snapped, still rattled by the voicemail as well as Roy's sudden appearance. 'I can't see that far ahead. Amy is in very good health. She could go on for years yet.'

'She's in a care home. There's a statistic about how long people live when they've moved into care.'

'Amy wouldn't hold with statistics. You'll understand that when you meet her.'

They'd timed it right. Amy was in good spirits and when Fran introduced Roy, sat up straighter and inspected him.

'Why didn't you answer my letter when I wrote first?' she asked, without bothering to say hello.

Roy smiled, and managed to make it very charming, Fran noticed, while she fussed around checking Amy had everything she needed. Roy pulled up a chair and sat down.

'I didn't get it originally, Great-Aunt Amy,' he said. 'When I found it and realised what it said, I was devastated and rushed over here straightaway. I was lucky, I got a good flight and it only took me twenty-four hours.'

Fran knew he was lying about not getting the letter but she could hardly say so. She had no evidence.

'I was made up when I heard about you and the farm,' Roy went on. 'I've been a farmer all my life so I know how important it is to keep the bloodlines going.' He smiled again. 'In people as well as in cattle.'

Amy almost smiled. 'Tell me about your farm in Australia. How did you manage to come away at such short notice?'

'I farm with my dad and we have a couple of men helping us. It's a big farm but we manage to keep it all going with just the four of us.'

Fran had to give Roy credit. He told a very appealing tale of how his father had built up the farm from nothing, working from dawn to dusk. He painted a picture of how beautiful the Outback was until even Fran wanted to jump on a plane and go there, just to listen to the kookaburra and see kangaroos bouncing over the plane. Her knowledge of Australia was extremely sketchy but she supposed what he was telling them was feasible.

Amy, possibly less gullible, said, 'You wouldn't want to come here and farm then, if your family has worked so hard to build up that big farm from just a few acres.'

Roy appeared prepared for this. 'I have a younger brother. He'd love to take over from Dad when the time came.'

Amy frowned. 'When I was looking you up I don't remember a brother.'

'He's my half-brother. He's like a proper younger brother to me.'

He went on about how much he'd appreciate carrying on from such a proud dynasty of farmers and making the farm profitable and safe for the future until Amy stopped him.

'How nice,' she said, and closed her eyes briefly. When she opened them again after a few seconds, she said to Fran, 'Is that friend of yours still staying at the farm?'

'Yes she is.'

'Good. Otherwise it wouldn't be right for Roy to stay there too.'

'Fran might have to move out,' said Roy.

'Francesca is looking after the farm,' said Amy firmly.

'But I could do that – piece o' cake! Little place like that, after the acreage I'm used to.'

Amy frowned as if she didn't quite understand what Roy was saying. 'Francesca is in charge of the farm,' she repeated.

Fran ended the visit quite soon after this as Amy obviously wanted her nap. But she could see Amy was also animated. She'd enjoyed Roy's visit, and Roy had come across as a dedicated farmer who would put his heart and soul into Hill Top.

'Now I have things to do. Why don't you have a look round the town a bit?' She was half expecting him to insist on coming to make an appointment at the bank with her, but she was not having that.

'Can you show me to the nearest pub that'll have Sky? I'm a big sports fan and I'm guessing you don't have Sky up there at the farm.'

'You guessed right! I don't know much about the pubs but there's one there. You could ask them. I'll meet you there after I've had my appointment.'

'Great. There's a match I want to see tonight.'

'You don't seem to be suffering from jet lag,' said Fran, reluctantly impressed. 'I'd want an early night if I'd flown halfway round the world.'

'You're only a girl, you don't have the stamina blokes have.'

She made a face at him and set off for the bank. She may be 'only a girl' but he would find out what she was made of soon enough!

Chapter Twelve

It was a relief to spot Tig's car and to see Issi coming out of the house to welcome them.

'You must be Roy,' said Issi, holding out her hand. Her smile was a little grim. Fran had packed a lot into her panicky texts. 'Good to meet you.'

'Good to meet you too,' said Roy, clasping Issi's hand with a friendly leer. 'I gather you're living here with Fran to keep her company?'

'That's right.'

'And now you're my chaperone!' said Fran gaily, hoping her desperation wasn't audible. 'Amy checked you were still here. Otherwise Roy would have to live somewhere else.'

'To be honest, ladies,' said Roy, sounding reasonable, 'we can do what we like up here. She's never going to know. You can move back to London, Fran, leave everything to me.' He grinned. 'Just like the old lady's going to.'

Issi bristled, but Fran raised a hand. 'Let's go in the house. I'm desperate for a cup of tea. And, Roy, make no mistake, nothing happens on this farm that Amy doesn't find out about. You either live here with us both, or you go elsewhere. We're staying put.'

'Fair enough. Don't blame you for fighting as long as you know who's going to win. Now, have your cup of tea and then give me a guided tour.'

He insisted on being shown everything, and commented on everything, from the ancient shelter on the hill ('Nice roof tiles on there. Bet you'd get a few bob for them. I'll find out how much they're worth') to the new cheese room ('Bet this cost a pretty penny. How'd did you finance that? I know it wasn't the old lady.') By the time Fran steered Roy back to the house, having heard him put a price on everything, she needed more than tea. Luckily Issi had a meal on the go and a bottle of wine open.

After supper, when they were clearing up and Roy had gone off to the pub to watch the match (what kind of match they hadn't quite grasped and didn't want to ask), they discussed him.

'I've worked with and known loads of Australians,' said Fran, scraping the crispy bit from around the cottage-pie dish. 'And they've all been great. Hardworking, great sense of humour, generally terrific. Why can't he be like them?'

'Well, to be fair, and I do hate to do that in this instance,' said Issi, 'but he may be hard-working. He may have a sense of humour. We just hate him because he's here, threatening to take all this' – Issi gestured – 'from you.'

'Hate is a strong word.'

'Yup!' Issi agreed. 'And I hate him too, because if he's a bastard and sells the farm as building land as you said he told you he would, what'll happen to Tig's job? His home? It wouldn't just be you going back to London, it would be me and Tig, too. And I don't think he'd transplant.'

Fran put the kettle on, more from habit than anything. 'In some ways you're in a worse situation than I am.'

'It's Tig I'm worried about. He loves this land as much as Amy does.'

'So do I,' said Fran. 'Oh God!'

'More tea. In front of the fire. You go through. I'll bring it.'

'And if all that isn't enough,' said Fran, having sipped the tea, 'the bank want to see me. It'll be about Amy's loan. When I came everything was supposed to be OK for six months, but I think she forgot about the loan when she arranged everything.'

'Oh, Fran! When are you going in?'

'I've got an appointment in a week's time. I wish I could have seen him today but it's a small branch; the managers don't visit often.'

'Well,' said Issi, 'plenty of time to earn a bit of money by then. We could do another supper club, or even open a pop-up restaurant in the barn!'

Fran had to laugh. The barn was made of corrugated iron, open to the elements on two sides, and full of machinery. 'Get that organised in a week? Easy-peasy!'

The following week, Fran noticed Antony in the car park while she was getting her ticket before her meeting with the bank. To her delight, he came up to her.

'Hey!' he said. 'What are you doing here?'

'Nothing nice. The bank have summoned me. That's never good news, is it?'

'Probably not.' He cleared his throat. 'Have you any idea what it's about? Are you in a hurry, by the way? Time for a coffee?'

The best coffee shop in town was a step away. 'Well, I have actually. I escaped early so Roy wouldn't notice I was going.'

'Come on then.'

They found a table and ordered drinks. As it was early, they came quickly and soon Fran was drawing patterns in the foam on her cappuccino. She wished she could just enjoy being with him while not surrounded by people, and didn't have the meeting of the bank hanging over her.

'So,' said Antony, putting down his espresso having taken a sip. 'How's it going with Roy?'

'Actually, awful. He's vile. And now I've got this meeting.'

'Do you know anything about it?'

'I can guess. When I first arrived here it was implied that all the financial stuff was sorted. But it wasn't. I discovered there's a loan from the bank which I think Amy must have forgotten about.'

'Is it due to be paid back?'

'No, but they are due a payment.'

'Are you in a position to make one?'

She looked at him. 'Of course not. Well – I doubt it. I don't know how much—'

'Would you like me to—'

'No! Absolutely not. I owe you far too much anyway.'

He smiled at her outrage. 'I wasn't offering to lend you money. I was going to offer to come into the bank with you.'

'How would that help?'

'It'll make the manager or whoever you're seeing think you're not just a girl down from London who doesn't know anything about farming, let alone how to raise enough money to service their loan.'

'Oh God, he will think that about me, won't he?'

Antony nodded. 'So what had you planned to tell him?'

'I'm going to tell him how amazing the cheese I'm making is going to be and for what a lot of money I'm going to sell it for. I hope if I'm convincing he'll let me extend the loan.'

'On cheese?'

'Erica said the other day that she thinks our milk could make a really good hard cheese, which I realise is long term – up to a year even – but until then I'll have the soft cheeses, and I'll do more supper clubs.'

'So what will you say when he asks what you'll do when the cows are dried off?'

Fran bit her lip. 'You know, I'm kind of hoping he won't know that cows do dry up.'

He laughed, softening his naturally rather severe expression. Fran couldn't help thinking how very attractive it made him. 'I think there's a good chance he won't! But please let me come in with you.'

'You must have been going to do something or you wouldn't have been in town. I don't want to take up your time.'

'Nothing I can't do another time.'

'Why do you keep saving me, Antony?' It was something Fran had often wondered about but it was only now, in these slightly strange circumstances, that she felt able to ask him.

He raised his eyebrow. 'I'm looking after my future interests, of course.'

She tutted and sighed. 'Honestly! You and Roy, both after something you don't deserve and aren't going to get. Although I'd rather you had it than Roy, any time.' She paused and looked up at the man beside her. He was wearing a suit, although not a tie, and seemed perfectly comfortable in this somewhat formal clothing. She thought maybe she shouldn't have said that last bit out loud. 'Come on then. It's time we went in.'

Fran was glad she had Antony with her. The man they were ushered in to see did not look friendly. He was young, probably highly qualified, and low on people skills. He frowned when he saw Antony.

'I'm Jeffery Partland, and here to see Miss Duke? Are you her partner?'

'In a manner of speaking,' said Antony with quiet authority. 'I sometimes advise Miss Duke on business matters, but not in a formal way.' He smiled and sat down.

Apparently content with this, Mr Partland turned to Fran, who hastily sat down too. 'So, Miss Duke, you're here on behalf of Mrs Flowers?'

'Yes. She's in a care home.'

'And you've taken over her farm?'

'For the time being, yes.'

'What do you mean? Is Mrs Flowers going to go back to the farm?'

'No, not from her care home. She's quite elderly. I'm a – relation – and she said if I could run the farm for a year she might leave it to me in her will.'

Mr Partland raised an eyebrow. 'Lucky you.'

Something in the way he said this seemed to emphasise that it wasn't a very secure arrangement, either for her or the farm. But she had given up her life in London for a farm she may not inherit. She must have been mad.

'Yes, lucky me.'

Mr Partland looked down at his papers. 'So, this loan. Mrs Flowers took it out, putting the farm up as security. The next payment is due now. Can you let me know when we can expect payment, bearing in mind the longer you leave it the greater the interest?'

'How much do I owe?'

'Don't you know?' He looked down at the papers to check. 'Eight hundred pounds.'

'Oh my God,' said Fran before she could stop herself.

'How many more payments are due?' asked Antony, who also seemed alarmed.

'Currently there are ten payments of eight hundred pounds due.'

'Can I renegotiate the loan?' asked Fran. 'Make the terms a bit easier?'

'Are you going to find it difficult to pay the eight hundred?' Mr Partland asked.

'Yes, very difficult!'

He frowned. 'It appears that this loan shouldn't have been granted in the first place. Obviously I had nothing to do with that.'

'Nor had I,' said Fran, 'but as we're both stuck with it, maybe we could make it possible to schedule the payments over a longer term.'

'So you could make lower payments, less than eight hundred pounds?'

'Yes,' said Fran, crossing her fingers under the table.

'How does your farm make money, Miss Duke?'

'It's a small dairy farm,' she said. 'I make cheese with the milk.'

'And how do you sell it? Do you have a shop?'

'I share a friend's farmers' market stall.' She still had her fingers crossed as this hadn't happened yet. 'I have very low overheads.' She didn't know what the overheads were but they would have to be lower than a shop.

'So it's mostly profit?' Mr Partland seemed a little encouraged.

'I don't charge for my time, so yes.'

Antony made a noise that made Fran look at him. She knew he was saying she should charge for her time, but how could she?

Fran felt she was the British underdog in a tennis final at Wimbledon. Mr Partland would serve what might be an ace and she would have to run desperately to think of an answer to his question. Somehow she managed to do it every time. And while she wasn't panting hard, a trickle of sweat had run down her spine and she was concentrating on looking relaxed and confident.

Antony gave a very small, slow nod, to indicate he thought she'd done it. If it had actually been tennis he'd have been on his feet waving and cheering. At least, Fran hoped so. You could never quite tell with Antony.

'Right, Miss Duke, you seem to know what to do but of course you'll need to produce a proper business plan.'

'I can help with that,' Antony murmured.

'As well as the payment that is currently due...' Fran stifled a small scream. 'And then we can think about renegotiating the terms.'

Fran got some moisture back into her mouth so she could speak. 'So, when do you want all this by?'

'The payment in a week, say, as it's already overdue, and then we can make another appointment for when I'm next back in branch.'

'OK,' said Fran and wished she'd sounded more confident.

'So? How do you propose to make the payment? I'm assuming you don't have a separate account with the money in it?'

'No.'

'So what will you do? Sell a cow?'

'That would be a ridiculous thing to do,' said Fran, suddenly angry. 'The cows are irreplaceable and how I make money!'

Mr Partland shrugged and got up. The meeting was over and he probably had a few more to do while he was 'in branch'. 'Well, as long as you make the payment next week I really don't mind how you do it.'

Fran wasn't quite sure how she got out of the bank but she found herself blinking in the sunshine as if she'd been in a very dark place for some time.

'I've got time for another coffee if you have,' said Antony, 'unless you need a stiff drink.'

'I definitely need a stiff drink but I can't have one. I'm seeing Amy soon and I'm driving.'

'Double espresso and a chocolate brownie, then?'

Fran smiled. 'Actually I think a sparkling water would do it. I feel like I've run a marathon – well, a half marathon anyway.'

'Let's go to the pub. We're rather on public view in the café.'

'Why is that a problem?' Her nerves were already rattled by the in branch meeting, so this made Fran jump.

'We don't want to be seen together again by someone who'll rush in to tell Amy we're in cahoots. Come.'

He took her arm and led her through streets Fran hadn't discovered yet to a lovely old-fashioned pub. 'No one who knows Amy will see us in here.'

While he ordered the drinks Fran sat at a table, wondering how on earth she was going to find eight hundred pounds in only a week. She had her own dwindling savings but she'd been living on them.

Her mind kept going back to the roof tiles Roy had mentioned.

'Well,' said Antony, coming back to the table with her water and a cup of coffee for him. 'At least he didn't ask what you'd do when the cows went dry.'

Fran found herself laughing. 'I don't think he knew much about cows. Only a bit less than I do, obviously.'

'With Tig you don't need to know much though, do you?'

'I must learn. Tig might not stay on the farm forever.' She suddenly felt a pang of sadness. 'I might not either if Roy gets it. In fact I definitely won't.'

'Come on! It's not like you to be pessimistic. There's a way of paying the instalment if you only think.' He cleared his throat. 'Of course—'

'No. Thank you. It's very kind of you, but you've already done so much for me, with the track and the cheese room and stuff.'

He smiled again and Fran's stomach did a little flip. She wished it wouldn't do that. She had enough to think about without falling in love. She needed all her wits to look after the farm.

'Only looking after my own interests,' he said casually.

'You don't want a cheese room! And I am going to pay you back. I just need to sort the bank out first.'

'You seem a bit more positive than a second or two ago. Did the water revive you?'

Fran managed a small chuckle. 'It did. I think I have an idea of how I might be able to find eight hundred pounds, but I'm cross because it was Roy who put the notion into my head and sad because it's selling off a bit of the farm.'

'Not land?'

Although his expression didn't really alter she could tell he was horrified. She shook her head. 'Not that bad.' She went on to tell him about the little shelter Roy had spotted, all fallen down, and the stone tiles that had been its roof.

'Well, if you don't think I'm butting in, I have a mate in the reclamation business.'

'Really? That would be amazing. If I tried to arrange it myself I'd be sure to get ripped off.' She sighed, suddenly exhausted from all her responsibilities. 'I don't know how I can ever repay you.'

'There'll be a way,' said Antony, quiet but firm.

'Although I'm not—'

'Selling me the farm? I think I've got that now. I promise I won't force you to should the time come.'

'Thank you for that too. Now I must go or Amy will be asleep when I get there. She takes a lot of naps,' she added. 'Email me the name of your contact, will you? I'll have to try and do it when Roy's not there.'

'Is he out often?'

'He goes to the pub a lot. Apparently to watch sport.'

Antony laughed. 'The way you said that it could have been pornography.'

Fran smiled back at him. 'It's not that. I'm just not sure he does go to the pub to watch sport. He might be doing anything and I wouldn't trust him—'

'As far as you could throw him?'

Fran nodded. 'I banished that thought when I realised that throwing him would involve actual physical contact. Now I'm off.' She paused, half out of her chair. 'You promise you'll tell me if there's anything I can do for you?'

'I promise,' he said solemnly.

But as she left the pub Fran knew there wouldn't be anything she could do for Antony. How could she, penniless, pay back someone who appeared to be so well off?

She was nearly at her car when she saw Erica, waving wildly. 'Fran! So glad I caught you. Farmers' market this Saturday? I've sorted the formalities; you're fine to have cheese on my stall. So good you're a chef.'

'Why? Are we doing a food demo?'

'No, but it's a good idea for another time. I'm thrilled because all your certificates are up to date and you're safe to sell cheese.'

'When I've seen Amy, I'll go home and make some more,' said Fran, trying to match Erica's enthusiasm.

She would have been excited if she hadn't had to worry about selling antique roof tiles to raise a quick eight hundred quid.

Seeing Amy wasn't very cheerful, either.

Amy was tired and grumpy and spent most of the minutes before she fell asleep saying how wonderful Roy was. To add to Fran's discomfort, she nearly ran into Amy's solicitor on her way out.

'Hello, Mr Addison. Why are you here?' she asked.

He smiled back. 'Sorry, can't say. Client confidentiality.'

'Of course. How silly of me,' said Fran. 'Anyway, hope you're well.'

She wanted to add that Amy was asleep and he wouldn't get anything useful out of her, if it was indeed her he was hoping to visit.

But as she walked away she couldn't help wondering if Amy had summoned him so she could alter her will in favour of Roy. She knew she was being neurotic – it was a care home, after all. Any one of the clients could have asked him to call. It was only too easy to think the worst, however.

When Fran was finally home, after the stressful visit to the bank and the dispiriting time with Amy, she found it was wonderful to take herself off, alone, to her cheese room and concentrate on producing items for Erica's stall. She put the radio on and heated, stirred, cut, flavoured and let stand several gallons of the very best milk there was. She realised this was not an unbiased opinion, but when, a few hours later, she tasted the mascarpone – which needed no flavouring to make it heavenly – she felt it was not unjustified.

Chapter Thirteen

On Saturday morning, the day of the farmers' market, Fran got up horrifically early. She loaded her car and set off down the track.

She was a little worried about what Roy might get up to while she was out all day but decided there couldn't be too much. Antony's friend had come out and valued the tiles, which turned out to be reassuringly valuable. His visit had coincided with one of Roy's frequent trips to the pub and that had been very convenient. She and Issi had decided that as she had practically sold the tiles already, if Roy tried to sell them too, behind her back, it would be too late. And, Issi had pointed out, only a very neurotic person (she nodded at Fran) would worry about such things.

As Fran turned into Erica's drive so they could put all the cheese into her refrigerated van, she decided that today was going to be fun, and she'd put all her concerns behind her and focus on the cheese.

Even though it was too early for it to be full of busy shoppers, the sight of the market was very cheering. There were stalls with piles of vegetables smelling of newly turned earth and freshness. Every size and shape of bread you could imagine – from spelt loaves studded with pumpkin seeds and glazed with honey, to rustic rounds of rye, nobbly and appealing, and everything in between – took over two stalls. Honey, beeswax polish and candles gave off the scent of wax and turpentine. There were buckets of cut flowers, including foliage gleaned from the hedgerows, and a stall selling products from goats milk including soap and cosmetics. A local pottery had a table full of bowls, plates, mugs and jugs, all in the most beautiful blue. The bright awnings, the cornucopia of produce (all local and high quality) coupled with the banter of the other stallholders lifted her spirits. That, and the wonderful waft of coffee that floated towards her from the café, already serving bacon baps and toast to the stall-holders. Fran smiled.

'Oh my God, I can't believe this cheese!' said a woman, tasting some of Fran's garlic- and nettle-flavoured cream cheese a couple of hours later. The nettle was more for the look than the taste, but Fran was very pleased with the effect.

Thanks to Erica's imaginative signs advertising Fran's guest appearance, the stall was attracting a lot of attention. A few supper club people came, most of them buying something from both Fran and Erica. Megan was the exception. She was wearing cigarette pants, a shearling body warmer with high-heeled boots and an Hermès scarf. She looked as if she belonged in Sloane Square, not a country market.

'Tastes of compost heaps, if you don't mind me saying,' Megan announced.

'How do you know what compost heaps taste of?' asked Erica.

'You know what I mean!' said Megan, rolling her eyes and flinging her hands about in an artistic way.

'Actually I do know what you mean,' said Fran. 'I don't agree that my cheese tastes like that, but you can imagine what a compost heap tastes like.'

Megan's expression softened a little. 'So how are you getting on with Roy? He's such fun, isn't he?'

Fran smiled and nodded. 'Barrel of laughs.'

'And he's so caring of Amy, isn't he? I think he must see her almost every day,' Megan went on, managing to make Fran feel she neglected her.

'I hope he doesn't overtire her,' said Fran.

'Oh, I'm sure he wouldn't do that. He's very considerate of her age, he told me. But she likes to know everything that goes on on the farm.'

'She might get a little bored with being told about it,' said Fran. 'I keep her pretty well up to speed.'

'Yes, but do you tell her everything?' asked Megan. 'I mean, Roy said there was a reclamation man visiting the other day. Did you tell her about that?'

Wondering how on earth Roy knew, Fran said, 'Well, no, I didn't tell her about that. I thought it would worry her.'

'Very considerate of you, but Roy feels that because she's still got all her marbles, she has a right to be kept informed.'

'Well, Roy obviously keeps you well informed, Megan,' said Fran.

'It goes both ways.' Megan shrugged as if she was doing everyone favours. 'I was able to tell him that I'd spotted you and Antony having coffee together the other day. Amy was very interested to hear that, I assure you!'

'She didn't say anything to me about it,' said Fran, truthfully. 'I tell her about the farm and anything I think she would be interested in, but not my every move.'

'You know how she feels about you spending time with Antony—'

''Scuse me, you two,' said Erica. 'But there are customers waiting. I'll catch up with you soon, Megan. We'll do lunch.'

This made Megan move away but without noticing that there weren't customers waiting at all.

'Thank you so much for getting rid of her,' Fran said. 'She's got it in for me.'

'And we all know why,' said Erica.

Erica had restocked the stall from her van but they were getting low on cheese when Fran looked up to see a familiar face coming towards her.

'Hell! It's Fran!' said a large man with a lot of curly hair.

Fran came out from behind the stall so she could hug him. 'Roger! It's you! What are you doing here?'

'What are *you* doing here is the question. You should be in my restaurant kitchen!'

'You would never have offered me a job in your kitchen, you're far too snooty,' said Fran, so thrilled to see her old friend and former boss she could hardly contain herself.

'Not as a chef, obviously, but as a KP...'

Fran punched him in the arm. 'My kitchen porter days are over,' she said. 'I am now a cheesemonger and maker.'

'Really? Let me taste some.'

Fran loaded up a cracker with her special cream cheese.

'Oh my sweet Lord. I've died and gone to heaven!'

'Don't exaggerate, Roger,' said Fran, who was used to his hyperbole.

'I am not exaggerating. For once, I'm not. Let me taste everything! If I like it, I'll sell as much of it as you can provide.'

In the end they had to stop him not only tasting, but buying everything. Erica said she had regular customers who had to have their orders but he bought almost every scrap of cheese on the stall.

Exhausted, and pleased they could pack up early, Erica said, 'Well, who was he, then?'

'Shall we pack the van and go for a coffee? I'll tell you everything I know about him.'

Fran told Erica exactly what she used to do for Roger when she worked for him, and also what a lunatic he was.

'Let's google him!' said Fran, wiping butter off her fingers, having eaten a toasted teacake in record time.

'Good plan,' said Erica. 'Here, use my phone.'

'My goodness,' said Fran a little later. 'He's gone up in the world. Look! He's going to have a TV programme and he's involved with a new deli opening in London.'

'Not just London, Belgravia,' said Erica, impressed.

'So it is. I call myself a Londoner but that bit of London is not on my radar.'

'Well, maybe it should be!' said Erica, delighted. 'It would be so brilliant if you could get your cheese in there.'

'He certainly seemed to like it.' Fran bit her lip. 'This could be a really good opportunity, couldn't it?'

'It could put you on the map as a cheesemaker and it could get me some very valuable extra sales.' Erica paused. 'More teacakes all round, I say!'

Chapter Fourteen

Fran drove back to the farm full of optimism. She could make a living out of cheese – if she sold it to the highest-end shop there was. If Roger could persuade his customers to like it, it could really put her on the Posh People's Foodie Map.

She arrived in the kitchen with a load of empty containers to discover Issi, just as upbeat.

'Hey!' said Issi, clicking on the kettle. 'Good day?'

'Amazing, actually. We sold everything and an old chef friend from London was there. Sold most of it to him, actually. But you're looking pretty happy yourself.'

'I am! Guess why?'

'Too tired for guessing. Give me a cup of tea and tell me. Please?'

Issi relented and also handed over a piece of cake. 'Present from Tig's mum – who's told us we have to call her Mary by the way. And the news is...' She waited.

'Ta da?' suggested Fran feebly.

'Roy's gone!'

Fran's mouth fell open. 'Gone? What do you mean, gone? Forever?'

'No, sadly,' said Issi. 'But for a while.'

'Why?' asked Fran, unable to enjoy the cake until she knew more.

'Because he was bored. He actually said that Amy was taking too long to die and so he's gone off with his mates from the pub – some sort of sporting tour, I think – to pass the time.'

Fran bit into the cake, full of fruit and tasting of cinnamon – utterly delicious. 'He could go back to Australia and wait for her to die, couldn't he?'

'Just what I suggested, but no, he said he didn't want to be too far away because he didn't trust you not to get up to something.'

'Just what could I get up to, I wonder?' She took another mouthful of cake. 'I'm open to ideas.'

'He thinks you'll be influencing Amy to leave the farm to you and not to him.'

'Too right, I will.' Fran sipped her tea and sighed, unable to put Mr Addison's visit to the care home the other day out of her mind. Was he visiting Amy? Or someone else? 'Not that Amy is exactly influence-able, if that is a word. She has a mind of her own and it's very strong.' She paused. 'Although I must

187

admit, she does seem to have taken to Roy. But this is perfect – him being away. I can sell the roof tiles, and with the cheese going so well, we're in with a chance, Is.'

'Sell the roof tiles?'

'To pay off the bank, hold them off, really. I told you, Is.'

'Oh yes, sorry,' said Issi.

'But I'm feeling really optimistic. We're on the up.' She frowned. 'Of course I owe Antony big time, which does worry me. I hate owing people things.'

'He has loads of money, Fran.'

'That's not the point. And besides, he's given me support and information and has just been great—'

'Because he likes you.'

' —and I want to pay him back.'

'There will be a way, I'm sure. But hey! You must get up early tomorrow and see the cows.'

'Really?'

Issi nodded her head enthusiastically. 'It's their coming-out day. Tig says the fields have dried out enough and the grass is really coming through. They're going into the pasture for the first time for months. Tig says it's a sight to behold. He usually leaves Sunday milking to Ed or Phil but he's keen to do it tomorrow.'

The following morning, Issi encouraged Fran out of bed with a cup of tea and the suggestion that she dress up warmly. 'It's going to be a lovely day but it's a bit chilly at the moment. You know what spring is like – fickle.'

Fran found thick socks and scarves to go over her usual jeans and jumpers and joined Issi in the kitchen. She accepted the toast her friend handed to her, aware that Issi really wanted her to enjoy the cows. It had been a joke between them that Fran was frightened of them and, as jokes often do, it had an element of truth. It was ridiculous, here she was, trying to be a farmer – a dairy farmer – and she was nervous about getting too close to the creatures who produced her living. She resolved to toughen up.

She followed Issi out of the back door and along towards the milking parlour. There were threads of mist in the air and the promise of sunshine gave everything a magical quality. The hedges were fuzzy with leaves about to open and splashes of white, which, Issi had told her, having been told by Tig, was blackthorn, which would turn into sloes in the autumn. There'd be wild garlic to make pesto with in the woods very soon, and the birds were singing.

'It doesn't get better than this,' Fran said.

'It doesn't, does it?' Issi agreed. 'It's so wonderful hearing birds instead of police sirens.'

'It is. I'm going to learn which bird makes which sound,' said Fran. 'There's an app you can get.'

Issi giggled. 'I don't suppose Amy would approve of apps to learn about birdsong.'

'As long as I learn. I won't tell her how.'

There was so much about the countryside to love, she decided, and it would break her heart if it was all taken away from her.

Tig came over.

'Fran,' said Tig.

'Tig,' said Fran.

'Come to see the cows?'

Fran nodded. She looked nervously at them. They seemed to know something special was about to happen and were stamping and huffing in a slightly terrifying way.

They stood well back as Tig opened the huge gate that opened on to the field. The cows came out, bucking and leaping like lambs, so excited they didn't know what to do with themselves.

'I'll bring them in at night for a week or two maybe, but after that they'll be out all the time,' Tig said.

Seeing such large animals cavorting about in the spring sunshine, surrounded by birdsong and the acid green of newly emerged foliage, made Fran want to laugh and cry at the same time.

'Cool, isn't it?' said Issi with a sigh.

'Super cool,' Fran agreed.

Then Fran glanced at her friend and noticed she was looking at Tig, not the cows. While they were both city chicks, they had both found happiness back on the land. Although she adored the fact her best friend from school had come to share her adventure and was possibly falling in love, it added hugely to her sense of responsibility. It wasn't just her home that could be lost if Amy left Hill Top to Roy. It was Tig's and possibly Issi's.

Still, it was spring, Roy had left – for a little while at least – and they had the place to themselves.

'I wonder if Roy is feeling like the cows, all bouncy and with that "let out of school" feeling?' said Issi.

'I'm definitely feeling as if the class bully has gone away for a bit. Let's ask Tig if he'd like to come for breakfast.'

'Good idea,' said Issi.

'I bought some amazing bacon at the market yesterday. I'll make fried bread,' said Fran.

'Bit fattening, isn't it?'

'Not for Tig. Agricultural workers use up a lot of calories, they need the fat.'

'Hmm,' said Issi, 'I'm sure that was true back in the nineteenth century, but he does spend quite a lot of time driving around on that tractor.'

'You don't want me jeopardising his six-pack?'

'Oh, I'm sure it's fine,' said Issi, blushing, possibly at the thought of Tig's finely honed torso.

When the cows were all getting down to the business of eating the fresh young grass, Tig walked up the field to join them.

'Did you like that?' he said to them.

'Loved it,' said Fran and Issi more or less together.

'Breakfast? Bacon? Fried bread?' Fran added.

Tig nodded.

As they walked back together Fran asked, 'Tig, are you very strong?'

'Why do you want to know?' he answered.

'Nothing really, it's just you're very silent.'

Tig laughed. 'I'll say anything I think needs saying, don't you worry.'

Fran saw him put his hand on Issi's shoulder. That said a lot, she thought.

The next few days were joyful. Although she was working as hard as ever, without Roy it was easier and more fun; and of course, as she became more practised, the cheesemaking went more quickly.

The man from the reclamation yard came, and paid Fran a very nice amount for the Cotswold stone tiles.

'That seems an awful lot!' she said, forgetting she should be edging up the price, not the opposite.

'It is an awful lot,' the man agreed, 'but I daren't give you less than they're worth. Antony would be furious.'

'Oh, well. As long as you're making a profit...'

'Don't worry, I am. And there's a fair bit here. I'll send the lorry up tomorrow to collect the tiles, if that's OK.'

'More than OK. The sooner the better as far as I'm concerned,' said Fran.

'Right. Cash suit you?'

'That's fine,' said Fran, wondering briefly if she had to worry about tax and decided not to bother.

She watched as the man peeled fifty pound notes off a wodge he produced from his back pocket and put them into her hand. She offered a quick prayer of thanks that Roy wasn't here to snatch the money away, or at least threaten to, and reckoned she had enough for one bank loan payment and a bit towards the next. She'd pay it into the farm account today, when she planned to see Amy.

Amy was on good form when Fran went in to see her later that afternoon.

'Roy's gone away for a little break,' Fran said to Amy, who nodded. As Fran had only had to say it once, it indicated that Amy was wearing her hearing aids, which helped communication.

'Good idea. He should see a bit of the countryside if he's going to live here.'

'I thought he should go back to Australia and look after his farm there,' said Fran, her good mood waning a bit.

'It's a long way away, Australia,' said Amy.

'He wouldn't need to get there by sailing ship,' Fran countered. 'It's only a day and a night on a plane.' She was a bit vague about this but felt she didn't need to be too precise.

'Getting under your feet, was he?'

'He was really. He doesn't do much but he complains about what I do.'

'Well, a man isn't going to like taking orders from a woman, is he? Suffered from that half my working life.'

'I don't give him orders.'

'But he's not in charge. He's won't like that.'

Fran swallowed. Amy could be contrary. She was quite likely to put Roy in charge just to keep him entertained, or to keep her on her toes. She decided to change the subject. 'Tig put the cows out this morning. It was so lovely to see them all springing and bucking around the fields.'

Amy softened. 'Ah, I used to love this time of year. Me and my husband used to watch them as they came out of the pen together. It was as if the cows were our children and we were watching them play.'

This took Fran by surprise and sentimental tears caught the back of her throat.

'Mind you,' Amy went on, 'it's a bit early, isn't it? Tig always wanted to let the cows out too early. You tell him. Tell him it's too early. He should leave it another fortnight.'

Fleetingly, Fran imagined herself telling Tig what to do with his beloved cows and now it was laughter threatening to embarrass her. She cleared her throat. 'You picked a brilliant herdsman in Tig. He'll never let you, the cows, or the farm down. You don't need to worry about anything he does, I know that.' She spoke emphatically, and was rewarded by a slight nod.

'Yes, I did pick a good herdsman. But he'd never take being bossed about by a woman.'

Fran had gone from tears to laughter to feminist outrage in a very short space of time. 'Amy!' she said indignantly. 'You're a woman! Surely he took orders from you?'

'But I was over eighty when I took Tig on,' as if this somehow meant she wasn't a woman. 'You're just a slip of a thing from London.'

Fran laughed openly. Amy was outrageous, but she was also brave and hard-working and had devoted her life to her farm. She had to remember that. 'Honestly, Amy, I don't know what to say. But did I tell you about how well my cheese sold at the farmers' market?'

'Very hard to get a stall at a farmers' market.'

'I know but I was a guest, on Erica's stall. And an old friend from London—'

But Amy was asleep.

She drove back to the farm, still chuckling gently about Amy and her many contradictions, to find Issi looking out for her.

'What's up?' said Fran as she pulled up.

'It's Antony. He called on the landline. He sounded – well – fairly desperate considering how reserved and buttoned-up he is.'

Fran had only just got out of her car before Seb drove up.

'Fran,' he said. He sounded extremely earnest for Seb, who usually took a lighthearted view of life. 'Ant needs you. Can you come with me now? Maybe pack a few things?'

'Oh God, Seb, what is it? Is he ill? Has he had an accident?' Fran's heart was pounding and she felt sweat break out on her forehead.

Seb's expression softened just a little. 'He said to tell you, it's payback time.'

Fran licked her dry lips. 'For all that he's done for me?'

Seb nodded. 'But don't worry, it's not life or death – well it is, but only – well, you go and pack an overnight bag and I'll drive you over to the house.'

Fran shook her head. 'I'll drive myself. You go and tell Antony I'm on my way.'

Fran concentrated on driving safely and not letting her desire to get to Park House at top speed make her hit a wall on the way.

Seb was waiting for her. 'Come in. It's OK!' he said, seeing Fran's anxiety. 'It's actually lovely.

But I've got to go now, which is why Antony needs you.'

'Where are you going?' asked Fran, more confused than ever.

'Old friend's wedding. I'm the best man. Here...'

He opened the door to the big sitting room and Fran was instantly struck with how warm it was. Antony got up from the sofa where he'd been sitting and came over.

He hugged her, hard, as if he needed comfort. 'You came. But I'm going to tell you what you're in for so you can go home again, and Seb can miss the wedding.' He took her by the arm. 'Come and see.'

He led her to the fireplace where the wood burner was blasting out heat. There was a large cardboard box. In the box were lying several very shiny black tubes. She realised what they were after a second.

'Oh my God,' she whispered. 'Puppies!'

He nodded. 'Only a few hours old.'

'But where's their mother?'

'She had a caesarean and rejected them, unfortunately. It happens. We're having to hand-rear them.'

'We?'

He laughed softly. 'Currently, you and me. Come with me into the kitchen and I'll explain while I get the next feed ready. They have to be fed every two hours and it takes an hour.'

Fran bit back her second 'Oh my God' since she'd got there.

Antony's huge kitchen had acquired a few new bits of equipment since she'd cooked in it. There were several tiny bottles, scales, a large tub of puppy milk, plastic jugs and a couple of thermos flasks.

She watched as Antony measured out spoonfuls of dried milk into a jug and set it on the scales.

'The pups belong to some very old friends who were almost like parents to me when I was growing up. Their daughter was like my younger sister. Their dog – the pups' mother – is a brilliant working collie, so apart from anything else, these puppies are potentially very valuable.'

He went over to the kettle and poured a little of the water over his wrist. 'If you use boiling water it doesn't mix properly,' he explained. 'June and Jack had to go to their daughter's, who's just had a baby. Unfortunately there are a few problems with the baby. They were torn, so I said I'd do the pups.'

'And you can't manage on your own? I can imagine! Well, I'm more than happy to help.'

He looked at her intently. 'Tonight you help, but tomorrow – well, I've got to go to London. You'll be on your own for twenty-four hours. This is a major favour I'm asking, Fran. It's more than anything I've done for you.'

She shook her head. 'I don't agree. You've done so much: the track, the cheese room—'

He interrupted her. 'If you've got more than enough money, spending a bit of it isn't any hardship. I'm asking you to give me hours of your time and to go without sleep.' He paused. 'Looking after these puppies is very labour-intensive. I'm going to get you to help me with one feed and then we'll see how you get on. It's not only feeding we've got to do. They can't wee and poo without help. We have to get them to do that too.'

'So when did you learn to do all this?' she said as between them they carried the hot water, the bottles, a jug of milk and the thermoses through to the sitting room.

'Today. June took me through it. She's done it before when Millie – that's the mum – had a huge litter and they had to hand-rear a couple. But this is something else.'

'Goodness.'

'Their vet didn't recommend them hand-rearing those pups but not even the hardest-hearted vet would let a whole litter die.'

'Of course not! Not even if they weren't remotely valuable. They're new life!'

Antony nodded and just for a moment it looked as if he wanted to kiss her but something made him hold back. 'I knew you'd get that. I really don't know anyone else who'd understand and be prepared to do it all for these tiny little creatures. They're so ... dependent.'

Fran cleared the gathering tears from her throat. 'I'm so glad you asked me.'

'Oh, I forgot,' said Antony. 'We have to wash our hands before we start.'

As Fran scrubbed her hands in the well-tiled but slightly chilly downstairs loo, she reminded herself that Antony had chosen her because she was kind and efficient, not because he liked her – not in that way.

Chapter Fifteen

Fran and Antony were in the sitting room, about to start the feeding session.

'Here's a clipboard,' Antony said. 'It's got all the pups' markings on it so we can tell them apart. Thank goodness they're collies and have white patches. We'd have to put nail varnish or something on them if they were Labs.'

'It's sort of cosy, isn't it?' Fran paused. 'And yet a bit like a hospital ward. Cosy because of the warmth and the low lighting, I suppose, but also efficient.'

'I think I see what you mean,' said Antony.

Fran didn't think he knew what she meant at all, but appreciated him trying to understand.

There was a small table loaded with thermos flasks of boiling water, another jug of cold water, and jug of milk and a couple of feeding bottles.

'Right, let's get the bottles filled. Well, only about halfway up.' He watched her. 'That's perfect.'

'They drink half a bottle of milk? I know the bottles are only dolly size really, but—'

'Ideally, we'd have a newly sterilised bottle for each puppy, but June told me they couldn't buy enough bottles for that. Instead, we pour boiling water over the teats in between each feed.'

'What's this?' Fran was looking at the clipboard. 'I get the markings and love that they've got names, but weeing and pooing? Really?'

Antony nodded ruefully. 'A bit coy, I know, but it's what June put when they made the chart. I'll show you.'

He picked up a cotton-wool pad and dipped it in the lid of a thermos into which he'd poured some boiling water and a little cold. Then he wrung out the pad over his wrist to test the temperature. Satisfied, he reached into the box and picked up a puppy.

'There's a heat pad under the Vet-bed in the box,' he said, holding the squirming little creature, 'it's vital to keep them really warm. It's why I've got the wood burner stoked and the heating turned up.'

Then tenderly, he began to dab the pad between the puppy's legs. 'Can you make a note of his markings? I can see it's a boy.'

Fran picked up the clipboard. 'Long white streak? Patch of white on the ear? That's Billy.'

'Great,' said Antony. 'And he's just weed, so put a tick in the box. I'll feed him now, poor little starving thing, and then we'll do the poo bit.'

He looked up at her. She was gazing at the tiny pup he now had in the palm of his hand. Antony supported Billy's head with his fingers and put the teat into the gaping mouth. Billy latched on and began to suck lustily.

'June told me that the advantage of puppies over human babies is that when you've fed them and they've weed and pooed, you put them back and they go straight back to sleep. None of that trying to settle them that apparently goes on with ordinary babies.' He paused. 'Now you feed one.'

Concealing her nervousness at picking up such a vulnerable creature, Fran reached into the box. Although the pup seemed to be completely asleep, the moment it was in her hand it squirmed into life. Instead of a little black and white tube, it was a puppy.

'Oh…' she whispered, cradling it.

'You don't have to be frightened of it. They are surprisingly tough. Now, who've you got there?'

Fran examined her wriggling handful. 'It's got three white feet so that should help.' She looked at the chart. 'Oh no, there are two with three white feet and two with a bit of white on their backs. Oh, Antony! I don't know which one it is.'

'There's something you haven't looked for. Turn it over. Is it male or female?'

Fran, feeling incredibly stupid, inspected the pup. 'I still don't know!'

Antony didn't mock her. 'It's a boy. See? It's surprisingly far up, away from where you'd expect it to be.'

Fran was abashed. 'Honestly, the most basic thing. I just hope I can do this.'

'You can. Really, if I can, it can't be that hard.'

Fran mentally put her shoulders back and started on the pup. First she persuaded it to wee, and then she fed it. That was the most satisfying, seeing the little thing full of a lust for life. Lastly, watching what Antony did (he'd fed another pup while she was still on her first), she got a little cylinder of yellow poo from him.

'I can't believe how satisfying that was,' she said. 'It was like watching paint coming out of a tube.' She put the puppy back with its siblings and it promptly fell asleep. Then she blushed. She wasn't sure she knew Antony well enough to talk about poo.

'I expect there's a posh paint colour called "Puppy Poo".' he said. 'I might have it in here when I get round to redecorating.'

She relaxed and picked up another puppy. 'Hmm, not sure it would work in here. You might be better with "Elephant's Belch" or whatever it is. Now.' She inspected her new captive. 'Who have I got here? Oh, you're a girl!'

When all six pups had been fed, and their various accomplishments had been marked off on the clipboard (ticks in all the boxes), Antony and Fran sat on the sofa together, looking at the sleeping litter, all close together in a heap.

'I swear their tummies are all a bit bigger now,' said Fran, 'although I'm sure they can't be really.'

'Apparently they're very tube-like when they're first born and their stomachs swell as the days go by. Now, let's a have a drink or a cup of tea or something before the next feed.'

A few minutes later, Antony put a mug of hot chocolate in front of her. 'It's so much quicker with two,' he said.

'I can imagine.' Fran sipped her hot chocolate. 'How long were you doing it on your own?'

'They arrived at eight this morning. I put off asking you for help as long as I could. And seriously, I wouldn't have done that at all if I didn't have to go away tomorrow. Although it's only for a night,' he added.

Fran managed not to gasp in horror at the prospect of being in sole charge of so many helpless little creatures. She turned the subject to something she knew about: food. 'Have you eaten much today?'

'A lot of toast. There's more bread in the freezer.'

'Why don't I make us supper? We've got just over an hour before the next feed. There'll be time.'

'That would be amazing. Cooking has been the last thing on my mind. I'm not sure what there is...'

'Don't worry. I'll find something.' When Fran had used Antony's kitchen to cook her pies, she discovered that there were good basic – and less basic – ingredients in his fridge. And if all else failed, she'd do omelettes.

An hour later she went quietly back into the sitting room to find Antony stretched out on one of the sofas, fast asleep. In between making supper (sausages and mash) she had prepared the boiling water, mixed up a double batch of milk and sterilised all the bottles. She reckoned they just had time to eat before the next feed.

She cleared her throat and, obligingly, Antony opened his eyes.

'Let's eat,' she said. 'The pups are already getting restless, thinking it's time for their next meal.'

'That's amazing,' said Antony, looking at the loaded tray and swinging his legs down to the floor.

She handed him a plate.

'Would you like a glass of wine with it?' he asked.

'I'd kill for a glass of wine, but honestly? I think not while I'm in charge of puppies,' Fran replied.

He laughed. 'I'll be in charge. You could have a glass.'

She shook her heard. 'I'd rather have a cup of tea, frankly. I'll make it afterwards.'

They didn't speak, both appreciating the sausages, which had just the right combination of meat, fat, cereal and spice, and the creamy mashed potatoes.

'That was heaven,' said Antony when he'd finished. 'Now I'm going to make tea.'

The puppies were stirring properly now so Fran measured milk into all the bottles. Then she went and washed her hands. The tea was waiting for her when she got back.

'I should probably feed the pups before drinking the tea,' she said, 'but I'm afraid I'm going to look after myself first.'

'Quite right,' said Antony, having taken a sip of his own tea. 'Now, shall we get started?'

And so it began again.

For the night shift, they took a sofa each, neither of them wanting to go to bed properly for less than two hours' sleep. Although she had set her phone to wake her, Fran slept through an entire feed. This meant when she heard her phone alarm again, she'd had four hours' sleep.

'Antony!' she reproached him as he came back into the room with the thermoses and milk. 'You should have made sure I woke up!'

'You've got to do a whole day and night on your own tomorrow,' he said. 'I thought I should let you miss a feed. Now, there's more tea on the counter in the kitchen. Would you care to bring it through? And home-made shortbread that June made for us.'

They didn't talk very much through the feed, mostly just commenting on how the individual puppies were doing. There was one, a bit smaller than the rest, who, though keen at first, tired quickly, that Fran took on as a challenge.

'I'll feed Betsy first,' she said, 'and then when she's had a nap, after all the others have fed, I'll do her again.'

'You're really into this, aren't you?' said Antony, stroking a tiny tummy with damp cotton wool.

'I've never really looked after an animal – animals plural, I suppose – like this before. It does make you really care about them. As you said, they're so dependent.'

'Even big animals, like cows, are dependent,' said Antony. 'Ask Tig.'

Fran was beginning to understand a bit better now how Tig felt about his cows, and how, presumably, Amy had also. It wasn't just because they were valuable and produced wonderful milk, it was because without care and attention they wouldn't thrive. And caring for them made you love them.

'I will talk to him about the cows a bit more,' she resolved. 'Apparently cows form family groups that it's important to recognise. I'd like to know more about that.' She took a breath. 'Now, have we done all the others? Pass me Betsy. Come on, little girl, let's get a bit more into you.'

Fran insisted that Antony missed the 6 a.m. feed and went to bed properly, so he could sleep until he had to leave for London, shortly after eight. He was driving himself as Seb was still away at his best friend's wedding.

She was just preparing for the 8 a.m. feed in the kitchen when he appeared, fresh from the shower, shaved and smelling heavenly. When she turned to look at him, she saw he was looking wonderful too.

'You don't look like someone who's only had four hours' sleep,' she said, taken aback by the impression he made on her.

'I don't know if people who've had very little sleep always look like you do,' he responded, 'but I must say, it's a look I like.'

Fran paused, halfway through filling the kettle. 'Are you paying me a compliment?'

He laughed gently. 'I realise to the sleep-deprived that probably sounded a bit obscure. But yes. You look lovely. Rumpled, not remotely "groomed", but delightful.' He frowned. 'I've probably stepped over a boundary when I shouldn't have. Sorry. Forget I said anything.'

'I'd rather remember, if you don't mind,' she said, suddenly shy. 'And have you time for tea?'

He walked over to his coffee machine, which was the size of a small car. 'I think I need something fairly high-octane. Which is a double espresso.'

'Toast? I could slather Marmite on to it to make it almost inedible? I'm afraid the thought of a double espresso at this time in the morning gives me a headache, but if that's the sort of thing you like...'

'Toast, with butter, and just the usual amount of Marmite would be heavenly.'

'I'm on to it,' she said.

Seemingly seconds later, Antony said, 'That was delicious,' wiping his mouth. He cleared his throat. 'I can't decide which would feel weirder, kissing you goodbye or not kissing you goodbye.'

'Oh...'

'Actually, it's probably wrong to kiss you in any case, but I'm going to do it anyway.'

And he did. Not the peck on the cheek she was expecting, but on her mouth, firm and meaningful enough for her to remember for the rest of the day.

Fran spent the day watching daytime television and dozing in between feeds. She was better at identifying the pups now, and had the knack of getting them to wee and poo quickly. Betsy, the little one, seemed to be thriving on her two-tier feeding system. Fran was quicker at measuring out the powdered milk, too. But she was a zombie really: the outside world seemed irrelevant. All that mattered was feeding the pups on time and getting ticks in all the boxes on the chart.

The pups always weed, but sometimes they missed the other bit, which was worrying. Fran wished she'd clarified with Antony on how many boxes could have crosses in them, consecutively, before the vet should be called. While this hadn't happened yet, she did look up the number of the nearest vet so she'd have it handy.

Issi came over in time for the four o'clock feed. She was instructed in puppy hygiene and – as a huge concession to the fact that it was so time-consuming, and it was Issi – was allowed to help with the feeding. Being short of sleep and making the little family the absolute focus of her attention had given Fran lioness tendencies when it came to protecting them.

'You probably don't want to hear this now,' said Issi, watching in admiration as Fran deftly produced wee from a puppy as if she were pressing a button and not just dabbing with damp cotton wool. 'But Roy is due back later this evening.'

'Oh no! I was hoping he'd spend a bit longer on his whirlwind tour of the British Isles.'

'He went to Cornwall.'

'Good choice.'

'But now he's coming home today. Not sure why but he muttered about B and Bs being expensive.'

'Oh God, I've been dreading this. Because I live at the farm, he's going to think that he has the right to as well. But I'm living off my savings. I'm not going to support him.'

'Of course not! I do what I can with my rent but I've seen you worry about all the expenses.'

'It'll be OK,' said Fran. 'Honestly, as long as we keep these puppies alive until they're collected, nothing else seems to matter. See little Betsy?' She pointed to the pile.

'You mean the black and white one?'

'No need for sarcasm. She's smaller than the others. Look!' Fran offered the minute pup for inspection. 'I'm feeding her twice, once at the beginning and once at the end of the session.'

'Should you force-feed them? Isn't that like what they do to geese to make foie gras?'

'No, it isn't at all like that!' Fran was indignant. 'But I'm not sure I should be doing it. She feeds well for a little but gets tired. By the time she's had a rest she's up for some more.'

'I'm sure it's absolutely fine,' said Issi.

Fran dragged her thoughts away from the little family that was currently her obsession. 'About Roy. I really don't want him poking round while I'm not at the farm.'

'Don't worry,' said Issi. 'I'll be there. I'll guard your territory. And you will be back soon, won't you? Aren't the pups being collected tomorrow morning?'

'I think so, but when is Roy coming?'

Issi shrugged. 'Not sure exactly. Late afternoon, early evening is what he said.'

Fran looked at her watch. It was nearly five. 'Maybe you should be getting back then?'

'I'll make you tea and toast and then go,' said Issi. 'I do understand, but you look exhausted. You should let me do a shift so you can get a proper nap.'

'I'm coping! It's hard but I'm coping.' Fran forced a smile. 'I can manage here if I don't have to worry about anything else. If you cover my back at home, that will be wonderful.'

'Then that's what I'll do. Tea and toast first though. Would you like me to make you dinner and bring it over?' suggested Issi. 'My pasta sauce is fairly edible.'

'Your pasta sauce is great but really, please, all I want you to do is guard my farm. There are cold sausages here, and leftover mash. I won't starve.'

'I do hope it becomes your farm!' said Issi. 'And not just for your sake.'

Fran put her hand on Issi's. 'I know. I think about Tig too. Now if you're going to make toast...'

It was a long night. Fran felt she was constantly washing her hands, boiling kettles and measuring milk powder. In between she was studying little bodies so she could identify them, rubbing them with damp tissue and – the least part of it all – actually feeding the puppies.

She was washing bottles in the kitchen after the eight a.m. feed when she heard the doorbell ring. Somewhat anxious, she dried her hands and went to open it. Who could it be? Who would call on Antony at this time? Surely it couldn't be good news.

A couple in their sixties stood on the doorstep. 'I am so sorry,' said the woman. 'I know it's horrendously early, but we had to come and see about the pups?'

'We're Jack and June,' said the man. 'Antony's friends. We own the collie bitch who had the puppies.'

Fran opened the door wider. 'You must be desperate to see them. But they're all fine.'

She felt oddly proprietorial as she opened the door to the sitting room and ushered the couple in.

June went straight over to look in the box. Fran went with her. 'I'm looking for Betsy,' said June.

'Oh, there she is,' said Fran. 'Do you want her?' She picked up Betsy and handed her over.

'She's grown! I suppose they all have but it shows most with Betsy. She was the smallest.'

'I fed her twice – I mean each feed. Once at the beginning and then a top-up at the end. Was that wrong?'

'I don't think so,' said June. 'How kind of you.'

'Shall I make some tea or something? While you get reacquainted with the pups?'

The couple nodded and then sat on the sofa, peering with wonder into the box. She left them to it and went into the kitchen.

A little later, June said, 'I can't believe Antony found someone to take this on at such short notice. I just didn't know what to do. I couldn't not go to my daughter and baby granddaughter. When he said he knew someone who might help we were so relieved.'

'And was it all right to leave them now? They're both well?' Although to Fran the puppies were the most important thing, she accepted that human babies mattered too.

June beamed. 'They are! Both fit as fleas now; although the baby is small, she's doing really well. But you? Was it hard for you to drop everything for these little scraps?'

'I was only too happy to help,' Fran said. 'Antony has been so generous to me.'

'He's such a lovely man, isn't he?' Sipping her tea, with Betsy on her lap, June had relaxed. 'Not everyone sees that side of him. They think he's all business, business, business.'

'How did you get to meet him?' Fran was delighted to be able to find out more about Antony.

'He's friends with our son. He used to spend school holidays with us when his parents first went to live in Switzerland, where his mother still lives. Although he came from a very different background, he was always very happy to muck in. We farm in a small way and have always had collies.' She kissed the pup and put it back before picking up another one. 'He could never have a dog at home, so he had one with us. Great working dog, she was.'

'I'm sure he was only too happy to help,' said Fran.

'Antony, yes, but you? I can't tell you how glad I am—'

'June.' Jack's warning to his wife not to say too much was like the barely audible growl of a dog who has no desire to use force but could if it wanted.

'No, but, Jack, this lovely girl has dropped everything to look after our puppies – you wouldn't have got the other one doing that.'

'She means Ant's wife,' said Jack, apparently resigned to his wife's need to have a good moan about someone in Antony's past she'd never considered good enough for him.

'She was only interested in his money and his property,' said June. 'You're not at all like her.'

Fran couldn't help laughing. 'I'm sure I'm not! I'm sure she was well groomed and glamorous.'

'She was that all right,' said June, caressing a tiny black head with her finger. 'Spent a fortune on clothes and was far too thin. Not at all pretty, like you.'

'Well, thank you. But Antony and I – well, we're not together, we're just friends.'

'Huh,' said Jack gruffly. 'He must think a lot of you to trust you with these little perishers.'

'He's right, you know,' said June, patting Fran's hand. 'So I hope you're single. I couldn't go through Antony's heart being broken again.'

'He didn't make a big fuss about it,' objected Jack. 'Doesn't wear his heart on his sleeve.'

'No, but he was suffering,' said June. 'I knew it.' She put down her mug. 'Now, I'll just use the facilities and then we should get this lot home. We're hoping their mum will take more kindly to them now she's over the op.'

'I'm going to miss all this,' said Fran, suddenly aware it was true.

'Come and see them whenever you've a moment,' said June and got to her feet.

As well as feeling dizzy after two nights of very broken sleep, Fran felt a bit flat, packing up to go back home. She wanted to see Antony again, to share the feeling of satisfaction of handing the puppies back, safe and ever so slightly bigger than they had been. Instead she had the prospect of Roy to return to.

However, when she parked the car, a very excited Issi came to the door. 'Come quickly! The first calf of the season. It's being born right now.' Then her excitement faded. 'Oh, you'll be shattered. You'll just want a bath and a nap.'

At one time, not very long ago really, a shower and a nap would have been Fran's first option. But since caring for the puppies, so small and defence-less, the thought of seeing an animal being born wasn't faintly disgusting and scary: it was wonderful.

'Just lead me to the cow in labour,' Fran said. 'Although not if she'll be put off by my being there.'

'She won't notice,' said Issi, thrilled by Fran's willingness to join her. 'Come on!'

Chapter Sixteen

Fran took the time to put on her coat as a stiff breeze had got up, giving the emerging spring a reminder that winter still had some teeth. Then she followed Issi down the path to the shed.

'We have to be very quiet and calm,' said Issi. 'This is a first calving and the mother is very special.'

'I know about the very quiet and calm bit,' said Fran, slightly hurt that Issi had forgotten where she'd just come from but understanding that her friend was very caught up in the moment.

'We're hoping for a bull calf,' Issi went on, sounding touchingly proprietorial.

'Don't we want heifers? For milk?' Fran, fairly brain-dead through lack of sleep, was confused.

'We need a good bull calf for the sake of the herd. The cow who's calving now was impregnated with sperm from a very special bull that will refresh the gene pool.'

'You know a lot about it.'

Issi stopped walking and turned to Fran. 'To be honest, Tig doesn't talk much but when he does it's about the herd.'

'Isn't that a bit – boring?' Fran suddenly imagined her bright and funny friend, stuck on an old sofa with Tig, talking about cows.

Issi hesitated. 'Actually, I find it all fascinating. They are such an old herd, and have always grazed this really special, rare pasture. It's why the milk is so full of flavour, and why your cheese is so good. Now come on.'

They reached the cowshed. Fran had been expecting the cow to be on her own, but she was in with the others.

'Is she OK?' she asked, feeling hampered by ignorance and lack of sleep.

'She should be fine,' said Tig, 'but it's her first time and you never know.'

'How long will it take?' Fran went on.

'Again, you never know, especially with heifers.' He smiled quickly. 'She's a first-time mother. She doesn't know how it's done yet.'

'But she'll be all right?' Fran was thinking of the mother of the puppies, who'd had to have a caesarean and had then rejected her offspring.

'I hope she will. It's all going OK so far.' He smiled again and Fran could see why Issi liked him so much: he was calm, knowledgeable and kind. 'You don't have to be here, you know, you could go back to the house and wait for news.'

'No! I must be here. Cows are what this farm has; I need to learn everything I can about them.' Before Roy inherits and sells them all, she added silently.

Tig made a sound that could have signified amusement or admiration or indeed that he had a frog in his throat. Fran didn't seek clarification.

She found herself oddly fascinated. Although nothing much seemed to be happening – the cow was wandering around the enclosure, picking at the grass and occasionally mooing loudly – the thought that any moment she would give birth kept Fran's attention. Either that or she was so tired, she was happy just to be in the moment and be part of what was potentially so important for the farm.

'Tig told me she's been lying down and getting up for a while now,' Issi told Fran quietly. 'As long as the contractions don't stop it should be OK, but if they do, she'll definitely need help.'

A bit later Issi suggested they made Tig coffee and went into the house together.

Fran ate a piece of cake while she cut one for Tig. 'Good cake!' she said.

'Mary made it. She knew the calf was due soon and it's a special one. Tig may not get in for meals.'

'One of the sweet things about Tig is that although he's a professional herdsman, through and through, he cares about his cows as if they were pets,' said Fran.

'It's true. It's good that you appreciate that,' said Issi.

'Why, in particular?'

'Because you may be his boss one day.'

Fran laughed. 'I'll never be his boss in the ordinary way. I wouldn't dream of telling him what to do.' Then she yawned so hard her jaw cracked.

'Listen,' said Issi. 'You're half-dead. Go and have a nap.'

'I don't want to miss this, Issi. I feel it's important. And I can tell Amy all about it later.'

'OK. Go and sleep now and I'll wake you the moment it starts getting interesting.'

Fran wanted to resist but knew it was futile. 'Promise to wake me? Even if I'm deeply asleep?'

'I promise.'

It seemed like seconds later that Issi was shaking her shoulder. 'I've just rung the vet,' she said.

Fran shot up, instantly awake. 'Oh my God! Is it going to be all right?'

'We don't know.'

Fran realised that Issi was close to tears and that she needed to be up for her friend's sake, as much as for the cow and calf. Issi's happiness was very bound up with Tig's and she realised that if anything happened to any of the animals, he would be devastated.

She put her hand on Issi's. 'You go. I'll be with you in a minute.'

The briefest splash of water on her face to wake her up and Fran was on her way to the cowshed.

The heifer was on her side, mooing. Tig was lying on the straw at the back end, his arm in the cow, his expression intense.

'The vet's on his way,' said Issi, who seemed calmer now.

Tig looked up and saw her. 'Vets don't come cheap. I wouldn't have called him if I could have managed – Oh, hang on, I might have got something. Is? Can you pass me those ropes hanging there?'

'Tig, if you need the vet, call him! Don't hesitate. We'll pay him somehow.' Fran had no idea how much vets cost, but she wouldn't have let an animal suffer however expensive it was.

He nodded, and Fran knew he was reassured.

Fran couldn't decide if she was repelled or fascinated as she watched Tig put ropes round the tiny feet that now appeared from the heifer. The thought of an animal being born in this way was horrifying, but it was obviously OK or Tig wouldn't be doing it.

'I might need a hand, Is,' said Tig quietly.

Issi didn't hesitate. She was over the side of the pen and at Tig's side in an instant.

'Right,' said Tig, 'hold on to this, and when I say pull, pull.'

Fran couldn't bear to look at or even think of a baby creature being pulled from its mother in such a powerful, not to say violent, way. But she trusted Tig completely, and if he thought ropes and tugging were needed, they definitely were.

She was squinting through the corner of her eye at what was going on when there was a 'Come on!' from Tig and then the calf landed on the straw in a gush of blood and fluid.

'It's a bull calf,' said Tig. 'Now rub it with straw, quite briskly,' he said to Issi. 'I've got to see to the mother.' There was no time for celebration.

The calf stirred almost immediately but the mother seemed less happy. Tig tried to encourage her on to her feet but she didn't want to move.

'What do you think the matter is?' asked Issi.

'Not sure. Could be milk fever.'

Fran found she wanted to cry but bit her lip hard to prevent it. She knew her emotion was to do with the puppies and being so tired and the general stress of it all. But it was also something deeper, more primal. It was watching a fellow female doing what females were born to do: giving birth. And it was hard.

'I'll make more tea,' she said to no one in particular.

'Good idea,' said Tig, and his affirmation reassured her.

As she walked back to the house a million unconnected thoughts went through her head, like how she was still wearing unsuitable stripy wellies even though she'd meant to get proper farming ones when she first arrived; what, if anything, she'd say to Amy if the heifer died; whether Tig really wanted tea or if he just wanted her out of the way; and if she should make tea for the vet.

She loaded up the tray with cake and four mugs of tea, including one for the vet who should arrive at any moment. Then she unloaded it again, put the empty tray in the bottom of a large basket, one of the many that Amy had dotted round the kitchen, and then put everything back on it again. As she set off back to the cowshed she felt pleased that she still had some initiative left.

She'd done right to include the vet in her calculations. When she got back to the cowshed there was a man holding a bottle of clear fluid high up and a tube leading from the bottle to the cow, which now had a needle in one of the veins in her neck.

'Milk fever,' said Issi quietly. 'Andrew is giving her calcium. Andrew!' she said more loudly. 'Would you like tea?'

'I'll have it afterwards if I may,' he said. 'Don't worry though. I never get to drink a mug of tea while it's hot. I've stopped even liking it that way.'

As Fran handed Tig his tea she sensed the atmosphere was lighter now, though whether this was because Andrew was there or because the calcium was working she didn't know.

She and Issi sipped and watched in silence. The calf was on its feet now but the cow was still sitting on the straw.

Then suddenly something changed. The cow seemed to change her attitude to motherhood and, with Tig and Andrew there to assist, lumbered to her feet.

'Thank goodness,' said Issi to Fran and put her arm round Fran's shoulders and gave her a quick hug.

They both watched as the little calf staggered round to his mother's udder and tried to latch on. The mother swung her head round and began to lick him. Then cow and calf worked out what to do at the same time and the calf began to suckle.

Everyone watched in silence and wonderment at the miracle of nature. Fran noticed that Issi's cheeks were wet and swallowed hard to keep her own tears in check.

Andrew sipped his tea at last and Tig finished his.

'I'll get some hot water so you can have a wash,' said Tig.

'Or you could come up to the house?' suggested Fran, who thought washing in a cowshed was too James Herriot for words.

Andrew smiled. 'I'll get the worst off down here. But is there a chance of more tea? I was lying when I said I liked it cold.'

As Fran set off back to the house again, with Issi, she was aware that as a feminist she should object to being seen as a tea-maker, but as one who knew nothing about calving she felt grateful to have something useful to do. She'd clear it with her conscience later.

She swayed slightly as she put the kettle on.

'You're falling over you're so tired!' said Issi. 'Don't worry about the tea. I'll sort Andrew and Tig out. You go back to bed.'

'I think I will,' Fran said. 'I probably need a proper meal but, frankly, I'm just too tired to think about what I want. Much as I love cake, it's not quite doing it for me at the moment.'

'I'll make you an omelette when you wake up. Off you go.'

Fran went willingly, longing for another proper sleep in a proper bed.

Chapter Seventeen

꧁꧂

Fran was so deeply asleep it took her a while to realise that Issi was shaking her again and she wasn't on some weird fairground ride that had appeared in her dreams.

'I'm so sorry to wake you,' said Issi. 'But there's a message on the landline answerphone from Roger.'

'Do I know a Roger?'

'Yes you do! He's your chef friend from London who liked your cheese. He's left several messages.'

'What time is it?'

'Three in the afternoon. You've been asleep a couple of hours.'

'Thanks, Is. I'll call Roger. Oh, has Roy appeared? Wasn't he due last night?'

'Yes. He'll turn up any time now, I imagine.'

'Right. I'll get my act together.'

*

'Thank the Lord you've called!' said Roger, responding after the first ring. 'I was beginning to give up hope! I want as much mascarpone as you can make as soon as.'

'As soon as what, Roger?'

'Grr! Look, I've got a team of food critics, magazine editors, representatives of major shops – it's all a bit last minute or I'd have been in touch before.'

'I'd never be able to supply supermarkets, Rog, even if I wanted to—'

'Not supermarkets! Niche grocers and delis! What's wrong with you, Fran? These are influential people. They could make your brand.'

It felt a little odd to think of the cheese she made with such love and, initially, such difficulty as a brand. 'Sorry, just a bit tired.'

'But you'll make it?'

'If I can. But what kind of mascarpone do you want? I mean, the kind I make from a culture, which is the best, takes longer. And you know I use unpasteurised milk?'

'That's why it's so good! I need your best, and I need it by tomorrow afternoon if possible.'

'So I've got less than twenty-four hours,' said Fran slowly, doing some calculations in her head but knowing she didn't really have a choice. This was such an amazing opportunity. 'I'll do my best.'

'I'll send a courier. You just let me know when you're nearly done and it'll be picked up.'

'I'm on it. If I can't do it I'll ring you back.'

'You must do it!' said Roger and disconnected.

But as soon as she'd put the phone down she realised she couldn't make it unless she had cream. She didn't even know if any of the cows were still giving milk. She'd lost track of the farm a bit – looking after the puppies had been like living in another world – and being so tired didn't make it any easier to think. If there was no milk her brand wouldn't get this huge boost, and if she was going to get the cheese made in time someone would have had to make cream. It was probably all impossible.

She went to find Tig. He and Issi were back in the cowshed, looking at the cow and calf, who were now happily coupled up, looking the very picture of bovine contentment.

'They are beautiful,' said Fran, aware she was interrupting a special moment between Tig and Issi.

'They are,' said Tig simply.

'It was such a privilege to see the little one born. Do have a name for him? Or don't you give your cows names?'

'I certainly do,' said Tig. 'And I reckon Antony's a good name.'

Fran cleared her throat, not quite sure how to take this. 'I'm sure he'll be thrilled.'

'He's a very handsome specimen,' said Issi. 'And so is Antony.'

'Yes, well, maybe,' said Fran. 'Now, Tig? Issi may have told you that I've had a call from Roger, who bought all my cheese at the farmers' market.'

He nodded.

'I need to make a lot of mascarpone. Are all the cows dry? Have we got milk? And if we have, has anyone made cream?' She studied Tig's expression but couldn't read it. 'No, of course not, you haven't had time.'

Her spirits slumped. It was all too good to be true. A collection of people influential in the food business were going to taste her cheese – but only if it was possible for her to make it. And there was no cream. All the cows were dry.

Tig humphed and Fran looked up again. A slight alteration in his usually inscrutable expression indicated he was pleased. 'I've always staggered the calving a bit, so we always have milk. More now it's spring, of course, but yes, we've got milk.'

'Oh, Tig!'

He smiled properly. 'And my mother's been up to skim off the cream. We didn't like to waste it.'

'Oh, Tig! Oh, Mary! I love you both.'

She set off towards the house, her mood suddenly upbeat. She would have a quick bath, then she would gear up into her cheesemaking clothes and head for the cheese room. She would make the most of this marvellous opportunity.

She was glad she'd made mascarpone often enough now to feel confident about what she was doing, although she always concentrated really hard. It was vital that she didn't add too much culture as the unpasteurised milk has its own bacterial structure. But once she'd done the initial blending of milk and cream and got it to the right temperature, she could leave it for twelve hours. If she got up early, she could drain it until it was nearly the right texture, and then she'd get on to Roger and he could send the courier. Sleep wasn't far away, she kept reminding herself.

Once again the cheese room wrought its calming magic. She'd designed it, Antony had brought it into being, and she loved it. She also loved mixing the pale yellow cream and milk, stirring it, working her alchemy, transforming it into the most sumptuous cheese she had ever eaten. As she tested the temperature of the cheese, time and again, waiting for it to read the right number, she wondered if this could satisfy her. Maybe she didn't need to make a hard cheese? Maybe this was enough?

But later, as she finally finished cleaning down the cheese room, she realised it wasn't. She had to find that quarry and learn the proper skills of a cheesemaker.

It was just after 7 p.m. when she made her way back into the house, extremely tired but extremely satisfied. She could now leave her cheese to drain for twelve hours, set her alarm for seven in the morning, finish the cheese off and then ring the courier. What could go wrong?

Because life had a habit of going wrong, Fran paid attention to this usually rhetorical question and did more mental checks than usual. But it all seemed fine. Peachy, even!

She was humming to herself as she went in through the back door. Issi was there, stirring something. She turned round as soon as Fran entered.

'Hi! Cheese go well?'

Fran knew instantly that something wasn't right. Issi's words and voice were perky, but her face was a picture of terror.

'Yes, good, thank you. But, Is? What's wrong?'

Issi's expression was agonised. 'Roy's back!' She was obviously worried about being overheard. 'He brought a friend.'

Fran began to understand. There was more to it than just an extra person for supper.

'They're drunk!' whispered Issi.

Pennies began to drop like coins from a fairground games machine. 'Very drunk?' Fran whispered.

Issi nodded. 'I'm cooking a big meal!' she said loudly.

Fran wasn't sure what, if anything, could be overheard next door and realised Issi didn't know either. It was best to play it safe though.

She raised her voice: 'Great! You didn't invite Tig to stay?'

'No. He'd gone before I knew we had guests.' She rolled her eyes in the direction of the sitting room.

It was all a bit ridiculous and Fran was beginning to see the funny side.

'That's a shame,' said Fran. 'It would have been nice to celebrate the birth of the calf together.'

'I know but he had such an early start.'

Fran took a minute to work out when her own start had been but as she'd been awake feeding hungry puppies every two hours through the previous night it was hard to say. She decided not to comment. 'But the calf is OK?'

Issi nodded. 'They both are. Antony is just so sweet!'

Fran smiled to hear the calf's name. 'I wonder how the human Antony is?'

'You could ring him!' Issi seemed very enthusiastic about this idea. 'Invite him for supper?'

'Oh no. Honestly, I'm dead on my feet. I expect he is too. He was looking after the puppies as well before he went to London. God knows if he's had a chance to catch up on his sleep.'

'But you'll eat?' Issi still sounded a bit desperate.

'Of course. I didn't think I was hungry but now I've smelt food I'm starving.' Fran smiled, hoping to spread reassurance.

'It's chilli,' said Issi.

'It is a bit, for the time of year, but put a coat on, you'll be fine.' Not a glimmer of response from one of their favourite, oft-repeated, jokes. 'Issi? Shall I go and say hello to Roy and his guest?'

'That might be a good idea,' Issi replied, tasting the chilli from the wooden spoon she was stirring with and then throwing the spoon back in the pot. 'Offer them coffee?'

Fran knew that Issi would never have tasted the chilli and put the spoon back in front of her unless she was very rattled; it was one of Fran's pet hates. She lowered her voice. 'How drunk are they, then?'

'Extremely. It's one of the reasons I got the chilli on early. I thought it might help sober them up a bit.'

'Are they – you know – aggressive?' At the best of times, Fran's heart rate increased whenever she thought about having to deal with Roy; if he and his mate were fighting drunk, she might completely panic.

'Why don't you go next door and see? I'll get this on to plates. We can eat through there. Then if they pass out we can just leave them there.'

Fran nodded. 'I'll go and say hello.' She paused. 'Have you got any wine open?'

Issi nodded. 'Roy brought it. Sip?'

'Yes please.' She took hold of the offered glass and tasted the strong Australian wine. Delicious but potentially lethal. 'OK,' she said. 'I'm going in.'

Fran took a breath, drummed up a smile and opened the door of the sitting room.

The smell hit her. Alcohol was coming in waves from the two men who were half sitting, half lying, taking a sofa each.

'Hi, guys!' Fran said brightly, far more warmly than she would usually be with Roy. 'What have you been up to?' It was blindingly obvious what they'd been doing but it felt polite to ask.

'Gin,' said Roy. 'We went on a tour.'

His friend, who might have been slightly less drunk than Roy, struggled upright. 'Hi, I'm Barry.'

'Hi, Barry. So you went on a tour that involved gin?'

Barry and Roy both nodded. 'Lots of gin.'

Barry cleared his throat, obviously making an effort. 'It was a distillery.' The word didn't come out perfectly, but well enough. 'They had tours. Lots of samples, different sorts of gin.'

'I see. So how did you get here?'

'Left the car there,' said Roy, much to Fran's relief. Otherwise she'd have been scanning the news obsessively, waiting to hear of a hit-and-run accident. 'Walked here.'

'Oh my goodness! Where did you have to walk from?'

Barry waved an arm. 'Was quite local. Bloody taxi wouldn't take us. We weren't even drunk then.'

Fran thought about this. 'So when did that happen?'

'On the way home,' said Roy. 'We drank the bottle we'd bought. But it was all herbal, it said. I didn't expect it to have alcohol in it.'

'Really? Don't they have gin in Australia?' Fran asked, incredulous.

Roy nodded. 'Yeah, they do, but they went on and on about the botanicals, flowers and such, that was in the stuff, I thought maybe it was like Auntie Amy's cowslip wine. In fact,' he went on, 'we found a bottle of that and added the gin.'

'I thought you drank the gin on the way home from the distillery,' said Fran, no longer pretending to be nice about all this.

'Not all of it!' Barry was indignant. 'We bought several bottles.'

Fran's barmaid experience took her only so far. In a pub she could have ordered them (shoved them, with help from some hefty male bar staff) off the premises and there her responsibility would have ended. But these drunks were in her home and there were no hefty bar staff.

'OK, well, I think maybe your next drink should be black coffee. And then we'll eat. Issi's made a chilli. I'll just set the table.'

'Oh, we're eating in here, are we?' said Roy. 'Because we've got guests.'

Fran decided to tell them what Issi had said. 'No, it's so that if you pass out, we don't have to move you. Now I'll make the coffee. Roy? Have you shown Barry where the downstairs loo is?'

'Loo?'

'The dunny,' she explained, grateful for all the Australians she'd worked with in the past.

'Well,' she reported back to Issi who was cooking rice and grating cheese. 'They are dreadfully drunk, but, so far, not too unpleasant.'

'But you won't go to bed and leave me with them?' Issi said. 'I haven't had your experience working in bars. I don't really know how to handle drunks.'

'I certainly won't leave you with them. I am pretty tired, but I think they'll pass out fairly soon. Let's feed them and hope that sends them off.'

'Do you think we should put them to bed after supper?'

'We can try. Let's see if the coffee and food helps.'

Gin, it transpired, didn't make them nasty, it made them garrulous, very, very garrulous.

Fran, who'd found herself drinking a glass of wine although she'd tried not to, nodded off several times during the meal.

Still they went on, discussing the finer points of some rugby match neither of them had been to in real life but obviously obsessed them. They took ages to eat their food, but every time either Fran

238

or Issi suggested they'd had enough and offered to take their plates, they clung on to them, took another tiny forkful and then went back to the rugby match.

Eventually, Fran could stand it no more. She'd wasted enough of her precious sleeping time with these idiots; she would waste no more.

'So, Barry?' she addressed him firmly. 'Where are you going to sleep? Shall we make you comfy on the sofa? I'm afraid all the rooms are occupied.'

'Couldn't I share with you, Fran?' Barry asked.

'No,' she said brutally. 'Roy? Time for bed. Off you go—'

'Now, hang on! Who are you to tell me when I should go to bed?'

'Someone who has to be up very early in the morning,' she said.

'We don't need your permission. We can go to bed when we like!' Roy went on.

Fran was not letting up. 'Not tonight you can't. I've had no proper sleep for days and I have to be up at seven tomorrow to work on my cheese. You're both going to have horrific hangovers in the morning. The longer you have to sleep them off, the better. Now off to the bathroom' – she pointed in the direction of the door – 'and when you come back I'm going to make you both drink a pint of water and take some painkillers. That may stave off the worst.' They didn't move. 'Go on! Now!'

Barry caved in first. He shambled off in the direction of the loo. Roy got up too, muttering darkly about uppity Sheilas and feminism having spiralled out of control.

'God, you're good,' said Issi when they'd both gone. 'Who knew you could be so bossy? They went off like lambs.'

'I think the threat of the hangover helped. I'll just get them their water and paracetamol.'

'We should really give them milk thistle,' said Issi, who'd become a bit of a hippy since she'd moved to the country.

'I'd give them ketamine if I thought it would get them out of my hair.' Fran was not going to pussyfoot around with flower remedies or anything remotely natural and benign.

'The horse drug?' Issi laughed. 'You are one tough woman!'

Fran tried to stay awake until she could be sure that Roy and Barry were safely comatose but she couldn't. Her eyes closed and that was all she knew until her phone alarm went at 7 a.m.

She dragged herself into consciousness. Did she have to feed the puppies? Then she remembered. The puppies were back with their owners. What she had to do now was drain her cheese.

She'd remembered about Roy and Barry when she got her first foot to the floor but as the house was silent, she didn't worry too much. She had to keep focused. She couldn't be distracted by men with gin-overs.

She had the quickest shower on record, dragged on some clothes and then hurried into the cheese room. If she made herself a cup of tea she might find all kinds of destruction and have to get involved in tidying up, or making big greasy fry-ups for Roy and Barry. She could do that after she'd dealt with her cheese and was waiting for the courier.

The cheese room had its customary soothing effect. In here she was in control; she knew what to do. Drunken relatives and their friends were irrelevant. It was all about the milk, the cream and the magic they could create together.

The cheese was heavenly, she decided. There was no other word for it. It tasted like the very best clotted cream and although it was rich, its buttery flavour wasn't cloying because of the hint of tartness right at the end. Although she'd eaten a fair amount of it in her time – she'd worked in an Italian restaurant for a bit – she had never tasted cheese as good as this. Issi was right: the cows and the unique pasture they grazed had produced something really special.

She wrapped it in several squares of muslin, portioning it out, and then into the large, wide-topped thermoses that Erica had somehow left behind after they did the cheese stall together.

She was confident, happy even. She would ring the courier.

Then she remembered that, annoyingly, there was no phone signal. She would have to go back into the house to use the landline. When she got there she found the landline in use.

'Listen, mate!' Roy was saying forcefully. 'We need a taxi! And we need it now!'

Fran practised her breathing, in for five and out for eight – or was it the other way round? Rather than watch Roy insult people over the phone, she went into the kitchen. Issi was there. And she had a cup of tea.

'Can I just have a sip?' Fran asked, and purloined the mug.

'It's OK,' said Issi. 'Your need is greater than mine. The kettle's on anyway.'

'So?' Fran looked around. The kitchen was fairly tidy. 'I'm assuming they haven't had breakfast yet.'

'They've only just woken, although I'm surprised they're up and about so early. I can't decide if I should make them the works, including some black pudding I got in for Tig, or let them sort themselves out?'

'Tricky. But I think if we gave them a good breakfast it would at least get Barry out of our hair.'

'They want a taxi to get them to the distillery, where they left their cars. They asked me to take them but I said I don't drive.'

Fran was impressed. 'And they bought that?'

Issi shrugged. She drove perfectly well. 'They're not thinking terribly clearly and I haven't got a car.'

'Well, I hope they don't ask me to drive them,' said Fran, putting toast into the toaster, suddenly starving hungry. 'I'm going to sort out the courier for my cheese, and then I'm going to bed until further notice.'

'Is the cheese OK?' Issi handed Fran a fresh mug of tea.

'It's glorious, Is! Just heaven. I swear you can taste the wild flowers in it – probably pick out the individual ones and name them.'

'Did you keep any back, so we could have some?'

Fran bumped her palm against her head in frustration. 'Duh! I should have done. Although there wasn't a huge amount of it. We could steal some back?'

'No, don't. This is your big chance. Don't jeopardise it. Remind me how you're getting it to London? You don't have to take it there yourself?'

'No, thank the Lord. I'm really not up for driving to London today. I'm booking a courier. I'll just go and see if Roy's off the phone.'

Roy was off the phone and he didn't look pleased.

'Hi, Fran!' It wasn't so much a greeting as delight in seeing a solution to his problem. 'Can I have your car keys? I can't get a cab and we need to get my car back from the gin factory.'

Fran stared at him for a few seconds wondering where he got his effrontery. He was outrageous. 'No,

243

Roy,' she said calmly. 'You cannot have the keys to my car because I expect you're still over the limit. Now I'm going to use the phone and then you can try more taxi firms.'

She'd put the details Roger had sent on her phone and went upstairs to get it. When she got down again, Roy and Barry were walking out of the back door.

'Oh, they got a taxi, did they? And they're walking down the track to pick it up at the bottom? Remarkably sensible.' She said this as she passed the kitchen. 'And they didn't have breakfast first?'

Issi put down the fish slice. 'No! Just after I'd put a whole lot of bacon into the pan. But I can't say I'm sorry. Good riddance. And let's hope Roy stays away for a while.'

'So bacon butties all round, then?'

Issi nodded. 'They are my signature dish.'

Fran's good mood caused by an absence of guests and the promise of a bacon sandwich vanished when the courier firm Roger had told her to call said they couldn't come until the afternoon. Her protests produced nothing. She rang Roger, who swore.

She let him rant for a bit and then suggested they tried another firm.

'We've no time to mess about, Fran, we need this cheese by midday. You'll have to bring it yourself.'

Fran glanced at her watch. It was nine o'clock. If she set off now she'd just about make it, and Roger was right, unless a courier could come at this very moment, it wouldn't be there in time. Unless the car had a blue light and neenars and could go through red lights.

She swore a bit herself and then went to find her breakfast. 'I can't believe it, Is. I've got to drive up to London myself and take the cheese. There's no alternative.' She eyed the bacon sandwich sitting on a plate. 'Can that be my one? Then I must be off.'

'But you're so tired?'

'I know, but needs must. I'll be OK on the way there, I expect. Then I'll park somewhere and have a nap before going home. What a nightmare.' She took a bite of sandwich, her teeth going through the softness of the bread, the butter and then the crisp saltiness of the bacon. 'That is so delicious.'

'Have some tea with it. And I'll make you another to have on the journey. I'll find a bottle of water, too.' Issi had gone into mother mode and Fran found she was grateful. She needed a mother just now.

She collected her bag from the bedroom and then went back into the kitchen to pick up the promised supplies. Before she put the sandwich in the bag she looked for her keys. They didn't seem to be there. And yet she always put them in the same, dedicated key pocket. Where on earth were they?

'Oh no,' she said quietly and ran through to the sitting room to look out of the window. It wasn't only the two men who had disappeared, her car had too.

Chapter Eighteen

Fran went back into the kitchen slowly, hardly able to make her legs move. Roy had taken her car and, with it, the chance of getting her cheese on the culinary map. Everything she had worked so hard for had been for nothing. She wanted to cry.

'Roy's taken my car,' she said, barely audible. 'I can't go to London. My cheese won't be eaten by all those important people. It won't make our fortune and save the farm. It's all been a complete waste of time.'

'No!' said Issi, aghast. 'That *bastard*. How could he do that?'

'To be fair,' said Fran, 'and you know how I hate to be fair when Roy is involved, he didn't know I needed my car. I didn't mention it when he said he wanted to take it.'

'That's not the point. He's stolen it. Hey!' Issi became even more animated. 'Let's call the police. They'd bring it back for you.'

'Not in time,' said Fran, still quiet, still reasonable. 'And if Roy is arrested he'll be breathalysed.'

'Then it's our moral duty to tell the police,' said Issi.

'I know. But I don't have the heart for it. Everything I've worked for has been for nothing.'

'There must be something else we can do,' said Issi. 'Think!'

'I have thought,' said Fran, confused. 'And I haven't come up with anything.'

'Antony!' cried Issi delightedly.

'Is, I'm not asking Antony for any more favours. Besides he's—'

'No, I didn't mean that, I meant – Antony!' said Issi, jumping up and down as the back door opened.

'Oh, Fran,' said a deeply familiar voice. 'You are here. I saw your car was gone – Darling! What's the matter?'

Fran found herself in his arms, wrapped tightly against him, smelling his cologne, his body, him, and feeling utter comfort, in spite of his shirt button that was pressing into her cheek. There wasn't anywhere in the world she'd rather be. Her tension began to melt away. It didn't matter about her cheese, her car or anything. She was in Antony's arms.

Issi, not in a state of bliss, was a bit more on the ball. 'Fran has to get her cheese to London, now! It's terribly important. It'll be tasted by all sorts of

247

important people. A courier was supposed to come but couldn't, and Roy's stolen her car so she can't drive herself.' She paused for breath. 'Is Seb around?'

'Seb?' said Antony, into Fran's hair. 'Yes, he's back.'

Fran pushed herself away from Antony's shirt-front. 'Is he busy? Could he take me to deliver the cheese?'

'I'll drive you. It would be my pleasure.'

Fran sighed. Antony looked down at her.

'Oh, you two!' said Issi, seeing exactly how things were between them. 'Now go and get your cheese. I'll make up a goody bag for the journey.'

'When I got back and found the puppies gone,' said Antony, 'I was sorry. I know it was such hard work and everything, but I loved looking after them with you.' They were on the motorway, driving at speed towards London and Roger's food experts.

Fran sighed. 'Me too. I didn't want to let them go either. I know it was for the best and everything, but they were my whole reason for living for those hours. Have you heard from June? Are they OK?'

'Thriving. She was singing your praises very loudly.'

Fran blushed and really hoped June wasn't saying the sort of things she'd been saying to Fran, comparing her to Antony's wife. 'Really?'

'Yes. The little one, Betsy? She really turned a corner while you were looking after her.'

'That's very good to hear.' Fran felt a little bubble of pride rise.

'But I felt—' Antony stopped, as if not quite knowing how to express his feelings.

'That they were a bit like our children that we were looking after together?' Fran finished for him, really hoping she wasn't making a massive assumption.

'That's exactly it.' He glanced across at her.

He seemed about to say more but somehow Fran didn't feel ready. She was still glowing from the way he had embraced her when he first walked into the house. She was worried that if they went too quickly now, and moved from a couple of kisses to declarations, it would all disappear like candyfloss.

She cleared her throat. 'It was funny, when I went back to the farm after Jack and June had taken the pups, I felt different about things. I felt more capable. We kept those pups alive and it gave me confidence, about animals.' She smiled at the memory. 'Issi met me at the front door, all excited. A calf was being born, the first of the season. I went and watched.'

'Oh my goodness,' Antony said, as if understanding this was a big thing for her.

'It was fascinating, very primeval, but I suddenly understood how Tig and now Issi feel about the herd. It's more than just the milk and cream, which for me means the cheese. Now I feel much more connected with the animals that produce it. They're more like people than machines.'

He laughed softly. 'Somewhere in between, I expect.'

'I don't expect you to understand!' She was a bit indignant. 'You're not a man of the land, a farmer.'

'What we do in our lives doesn't necessarily reflect what we feel in our hearts.'

'Oh, that's deep!'

'But in this particular instance' – he made a gesture indicating the car and the fact he was driving her to London – 'this absolutely reflects what I feel in my heart.'

A rush of emotion threatened to overwhelm Fran for a few moments. 'I don't know what to say.'

'Don't say anything,' Antony said. 'I shouldn't have done. Forget I did.' He smiled at her. 'Look, don't dwell on it, or worry. Have a nap while you can.'

Fran smiled back and closed her eyes. She was sure she wouldn't sleep, not after what he'd just said, but she appreciated a chance to think about it.

He had to wake her up. 'Hey,' he said softly. 'The traffic's pretty bad. Not sure I can get to the venue on time. Are you up to getting out and walking?'

Fran's eyes shot open. 'Are we here?'

'Nearly. We have fifteen minutes. Do you want to walk or will you stay with the car while I go?'

'I'll go!' Fran got out of the car the moment Antony had pulled up. This was her chance; nothing was going to stop her now.

As she jogged through the streets, dragging the case on wheels Antony had lent her, her phone set to Maps, cutting behind Harrods towards Belgravia, she wondered if she'd slipped into a film while she'd been asleep. Here she was, with five minutes to get to a venue she wasn't sure how to find, with a product that could make or break her. Which was all crazy enough, but if you added to this that the man she'd been thinking about pretty well continually had made it fairly clear he had feelings for her too – it was almost too much to deal with.

Sweat trickled down her temples as she checked her phone and realised she was nearly at the pin that represented the hotel Roger had said she should come to. She looked up and there she was. Her tongue felt like carpet and she berated herself for not bringing water, but she took another breath and set off up the seemingly hundreds of steps that led up to this rather grand building as quickly as she had energy for.

It took a while for her to locate Roger, who was in a crowded room full of waiting staff.

'Roger, hi,' she said, panting hard.

'You took your time – it's nearly midday!'

She took a quick, indignant breath. 'Roger! Your couriers couldn't come. And someone stole my car.'

'How'd you get here, then?'

'Got a lift.'

'All the way to London? That's some lift.' Roger, who had been slow to notice how frazzled Fran was, now inspected her.

She nodded.

'Here.' Roger took a glass of champagne from a passing tray and handed it to her. 'Get that down you.'

Knowing it was the last thing she should be doing, Fran gulped down about half of it.

'What's the cheese like?' Roger asked.

'It's heavenly, Rog, and I'm not exaggerating. I just hope nothing bad has happened to it on the journey.'

He handed the case with the cheese in it to a passing waiter. 'Take that into the kitchen and give it to André. Thanks, mate.'

Fran watched Erica's thermoses disappear along with the case and realised it was forever. She gulped, hoping the cheese really was as good as she thought it was.

'I'd better go,' she said, wondering if she'd ever find her way back to where Antony had stopped the car.

'OK, well, thanks for doing this. You really did go the extra hundred miles or so.'

Fran smiled. 'Not quite that far. But I'll leave you to it. It's going to be a fantastic food festival.' She looked around at the beautiful room, full of beautiful people, interspersed with TV cameras setting up. 'On telly, too! I'm sure it's going to be absolutely amazing!' Then she was off.

She dodged her way through the smartly dressed people who were arriving, recognising some famous faces from the food world, including Gideon Irving, the food critic. So her cheese really was going to be tasted by important people. It was very exciting!

Antony's car was parked on some double yellow lines, hazard lights flashing. Fran almost fell into the front seat.

'I am so pleased to see you,' she said. 'I feel as if I've run a marathon!' The champagne, although nice at the time, had been a mistake.

'You have been through a lot,' he said, moving off. 'Can I suggest something?'

'Please do. I have no decision-making ability at the moment. Currently I just wait for what life throws at me and then try to duck.'

She caught his amused and possibly loving glance. 'Then I'll take you to my flat. We can order some lunch.'

'I desperately need a shower...' She really didn't want to be taken to some swanky restaurant when she was in jeans she felt she'd worn for weeks and a top that wasn't much fresher.

'You can have one. Lunch will arrive in the flat.'

'That would be lovely, I must say.' So much had gone on just recently, not just in actuality, but emotionally. Standing under a stream of hot water instead of dodging about under the hand held one at the farm would be bliss.

Antony might have Seb to drive him around most of the time but he still seemed very adept at getting around London, down the back streets used by professionals.

They pulled up in front of a fairly modern-looking block right next to the Thames.

'I bet you have amazing views,' said Fran. She was so disorientated by everything that had happened to her recently, she had to resort to small talk.

'We do. You'll see in a minute.'

A man in a uniform appeared at Antony's open window and took the keys, presumably so he could take the car and park it.

As her car door was opened by a similar man, Fran realised how different Antony's life was to hers. Although she felt she knew him a lot better now, this did make her feel shy.

She managed a tentative smile in the lift that shot up at an alarming rate. Antony smiled down at her. 'Nearly there.'

'Oh,' she said when the doors opened on to a corridor. 'I was rather hoping the lift would go straight into your flat.'

'Sorry to disappoint! But it's not far.'

'Oh my goodness,' she said when they were in. 'I know I said you must have wonderful views but I didn't know quite how wonderful!'

The wall at the end was glass and the whole Thames and every landmark on it, from Big Ben, the Houses of Parliament, the London Eye and in the distance the silver outline of the Shard, was laid out before her.

'It's why I chose this apartment. Now, let me show you where the shower is. Shall I order lunch? Is there anything you particularly fancy?'

'You order. I'll shower.'

The bathroom was twice the size of her bedroom at Amy's house and had enough towels to dry half a dozen people, it seemed. He had followed her into it. 'I'll turn it on for you. There. Take your time. And do use the shampoo and things.'

Fran took a moment to check out the toiletries; they were extremely good quality.

There's very little as wonderful as hot water coursing over you when you're very tired and feel sticky. She stayed in there longer than was necessary for cleanliness and washed her hair, mostly because she wasn't quite sure what was going to happen next.

Then she put on one of the bathrobes hung up behind the door and inspected her face. For some reason she was faintly surprised and a bit disappointed to see she had absolutely no make-up on at all. She hadn't put any on that morning, nor since, but somehow she still expected to see remnants of mascara or a smudge of colour on her lips, but there was nothing. She needed her handbag.

She opened the bathroom door a crack and couldn't see Antony. Feeling ridiculous, she nipped out and into the sitting room where she'd left her bag. She ran back into the bathroom with it.

She'd never been one for keeping an entire make-up kit in her bag – she didn't wear it much anyway – but she needed something to soften the 'just boiled' look her shower and hairwashing had given her.

Fortunately the wonderful toiletries in the bathroom included some sort of moisturiser and with the stub of kohl pencil and a dried-up mascara, she felt a bit better by the time she emerged again.

Antony was in the hall. 'Hi,' he said. He must have been waiting for her. 'I've ordered tapas. It should be here in a minute. I hope that's all right?'

'I love tapas!'

'Good. I'm glad I haven't made a mistake.' Then he took hold of her wrist and put his hand on her cheek. 'I hope this isn't a mistake either but I don't think I can put it off any longer.'

His mouth on hers took her by surprise but she was more than ready to join in. She felt she had never been kissed so thoroughly or so skilfully before and it set her on fire. When the doorbell rang meaning the food had arrived and they had to stop it was like pulling magnets apart.

Fran slipped into the bedroom to get out of the way. She trusted the food would either be taken into the kitchen or the sitting room. She didn't want to be seen by anyone in her current state – not when it must be perfectly obvious what she and Antony had just been doing.

She was looking at the view, trying to take it in, when Antony came to the door. 'You can come out now.'

Delicious aromas of spice led her to the sitting room.

The coffee table in front of the sofa was set out with little dishes, some of which were still sizzling. A bottle of wine was open and there were a pile of proper napkins along with a couple of plates and knives and forks.

'It smells really good,' said Fran.

'It will be good. Come and sit down.' He picked up the bottle of wine and half filled a glass, which he handed to her. 'Is there any reason why we should drive home today?'

Fran considered all her responsibilities waiting for her at the farm, including Roy. 'No.'

He smiled, and poured wine into the second glass. 'Now, what would you like?' He had a plate in his hand and seemed to want to serve her.

She couldn't think. She was so distracted by her need for Antony. She swallowed. 'Any of it, except octopus. I'm not keen on octopus.'

'Nor me,' he said, 'so there isn't any.

It would have been so restful, being served, she realised as she sat back in the corner of the extremely comfortable sofa, if she hadn't been on fire for him.

His every movement excited her. Seeing him put potatoes cooked with chorizo and paprika and tomatoes on to a plate with a little square of pork belly and some slices of *ibérico* ham seemed like the sexiest thing she had ever witnessed.

She sipped her wine and looked at him. When he caught her eye she looked at her plate and nibbled roasted almonds.

The food and wine were delicious but she couldn't eat or drink much. Antony didn't seem very hungry either.

Eventually, he almost threw his plate down, wiped his mouth on his napkin and got up. He crossed to her and held out his hand. 'I think it's time I took you to bed.'

Eventually, they were hungry again, and Antony fetched the leftover food. They ate it, cold and a little bit greasy, but it was still delicious. Not more delicious than what had gone on the previous hour, but still lovely.

'I've gone and got *patatas bravas* on the sheets,' said Fran.

Antony sighed contentedly. 'I couldn't care less. Do you want some more wine?'

'No thanks. I've had enough.'

'Not enough of me, I hope?'

'No,' said Fran, reaching for him. 'Never that.'

Chapter Nineteen

Fran was in the kitchen the next morning, wearing one of Antony's shirts and nothing else, making sense of the coffee machine, when she heard her phone ting in the bedroom, indicating she had a text.

When the coffee was doing what it was supposed to do she went into the bedroom to look at her phone.

Antony was in the shower. She allowed herself a couple of seconds to wonder what might happen if she was still in the bedroom when he came out of it and decided to find out. But first, the text.

It was from Issi.

Can you give me a ring, soonest? It's urgent.

She ran from the room to the hallway, finding Issi's number. Issi answered instantly. 'Is? What is it?'

'It's Amy. She's in hospital. She was taken in during the night. It's not looking good, Fran.'

'Oh God! I should be with her.'

'Well, yes. As soon as you can. Roy's on his way there now.'

'Oh no. He'll tell her how I'm in London with Antony, the man she loves to hate.'

'She's not making a lot of sense apparently, so don't worry about that. They think it's probably a UTI – urinary tract infection, in case you don't know. My grandmother kept getting them. They make you doolally for a bit but she should be OK once the antibiotics kick in.'

'But you think she'll be OK permanently?'

'Hon, I'm not a doctor. Just get here.'

Fran ran back into the bedroom. Antony was getting dressed. 'What's up?' he asked, buttoning his shirt.

'It's Amy. She's in hospital. I need to go to her.'

'Fine,' said Antony. 'Then I'll take you there. You get dressed; I'll order some breakfast which we can pick up from reception and eat in the car.'

He was so calm, so in control; his clear instructions made her feel less panic-stricken.

'Keep my shirt on,' he added with a smile. 'It suits you. I'll find you a jumper to put on top. It may be a bit fresh out there.'

Everything happened very smoothly after that. Wearing Antony's shirt and one of his cashmere sweaters over the top of her own clothes, Fran got into his car, which had been brought to the door by the parking valet, clutching a cardboard carrier with coffee and a bag with croissants. Her belongings were on the back seat.

'I'm so grateful, Antony,' she said when she'd taken a sip of the strong, but very good coffee.

'You don't ever need to feel grateful for anything I do for you. I love you, therefore I look out for you. Simple as that.'

Fran couldn't speak. She thought she might cry, which would be ridiculous. She cleared her throat, but still couldn't utter a word. She patted his hand instead, hoping he'd understand. Part of her was so happy, but the other part was desperately anxious. She couldn't help remembering what the nurse had said about Amy's heart condition. Supposing Amy died before she got there?

She bit her lip hard and tried to focus on the passing streets. Never to see that often-cantankerous old lady again was a horrible thought. It hadn't always gone well. It had taken them both a little while to get the measure of each other but Fran realised she now loved her, for all her cranky ways. And she sensed that Amy liked her back. Fran couldn't assume she was loved, but liked, certainly.

But did she like her as much as the oleaginous Roy? Roy, who put on the charm, suppressed his less attractive characteristics and claimed to be a farm boy who'd always wanted a little spot in the Old Country?

The staff at the care home had told her, and she had sometimes observed it for herself, that Amy liked men. She had very old-fashioned notions and in spite of her own life as a farmer, she did seem to think that men were better at it that women. Feminism seemed to have passed her by. And to be honest, Roy *was* a lot better qualified to run the farm than she was. She was a city girl who was afraid of cows. But she loved the farm and Roy seemed only to love its potential value.

They didn't speak much on the journey home, but as they started on the last leg, Fran said, 'Should I go home first and change, do you think?'

He glanced at her and smiled. 'I'd ask Issi. You do look – well...'

'As if I'd just got out of bed having had a very nice time?' Fran was relieved to have her gloomy thoughts sent in another direction.

'Let's just say you have a special glow about you.'

Fran glowed some more.

'I am so sorry about Amy being ill just at this minute,' he went on. 'We should be having a lovely time together; there should be nothing but happiness just now. But instead you're worried about losing someone who's become dear to you.'

'That's true, but I'm ashamed to confess I'm worried about losing the farm, too. I know it's awfully mercenary of me, but if Roy inherits, what shall I do? I really don't want to go back to London. I'm a country girl now.'

'You could consider moving but not very far from where you live now? My house is big enough for two.'

She laughed. 'Your house is big enough for two hundred.'

'Only if we hire a marquee...'

'You know what I mean!' The joy of it was, he did know what she meant. She felt he understood her in a way no other boyfriend had, really. But was he a boyfriend? It seemed too flippant a term, really, for Antony. And it felt too flippant a term for how she felt about him. 'Thank you very much for inviting me to stay,' she said seriously.

He laughed. 'It's an open-ended invitation. For as long as we both shall live, to quote a rather famous line.'

'Are you asking me to...' she paused, '... live with you?' Fran wanted to be clear about this. Getting it wrong would be dreadful.

He glanced at her again and didn't speak immediately. 'What I'm saying is, if you don't inherit the farm, you could come and live with me – there's no need for you to go back to London. I want you by my side for ever. But if the farm is yours, well, living arrangements can be discussed.'

'Right, just so I can get it clear in my head, if I inherit the farm you may be willing to move out of your house and share my rather small house, which hasn't got proper Wi-Fi and only a hand-held shower?'

'Darling.' He touched her knee briefly. 'What I'm going to say can easily be misinterpreted but I do hope you won't. You know I love you and also that I've always wanted Amy's farm. Not only for the potential south-facing vineyards' – he held up his had to stop her protesting at the thought – 'which I now know are never going to be there, but for the wonderful position of the house.'

'So you want me for my south-facing views?' Fran was joking but suddenly things did seem a little different.

'No! I'd want you wherever you lived. What I'm trying to say, rather clumsily, is that I don't mind giving up my house to live with you in yours.'

'OK...' said Fran slowly.

'But if you weren't there I wouldn't want your house. At one time, yes, but not any more.'

'Golly,' said Fran, knowing it was inadequate as a statement but unable to express herself properly.

There was a ping from her phone. It was Issi. *Are you nearly at the farm? Come as soon as you can.*

'We need to hurry!' she said.

'We're very close,' Antony said calmly. 'I'll have you there in ten minutes.'

Chapter Twenty

Amy was in the local cottage hospital, so finding her bedside wasn't as hard as it might have been. Fran ran after Antony who strode down the corridors as if he knew where he was going.

Amy was in a side ward looking heartbreakingly fragile. There were tubes giving her oxygen and a drip in her arm. She looked dreadfully old and ill and so tiny.

Roy got up when he heard their arrival. 'She's pretty much out of it,' he said, far too loudly in Fran's opinion. 'I'm off to the pub. I've told the nurses not to resuscitate.'

'What gave you to the right to do that?' said Fran, utterly outraged.

'I am her next of kin!' declared Roy. 'See you later.'

'*Is* he her next of kin?' asked Antony.

Fran shrugged. 'I have no idea, but we need to "un-tell" the nurses that this minute.' She dithered, wanting to stay with Amy but feeling it was essential she saw someone in authority immediately.

'Shall I go and find someone?' said Antony. 'Then you can stay here with her?'

She nodded, suddenly, embarrassingly, fighting tears yet again. It was partly gratitude that he had guessed what she wanted, and partly shock at seeing Amy so diminished.

She cleared her throat, pulling herself together at the same time as she pulled up a chair. Then she picked up one of Amy's hands, as small as a child's. 'Amy? It's Francesca. I've come to see you. I know you're asleep, but I'm going to wait here until you wake up.'

As she sat, waiting for Antony to come back with a nurse, or for some reaction from Amy, Fran felt strangely connected with the old lady. They hadn't always communicated very well, but here, holding hands, saying nothing, feeling seemed to flow between them.

Antony came back with a nurse who seemed pleased to see Fran. She introduced herself and then said, 'The trouble is, she's just not getting enough fluid. The care home said she didn't like the taste of the water. She missed the water she had at the farm.'

Fran glanced up at Antony.

'That's easily solved,' he said. 'I could go back and fetch some. I'll buy one of those dispenser things at the hardware store first.'

'Honestly, just a bottle would be fine,' said the nurse, 'but that might be really helpful. Even if she can't really taste the difference, it will encourage her.'

'Would she like some of her cowslip wine, do you think?' asked Fran.

'She might,' said the nurse. 'Again, she probably wouldn't have very much but it might cheer her up.'

'I'll ask Issi,' said Antony. He looked at Fran. 'Is there anything else you need from home? Or from the canteen?'

'I'm sure I'll be fine—' Fran began.

'I'd have a cup of tea now,' said the nurse. 'The canteen is staffed by volunteers and they'll close soon. And I do recommend the chocolate cake.'

Antony smiled. 'I'll get that and then head off for the farm.'

'He's nice,' said the nurse when Antony had gone. 'Is he your boyfriend?'

Fran felt put on the spot. 'Er, yes. I suppose so. It's all a bit new,' she explained.

'If it's new, he's being really kind – especially to an old lady he doesn't know.'

'Oh, he does know her, sort of. It's complicated.' Fran didn't want to say that they were neighbours, and Amy thought Antony was the spawn of the devil, particularly when he so obviously wasn't.

'Maybe he's being kind to her to help you?'

Fran nodded. 'I expect that's it. He is one of the kindest people I know.'

'Then hang on to him. Kindness and good looks don't always go together.'

The nurse left and Fran smiled to herself. If the woman had also known that Antony was well off, she'd have been even more insistent that Fran should keep hold of him.

Just under an hour later, Antony came back with the water and a care package from Issi: sandwiches, some make-up and a thermos of hot chocolate.

He kissed her cheek and they hugged briefly.

'You must go now,' said Fran. 'You've given up enough of your time for me and mine in the past two days.'

'Call me if you need anything. And I'll pick you up whenever you want.' He looked at her so intently there was no doubt that he meant it. It made Fran's heart skip a beat from relief and happiness. He was a rock when she needed one.

'I will call but I know you must have so much to catch up with.'

He hesitated. 'You're more important than work.'

She laughed gently, loving him more for saying that. 'You don't have to choose. Do your work. If Issi or Tig can't pick me up I'll get a taxi.'

'I'll allow Issi or Tig to pick you up, but don't take a taxi. It wouldn't take long for me to do it.'

She beamed at him, certain that love was radiating out of her, not sure if she shouldn't be a bit more circumspect about revealing her feelings but unable to help it. 'If I need you, I'll call.'

'Promise?'

'Promise.'

A quiet bliss settled over Fran, overwhelming to a large extent her anxiety for Amy. It was wonderful to be in love and feel loved in return.

Eventually, she began to talk to Amy. She really wanted to tell her about Antony and how happy she was, but Amy was really the only person she couldn't tell. She talked about the cheese instead.

'You have got to pull through this time, Amy. I know you can't live forever, none of us can, but I need to tell you about the cheese.' She cleared her throat. 'I've been up to London to deliver it to an old chef friend of mine. He tasted it when he bought some at the farmers' market and thought it was wonderful. Then I made a lot more for him so he could present it at a food festival to some very famous food writers and chefs.'

She thought she sensed a tiny squeeze from the bird-like fingers.

'It does have such a wonderful flavour. All those wild flowers and different grasses – you can really taste them.'

There was another tiny squeeze – this time there was no doubt about it. Amy seemed to want to speak, although her eyes were still closed. Fran tucked her hair behind her ear and leant in close.

'Too young,' breathed Amy, only audible because Fran's ear was practically touching her lips.

'No! I'm not too young. I'm loving the farm and making it all work. I'm not too young at all!'

'Not you, the cheese,' said Amy.

Fran laughed gently. Amy was not only able to talk, but to take in what she had been saying and make a sensible comment. 'Oh, it's not Cheddar, Amy. It's soft cheese. But I will make hard cheese. I really want to. But I need to find the quarry. Maybe you could tell me where it is?'

This had to be a good time to ask Amy. They were talking about cheese and she knew Amy wanted Fran's produce to be good. But Amy seemed to have drifted back to sleep.

When the nurse came, Fran stood up and stretched. 'I think she's a bit better. She spoke to me.'

The nurse checked all the various bit of equipment, and then she felt Amy's forehead with her hand in a genuinely caring way. 'I think you're right. I think she's a bit better!

The two women looked at each other, smiling delightedly.

Then Roy came back and while Fran wouldn't have said he was definitely drunk, he had the smell of pub about him.

'Amy's better,' said Fran. 'Isn't that great? She spoke to me.'

'Great,' said Roy, his expression not matching his words, still not moderating his volume. 'Then I can tell her all about who you've been sleeping with, can't I?' He leant into Amy. 'Aunt Amy? Can you hear me? It's Roy again!'

Fran took hold of his arm and pulled him back. 'Don't shout at her. She's ill.'

'I have to shout. She's deaf and out of it!'

How could he even think of troubling an elderly and very sick woman with gossip? And was there no depth to which he wouldn't sink to improve his chances of inheriting the farm?

'Don't shout,' Fran repeated. She was sure she saw Amy flinch away from the noise. Annoyingly she couldn't think of what else she could do to stop him. She wasn't strong enough to drag him away physically.

Thank goodness, obviously hearing raised voices, the nurse came back in. 'I think my patient would be better if her visitors went home now. She needs her rest. Thank you for getting your boyfriend to bring in the water from home,' she said. 'I'll tell you if she likes it.'

The woman had natural authority and a uniform. Roy calmed down and they both left the room, Fran having given Amy a quick peck on her forehead.

As they walked out of the hospital, Fran realised she needed a lift home. She could call Antony or Issi but why should she? Roy was here.

'Which car did you bring?' she said as they approached the car park. 'Yours or mine? Either way, I need a lift back to the farm.'

'I was going back to the pub—'

'Nope. You're taking me home first. You owe me. You took my car without permission.'

'For someone who was weeping at the bedside of an old woman you're hardly even related to, you've got quite a cob on,' said Roy as they walked.

'Because I care about Amy, it doesn't mean I'm soft,' she said.

'I just wonder why you care about a woman who's days away from death? Is it because you think you might inherit her farm?'

'I think it's blatantly obvious that's why you *don't* care about her. She's worth so much more to you dead!'

He shrugged.

To Fran's relief, it was Roy's car she saw, slightly askew in the corner of the hospital car park.

They were just turning out of the town when Fran saw Megan walking along holding bags from the town's dress shop. To her surprise and irritation, Roy pulled up.

'Hey, Megan!'

'Roy!' Megan leant in and kissed Roy's cheek through the window of the car.

They obviously knew each other well.

'Hello, Megan,' said Fran, trying to keep her voice neutral.

'Oh, Fran, I didn't expect to see you there.'

'Roy's giving me a lift back from the hospital. Amy's there, not very well.'

'That's kind of him,' said Megan. 'And I hoped we'd see you in the pub?'

Fran was surprised. She didn't think Megan was a pub kind of person. She'd be more into cocktail places, or wine bars. But maybe Megan was a regular down at the Wheatsheaf, or whichever of the town's pubs Roy frequented.

'I might be down later, but I'm rather under the cosh here.' He jerked a thumb in Fran's direction. 'Madam might want me to run another errand for her.'

'Right now "Madam" just wants to get home. It's been a very long day,' said Fran.

'And a long night too, I reckon,' said Roy.

He was about to expound on what she might have been doing when Megan broke in. 'So what's wrong with Amy?' she asked Fran.

'She has an infection. She was a bit better when we left her though.'

'I think it's cruel to keep old people alive beyond their natural lifetimes,' said Roy. 'We put down animals when they're in that state.'

'Amy is not "alive beyond her natural lifetime",' said Fran firmly. 'She could live for many more years yet.'

'Yeah, but in what state?' said Roy. 'She's already losing her marbles. We don't want a mad old biddy in an expensive care home.'

'Roy? Could we just go home? Nice to see you, Megan.'

Unfortunately Roy didn't pick up his clue to drive off.

'Have you seen much of Antony lately?' Megan asked, still leaning through Roy's window.

'Seeing him? She only spent the night with him. Dunno if the old lady would like to come and find out her beloved cousin is "sleeping with the enemy".' He waggled his fingers to indicate inverted commas as he spoke.

Fran wanted to groan but managed to keep it internal. 'Oh, Roy! Can you stop harping on? I want to get home. I'm sure Megan will save you a seat at the pub.'

Megan, who'd been doing a fairly good impression of a friendly person, suddenly tightened her mouth. 'Is this true?'

'I'm not answerable to you, or to anyone. My business is my business,' said Fran, exasperated.

'I think Roy's entitled to know,' said Megan. 'It's not a secret, is it? Oh yes, I remember – it is a secret! Amy would never leave you the farm if she knew about it, would she?'

Fran wanted to get out of the car and stomp off but she wanted to get home even more. Just then her phone vibrated in her pocket. It was Antony. 'Hi,' she said, before he could speak. 'Yes, I'd love a lift home, thanks.'

She opened the car door. 'As you would obviously rather spend time talking to Megan I've made other arrangements. And please don't come home drunk again.'

'Hello, darling,' Antony said quietly, and kissed her.

It was the slightest, most harmless kiss, but it conjured up all sorts of blissful memories and stirrings from the night before. It took a lot of throat-clearing and shoulder-straightening before she said, 'Hello back.'

He set off. They didn't speak for a while and Fran realised how much she loved watching Antony drive. She loved seeing his well-shaped hands on the wheel.

'What's been going on?' he asked.

'Well, I was going to get a lift with Roy but then we met Megan. Apparently they are now "bessie mates", although I can't quite think how. They can't have much in common.'

'I think you're overlooking one thing they very much have in common.'

'What's that?'

He didn't answer immediately. 'They both want something you have, or might have.' He looked embarrassed.

'You mean Megan's so jealous of me and you that she's prepared to chum up with someone like Roy to get back at me?'

'Exactly.'

'God!'

'This sounds awful, but she's had her eye on me for some time now. I'm sure not for me but for my money. You're standing in the way of what she wants – me – and what Roy wants – the farm. That could make for a very binding partnership.'

'But no one knows if I'm going to get the farm.'

'True, but you have got me.'

Fran allowed herself to sigh blissfully. 'And Roy wants the farm. From Megan's point of view there'd be satisfaction if she could stop me getting the farm as well.'

Chapter Twenty-One

A week after Fran and Roy had been called to her bedside, Amy was back at the care home. Fran had taken it on herself to make sure she had small, tempting morsels of food to keep her appetite from flagging. She was preparing to visit Amy now and Issi was making them a cup of coffee, having just given Fran an update on the latest calf to be born – a fine heifer with lovely markings.

'You're so good with the cows, Issi. I do admire you.' Fran put some little frangipane tarts into a plastic bag and tucked it into the box. There was another bag with finger sandwiches and yet another with some bite-sized pasties.

Fran knew Amy would never eat it all but she wanted to offer her a choice, and it made her feel positive, thinking of things Amy might like to eat.

The doctors had warned Fran and Roy that Amy would never get back to being quite as well as she had been before her infection. Fran found this desperately sad. Roy seemed to think that the dangling carrot of his inheritance had just got a bit nearer.

'Obviously I wouldn't have got so involved with the cows if I didn't have feelings for Tig,' said Issi. 'But now I'm interested because I really like them. Who knew there was a dairy farmer in me, struggling to get out?'

'I wish I was a bit more like a dairy farmer. I like what cows produce – very much – but as for looking after them? I am still a bit afraid of them.'

Issi put a mug of coffee on the table for Fran. 'It doesn't matter though. You've got Tig to look after them for you.'

'I know. I'm very lucky. Amy was very lucky.' Fran snapped the lid on the box of tiny comestibles. 'Although I do wish he'd told me he staggered the calving so we always had milk and didn't let all the cows go dry at the same time. I wouldn't have worried so much about what I'd do when there was no milk.'

'He's not a great talker,' said Issi.

Fran noticed she didn't seem unhappy with this state of affairs. Usually Fran would have made some vulgar reference to his other skills but today she didn't have the heart for it. Antony was abroad and Roy kept making snide remarks about him being an International Man of Mystery, implying what he did was somehow immoral if not actually illegal.

She knew that he was dripping this same poison into Amy's ears, too.

Amy was fairly bright when Fran arrived at her room. She was up and dressed and sitting in the chair for the first time since her illness. She was obviously peckish, too.

'What have you brought me?' she said, putting on her glasses.

Fran took the top off the box. 'Sandwiches, baby pasties and some frangipane tarts.'

'Very nice. Give me a pasty. Let's see how good your pastry is.'

As Fran knew her pastry was excellent she handed one over with confidence.

'Mm, very tasty.' But Amy put the pasty down half eaten. 'I'll try a sandwich now. What's in them?'

'Egg and cress.'

'What I would like to try', said Amy, when half a finger sandwich had been consumed, 'is some of the cheese you make, which is apparently so wonderful.'

'Oh, Amy, I can't give you soft, unpasteurised cheese! I'd be had for trying to murder you. You said so yourself!'

'What do you mean? What nonsense!'

'Seriously. Elderly people shouldn't have unpasteurised milk, or the products of it, you know that.' Amy had clearly forgotten accusing Fran of trying to poison her with her cheese. Then Fran had a thought and pursed her lips. 'However, a hard cheese might be OK. If you told me where the quarry was, for us to age the cheese in, you could taste for yourself how wonderful it is.'

'I know how wonderful the milk is. I drank it for sixty-odd years. And I don't think young people should be just handed things on a plate.'

As Fran had just handed Amy a plate with a frangipane tart on it, she couldn't help laughing. 'But it's different for old people?'

But Amy shook her head. 'You don't get out on the farm enough, my girl. You'd find the quarry for yourself soon enough if you did.'

'Roy hasn't found it either,' said Fran, resentment finding its way through her fondness for Amy.

'Then he's not going out enough.'

'But Roy—'

Before Fran could expound, there was a noise. It was Roy. 'What's that about me?'

'Nothing!' Fran felt childish and undignified. It was time to go. She got up.

Roy instantly took her seat and scooped up about three sandwiches. 'These are nice.'

'They were for Amy! For her to have later,' said Fran.

'They'll be stale later,' said Amy.

It was all Fran could do to stop herself sticking her lower lip out and stamping her foot.

'I've brought you some of that lemon water you like,' said Roy, putting a bottle on the table.

'Oh, Roy! You are kind,' said Amy, obviously delighted.

'I didn't know you liked that,' said Fran. 'I've just been bringing you water from the farm.'

Roy, looking extremely smug, ate a pasty in one bite. 'You should make a bit more effort to find out what Great-Aunt Amy wants,' he said.

Fran felt pushed out and insecure. Did Amy really want to be called Great-Aunt? Had she been misreading the signs about what Amy needed? She was trying so hard to get it right, to please Amy, to make her happy, and yet Roy seemed to manage this without really lifting a finger.

'I'd better go. Is there anything you need for next time, Amy?' she said.

'Roy will look after me,' said Amy.

Fran felt cut to the quick. Amy could starve to death as far as Roy was concerned. She struggled to sound nonchalant. 'OK, I'll see you tomorrow.'

As she walked out of the care home she felt desperately hurt. And she missed Antony terribly.

Issi and Tig were at home, drinking tea by the fire. Fran flopped on to the sofa.

'What's up?' said Issi. 'Hang on, don't tell me, I'll make you some tea first. Unless you'd prefer wine?'

Fran glanced at her watch. 'Wine, please.'

'I'll sort it,' said Tig. 'Unless you'd rather I went home?'

'No!' said Fran. She sighed. 'Roy came while I was with Amy. Amy seems completely besotted with him. I wouldn't mind, really I wouldn't, not inheriting Hill Top. But Roy only cares about Amy because he wants the farm.'

Tig came back into the room with a bottle of red wine and some glasses. When Fran was settled with one they sat in silence for a while.

'I try so hard to improve her life but no matter what I do, there's always something Roy can do that's better.'

'What she would really like, I think,' said Tig, 'would be to see the farm again. Don't suppose Roy could make that happen.'

'But could I?' said Fran, her spirits lifting a bit at the thought.

Tig nodded. 'All you'd need is an all-terrain vehicle.'

'A quad bike? But surely Amy couldn't go on one of those?' While she was denying it was possible, Fran was thinking hard. Of course Tig was absolutely right. Seeing the farm would be what Amy wanted most.

'I bet Antony has a quad bike that can take a passenger,' said Issi. 'Or access to one, at least.'

'I'll email him,' said Fran, excited at the thought. While her head believed he loved her, her heart was taking longer. It seemed so impossible that such a wonderful man could love an ordinary girl like her. She wasn't overly modest, she knew she was reasonably attractive, but with Antony, she felt out of her league.

'Shall I cook something?' said Tig.

'Yes please,' said Fran.

'I'll help,' said Issi. 'You get in touch with Ant.'

Fran wished she could text him instead of emailing, then she wouldn't have to write so much or wonder how to sign off. Sadly, the dodgy phone signal meant a text might not get through. She kept the email short.

Do you have access to a quad bike that takes two people? F x.

Who wants to know and why? A xx, he replied instantly, giving Fran a little burst of happiness.

Me, and it's complicated. F xx (two kisses when he'd given two kisses was definitely OK).

Can you talk if I phoned you? A xxx.

People are here, F xxx was her reply. She'd have loved to have a long conversation with him but he'd have to use the landline and so it would have to be fairly businesslike.

The phone rang almost immediately.

'What's all this about a quad bike?' he said.

Not the most romantic words ever heard but they made her smile inordinately.

A couple of weeks later, towards the end of April, Fran and Antony set off for Amy's care home. It had taken a lot of organising and preparation but the day had come for Amy's visit to the farm. And the sun was shining. Better even than fine weather was, in Fran's opinion, the fact that Roy had gone down to Cornwall with some mates to watch some sort of match – football or rugby, or possibly even darts. He would be out of the way all day.

There was only one small cloud of anxiety threatening Fran's happiness: how would Amy react to Antony? Roy had had ample opportunity to drip poison in Amy's ear and had even taken Megan in with him to bump up the dose. According to a nurse, who had become a friend of Fran's, Megan had pulled no punches, and had reported that Fran and Antony were living in sin (this expression had made Fran smile) with no regard to Amy's wishes in the matter.

However, Amy hadn't actually called Fran on this and Fran sensed that Amy didn't believe it. And given that Antony had been away so much, and Fran had been working so hard making cheese and selling it to Roger (her produce had been a *huge* hit at the food festival), when she wasn't making tasty morsels for Amy, it was very far from the truth.

'Remind me,' Fran said as they drove along the lanes towards town, 'what did your grandfather actually do to annoy Amy so much?'

'You'll have to ask her that, but I think it was during the war. My grandfather was something to do with the Ministry of Agriculture. Amy accused him of telling people about the farm. Had things gone differently Amy and her husband would have had to plough their pasture to grow vegetables, or other crops.'

'But that didn't happen?'

'No. I think the fields were too small and steep.'

'So why the grudge?'

Antony shot Fran a look she couldn't interpret. 'I think Amy and my grandfather may have had a bit of a thing for each other.'

'But they were both married!' Fran was shocked.

'No, no, long before that. I don't know who broke up with whom but it obviously wasn't great.'

Fran smiled. 'Maybe Amy preferred her husband's farm to your grandfather's?'

Antony shrugged. 'Anyway, it's water long under the bridge. We just have to hope that Amy won't slap my face and refuse to get into the car.'

The thought of tiny Amy, leaping the couple of feet necessary to reach Antony's face, or possibly climbing on a stool, made Fran smile.

Amy was in a wheelchair, waiting, when they arrived. She was excited but also a little frosty. Fran, wanting to avoid any awkwardness, hurried to greet her.

'Hello, Amy. Are you prepared for this?'

'I don't know why everyone is making such a fuss. I'm only going home for a day,' she said crisply.

'But I explained about the quad bike? It's so you can see the fields and things. Antony is going to drive you. Let me introduce him to you—'

'I know who he is, thank you.'

Antony, who had followed Fran more slowly, said, 'I am very pleased to see you again, Mrs Flowers. It's been a long time since we last met.'

Amy gave him a stiff little nod.

It took a while and a lot of patience to get Amy into the car. Fran held on to her stick, her handbag and her walker and eventually Amy was in the front seat. The walker went into the capacious boot. Then Fran got in the back of the car and Antony set off.

Fran's instinct was to make polite conversation but she sensed Amy was not in the mood for small talk. Antony took them the scenic route, which he had obviously thought Amy would appreciate. But no. In contrary mood (which made Fran's heart sink a bit) she said, 'Why are you going this way? It's far quicker up the main road.'

'True,' said Antony calmly. 'I just thought you'd like a bit of scenery on your way. This way you can see the bluebells in Winfield Wood.'

'I've seen more than enough bluebells in my life, thank you. I just want to get home.'

Fran began to fret. Supposing Amy was horrified by the changes she'd made to the house? Knocking out the fireplace? Putting away a lot of the ornaments and photographs? She and Issi had put back a few of the best photos but had agreed that Amy wouldn't mind a bit of decluttering. Now Fran wondered if she'd got it all wrong and Amy would be devastated to see her old home so altered.

It had been decided that Amy should come into the house and have a light lunch before setting off across the fields.

Antony and Fran got her into the wheelchair and trundled her through the yard towards the back door.

'Wait!' she said. 'Let me look at everything!'

After a little while Fran realised that Amy was nervous too. She didn't know what she was going to find and her beloved farm could have fallen into disrepair. She put the brake on the chair and let Amy look about her.

Tig emerged from the cowshed and came over. 'All right, Amy?'

'Tig,' Amy replied.

'Shall I bring you Flora's calf to have a look at?' he said. He looked at Fran. 'She's the mother of the calf you saw being born.'

'That would be nice,' said Amy.

Watching the two of them, who had until recently been colleagues, communicate, made Fran feel sad for Amy. She hadn't just lost her independence when she went into a home, she had lost her job, her status, her reason for living. She had been coping with it very well, she realised.

Flora's calf was duly presented, inspected and found to be good.

'I think it's time for lunch now,' said Fran. 'Time is getting on.' However, it wasn't time she was worrying about. It was Amy's energy levels. If she was too tired she wouldn't enjoy her tour of the fields. But she couldn't say that out loud.

'Well!' said Amy, when she had arrived in the sitting room. 'I must say, I quite like having the big fireplace back. We made it smaller during the war, you know, to save on coal.'

'But didn't you burn wood?' said Issi.

Amy shook her head. 'It took too long to drag it out of the woodland and chop it up. We were up against it, you know.'

'I can imagine,' said Antony and received an inscrutable look in recognition of the fact he had spoken.

'I'm glad you've kept the picture,' Amy went on. 'I'm very fond of that picture.'

The picture in question was the painting of hills, fields and a house that possibly represented the farm. Although Fran and Issi had agreed it was the worst form of amateur art it was doing a good job hiding some missing plaster.

'Who did it?' asked Fran, feeling there must be a sentimental reason for Amy's fondness.

'A friend of mine. She was always arty. Now,' said Amy, obviously thinking the conversation about the painting was exhausted. 'Did you say something about lunch?'

Amy did well. She enjoyed the quiches, ignored the salad and drank a glass of her own home-made cowslip wine. Then she said, 'Well now, I want to taste some cheese.'

Fran took a breath. 'Really, Amy, you know perfectly well that I can't let you have any.'

'They're still my cows, you know. My milk. If you've been making this fancy cheese I have a right to try it and I don't want to die not knowing what it tasted like!'

'But, Amy—' Fran, a chef, had been on courses; she knew about raw milk and its potential hazards.

'I think you should let Mrs Flowers try the cheese,' said Antony firmly. 'She can make her own decisions and take responsibility for her actions.'

Amy looked at Antony properly for the first time. 'That's the most sensible thing I've heard one of your family say in fifty years.'

Fran wasn't happy, but she had to agree. 'Just don't sue me if you get ill,' she said to her as she gave her a small blob of mascarpone. 'Have it on a biscuit with a drop of jam. It's delicious.'

But Amy didn't want crackers or jam. She took her knife to the cheese and lifted it to her mouth. She sniffed at it and then ate it, all on its own. 'Hmm, she said. 'Not bad.'

This was high praise from Amy.

Fran had intended to run alongside the quad bike while Amy had her tour of the farm but Amy, securely fastened next to Antony, had other ideas.

'Don't be ridiculous, child! You won't be able to keep up. Tig will come with me; he can run faster than you. Go back and make a cake or something. You're good at that. Oh and Tig, you'd better bring a notebook, there are bound to be instructions.'

Issi and Fran went back into the house together, both feeling a bit like schoolgirls dismissed from the head teacher's office.

'I was hoping they'd see the quarry so I'd find out where it is,' said Fran.

'I expect she'll grill Tig about the farm,' said Issi. 'I think it's all going quite well with the calving but she'll ask searching questions.'

Without consulting, Fran put the kettle on to make them both tea. 'Do you think I was wrong to give Amy that bit of cheese? I'd never forgive myself if she got ill. She's quite frail.'

Issi considered. 'She did know the risks and think how sad it would be if she'd never had a chance to taste it? You'd feel awful about that too.'

'You're right,' said Fran, sighing. 'I don't know why I'm so fond of her. She's not always very nice to me.'

'She's got character and I *do* think she's fond of you,' said Issi. 'She just doesn't wear her heart on her sleeve.'

'But supposing I've killed her!' Fran wailed.

'The sooner the old bird dies, the better,' said Roy, coming into the kitchen, looking annoyingly pleased with himself.

'Are you back already?' said Fran. 'I thought you'd still be away watching rugby or football or whatever.'

'It wasn't a match, sweetheart, it was a very successful meeting. Very successful.' He paused, and helped himself to a slice of quiche left over from lunch. 'So where is the old biddy? They told me at the home she'd come up here for the day.'

'She's having a tour of the farm,' said Fran. 'So who was your meeting with?'

He tapped the side of his nose with his finger in a way that made Fran want to punch him. 'You'll find out soon enough, sweetheart. And you won't like it!'

Roy insisted on driving Amy back to the care home, somehow fitting the walker and other bits and pieces on to the back seat of his car. Fran would have been quite happy to stop him doing so, but seeing how eager Amy apparently was to spend some extra minutes in his company she didn't feel she could argue.

Fran and Antony found themselves alone. 'Thank you so much for doing that,' said Fran. 'It was incredibly kind of you.'

'She did seem to enjoy it. She kept asking Tig questions and telling him things and he was brilliant. He wrote it all down, answered questions, set her mind at rest. All sorts.'

'Did you find the quarry?' said Fran. 'I really need to do so. I'm sure she would have said something. You'd think she'd want me to find it.' Feeling she was sounding a bit emotional, she fell silent.

'If we went near it, she didn't mention it,' said Antony, holding both her hands.

Fran sighed.

'You need cheering up,' he said firmly. 'Let's drive over and see the puppies. June asked me to bring you the other day but I've been so busy – as have you – but now would be a good time for some puppy jollity, don't you think?'

'I do certainly think! What a wonderful idea. But will it be convenient for Jack and June, do you think?'

'If you've got a litter of puppies in your house you don't go out much. I'll call them.'

'I'll go and tidy myself up – maybe change out of this dress and put my jeans back on,' said Fran.

Antony caught her wrist lightly between his fingers. 'Don't do that. You look lovely.' He kissed her temple.

A moment's reflection and Fran realised she was probably rather tousled and messy; she was touched. 'Oh, OK,' she said, resisting the temptation to glance in the mirror and check what she really looked like.

Chapter Twenty-Two

'I'm so sorry I've been away so much,' said Antony. They were on their way to see the puppies and Fran was excited at the prospect of having uninterrupted time with him, in his large comfortable car, for at least forty minutes. 'It's a bit hectic at work and it means you're having to deal with all this on your own.'

'Not at all! You've been amazingly supportive. What about today? Amy wouldn't have ever seen her farm again if it weren't for you.' She paused. 'Roy would never have done anything like that for her and yet somehow he always muscles in and takes the credit. He wasn't even due back from his sporting trip.'

'Which sport?' He sounded curious.

'Oh, I don't know!' She wondered if it was important and decided it couldn't be. 'I don't even care.'

She didn't want to waste precious moments with Antony talking about Roy. She looked across at him now. When she was with him she felt completely happy. But he was away a lot and she missed him.

Antony, as if he could read her thoughts, put his hand on her knee briefly, as if to reassure her. 'There's nothing like a litter of puppies for making you put all the bad stuff away.'

'How old are they now?'

'They must be about a month, I think.'

'I can't wait – they will have grown so much! Think how tiny they were when we looked after them.'

He glanced at her quickly. 'You were amazing. No one else would have done what you did.'

'Of course they would. Everyone loves puppies,' said Fran. 'I just wish I felt the same about cows. I mean I love them, I'd do anything to keep them from harm, but they're awfully big and they scare me.' She paused. 'Don't tell anyone. It's ridiculous for a farmer to be frightened of cows. Not that I am a farmer, really.'

'I think you are. You may not own the farm but you've been looking after it.'

'I'm doing my best.'

She didn't confess to her worries about whether she could really make the farm a going concern, even if she did inherit it.

'Oh my goodness, how you've all grown,' said Fran as she went into the room where the puppies were kept. 'Moving around and everything. And look! You've got a mum now!'

'Yes,' said June, obviously proud and delighted. 'It was worrying for a while but we got her interested in them again, and now it's as if nothing ever went wrong. Sit down on the sofa and I'll give you one to hold.'

'Which one is Betsy?' asked Fran. 'She was my favourite – not that I had a favourite really,' she added guiltily.

'Here she is,' said June and put a furry bundle in Fran's hands.

'You've changed so much! Open eyes, walking properly,' she said. 'I can hardly believe it.' She kissed the puppy. 'You are so adorable. They all are, of course.'

'We're very pleased with them,' said June. 'There are a couple who are showing signs of being really useful little working collies.'

Fran was about to ask if Betsy was one of them, when June went on.

'It's as if their bad start had never happened. And they're all spoken for now.'

'Oh, how lovely,' said Fran, hoping her disappointment wasn't obvious.

She'd been half hoping to stake a claim on Betsy; they'd shared some dark midnight hours together, and although logically she knew the little puppy could have no memory of their time together, she did seem very happy sucking at Fran's fingers and being stroked.

Antony sat down next to her and picked up another puppy. 'They are adorable, aren't they?'

Fran suddenly realised how very sexy seeing a strong man being tender with a tiny creature was. That little thing in large, capable hands. A pang of yearning hit her so hard she had to cough and clear her throat in case it was noticeable. 'Heavenly,' she said, but she wasn't only referring to the puppies.

'Would you like to stay and eat with us?' June asked when the puppies all indicated they'd like to go back to sleep now, thank you. 'I've got a shepherd's pie in the oven and it's huge. We haven't seen Antony properly for ages,' she went on. 'He's always gadding round the world being an international businessman.'

'Empire-building, that's me,' said Antony, laughing. 'It's hard get the proper respect from people who've known me since I was a boy with my front teeth missing,' he said to Fran.

Fran's decision was made. 'Shepherd's pie sounds delicious.' These were old and dear friends to Antony and it was a privilege to have supper with them, even though she had been hoping for some private time with him. 'And I'm longing to hear about your new grandchild,' she added.

It was a very jolly and informal meal, and June, who'd had a couple of glasses of wine by then, said, 'What you two did for pups that weren't even yours was off the scale of kindness. It meant we could be with our daughter when she needed us.'

And when Fran was helping clear up, June put her hand on Fran's arm. 'We're so happy to think he might have found a decent girlfriend at last. I always say finding a man who's rich and kind is like finding lovely shoes that are comfortable: it's really rare. But it does mean he attracts a lot of the wrong sort, who just want to take advantage of him. You're not like that.'

Feeling slightly guilty herself because June's inhibitions were down, Fran couldn't help herself probing. 'So it wasn't only his wife who was – not so nice.'

June shook her head. 'There've been a couple of shockers. Real gold-diggers. But fair play to him, he brings them over here and if they don't go down well with us, he backs off.' She frowned. 'Not always immediately, but eventually they get the heave-ho.'

'Oh golly, I hope I pass the test!'

"Course you have. When you slept on a sofa so you could feed our pups through the night, you proved you were a star!'

'Who's a star?' said Antony, coming in to the kitchen with another load of dirty plates.

'Fran is,' said June. 'For helping with the puppies.'

Antony smiled down at Fran in a way that made her stomach flip with lust and her heart leap with love. 'She absolutely is. And now I really must get her back. I've got a horrendously early start in the morning. I should have been in Lisbon yesterday for a meeting so I've got to be at the airport in the middle of the night.'

'Antony!' said Fran, aghast. 'You missed an important meeting so you could take Amy round her farm? We could have picked another day!'

'A meeting is only important when I'm there,' he said with a wink. 'And they arranged it at very short notice. I wasn't going to cancel Amy.'

'Quite right,' said June.

Antony turned to her. 'Thank you so much for supper, June. It was, as always, delicious.' He gave June a big hug.

When the farewells and thanks were finally complete and they were back in the car, Fran realised that Antony was a very private person and he only really came out of his shell with people he knew well and loved. It made her feel very special.

The following morning Roy was up before Fran and she felt resentful. It was bad enough having to share the house with him without him intruding on her early mornings, which she usually had to herself. She had to make cheese that morning and then she was going to see Amy. She wanted to see whether the previous day had completely taken it out of her and made her ill. If the cheese Amy had insisted on trying hadn't already done that.

'I thought I'd go and see the old lady this morning,' said Roy.

'I'm going this afternoon, when I've made cheese,' said Fran, 'so don't wear her out.'

'I don't know why you care so much about her. She's just standing between us and the farm,' said Roy. 'She's had a good innings – the sooner she pops her clogs now, the better.'

'I know you only say these things to upset me, Roy, but I do wish you wouldn't.'

'You're not saying you don't want the farm? Or is it just you don't want me to have it?'

'That's pretty much it. I don't want to see it all ruined.' Fran put her slices of bread in the toaster.

'You're too sentimental, Fran. This farm isn't a viable proposition unless it is "all ruined" as you say.'

'I'm selling my cheese for very good money,' she said, thanking her stars for Roger and his posh delis.

'That may be true but you need a hard cheese and even then it probably won't be enough. Farmers have to diversify these days.'

'That's what the cheese is. When Amy was in charge she sold it as milk. I'm adding a huge amount of value and selling it direct to retailers. Nothing could be more profitable than that.'

'It still won't pay the bills, mark my words. And supposing Amy does last for another ten years?'

'Well, you'd have pushed off back to Australia anyway!'

'I can stay for a year, no worries. And if she lasts much longer, you'd have to sell the farm to pay for her care home.' Roy crunched into his toast annoyingly loudly.

'Then neither of us gets to inherit. Big deal! And it's Amy's. It's only right that she should spend the money it raises on her care.'

In fact she knew that Amy didn't have to live very much longer before paying for her care home would be a real issue. Amy had pre-paid six months and that time was speeding by.

'And Antony only wants you because he wants the farm, you know. If I get it, you won't see him for dust.'

'That's not true!' Fran said, all interest in her breakfast gone.

He shrugged in a knowing way. She couldn't bear it.

'Well, I can't sit here chatting all day,' she said. 'I have cheese to make.'

'We should go through the books together,' said Roy. 'We should know what sort of a state this farm is in.'

Fran had the authority to look after the farm's finances and she didn't want to share it with Roy. But he was right. She should go through the books again, maybe with Antony who had experience of such things. She'd learned a bit about it all since she first arrived. And supposing she did inherit the farm and still couldn't make a go of it? How heartbreaking it would be to have to sell it. But she wasn't going to let Roy near the books. She'd hide them if necessary.

'Well, we're not doing it now, Roy. As I said, I'm busy.'

After she had made cheese and shared lunch with Issi and Tig, she went into town to see Amy and do some shopping.

She did the shopping first, buying Amy some of the lemon drink she liked. She added the bottle to the basket that held some miniature versions of the large quiches she had made the day before. She liked to bring presents – somehow she felt if she arrived empty-handed it would be a disappointment.

She nearly bumped into Mr Addison, Amy's solicitor, coming out of the door of the care home. 'Oh, hello!' she said. 'Is Amy OK?'

He shrugged. 'She is very elderly,' he said in case somehow Fran didn't know this. 'She's never going to be really OK, is she?'

Then he walked off, and Fran opened the door of Amy's room not knowing what she was going to find.

To her relief Amy was both still alive and awake, which seemed a miracle.

'Are you tired of visitors?' Fran asked as she kissed Amy's cheek. 'I won't stay long. I just wanted to make sure you were all right after yesterday. It was a long day.'

'It was. I'm not saying I didn't enjoy seeing the old place but that cart thing, whatever you call it, that I went in wasn't very comfortable.'

Fran exhaled, not sure if she was glad Amy was still her slightly difficult self or annoyed that something she had thought would be a wonderful treat turned out to be 'not very comfortable'.

'You haven't had any side effects from the cheese you tasted?'

'No. Why should I? It wasn't poisoned, was it?'

'Of course not, it's just it was made from unpasteurised milk...Oh, never mind.'

Fran kept her word and left Amy quite quickly. Amy was tired and needed to 'rest her eyes' as she liked to call a daytime nap.

She had parked her car in front of the house and was about to go in when she heard a noise. She'd lived on the farm long enough to know it was a cow – a cow obviously in distress.

She ran down to the cowshed to see if she could find Tig, although she knew if he had been around he'd have heard the cow himself and done something about it.

She went into the house and dialled his number on the landline. No reply. She left a message.

As a last resort she ran up the stairs and called Issi, hoping against hope she'd find Tig with her. But there was no reply, no sound. They were both out.

Just now, even Roy would have been something. He could have made himself useful for the first time and rescued the cow – at least he probably wasn't frightened of them.

Even through the walls of the house, the cow's distressed bellow was audible. She had to do something. She couldn't let it suffer. She pulled on her stripy boots. She really *should* have bought some proper farming ones by now.

She went back round to the front of the house and looked towards the bellowing. She spotted the cow. It was in the highest field and very near the hedge.

As she sprinted up the hill towards it, she did feel a touch of pride at how much fitter she was these days. There would have been a time when a hill that steep would have had her puffing a bit.

Her pride was short-lived though. There was a cow, in distress, and there she was, not knowing what on earth to do about it.

Nervously, she opened the gate, went in and set off towards the animal. As she got nearer, she recognised it. This was Flora, the cow who'd had the difficult calving that she'd watched. And there was no calf visible. That was the problem! The calf must, somehow, have got on the other side of the hedge. No wonder Flora was bellowing. But one of the few things Fran was certain about was that cows could be very dangerous if separated from their calves.

Without getting too near, and grateful that the other cows were way down the bottom of the field, she peered through a gap. Yes, there was the calf. So all she had to do was somehow get the calf back through the hedge. But first she had to get herself into that field.

Cursing herself for not having learnt the geography of the farm better, she tried to remember where the gate was to the field next to the top one. Then Flora gave another huge bellow and she decided to stop worrying about the gate and just go through the hedge.

She looked briefly for a less dense bit, squeezed her eyes shut and led with her elbows. Determination and managing to ignore the scratches got her through to the other side. She landed with a bump and immediately began rolling down the hill a bit. She sat up and saw the calf – and also realised that she'd found the quarry.

No wonder she hadn't found it before. It was small and in a bit of a dip, very out of the way. A small hawthorn tree had grown up in front of it, hiding the wooden door that seemed to have come off its hinges. Through the gap, Fran could just about make out a couple of shelves on the wall. This must be the place where Amy ripened the cheese all those years ago.

Hugely encouraged by this discovery, she turned her full attention to the calf.

Now she was the same side of the hedge she could see what had happened. It had somehow got through the hedge and had followed its mother's bellows further along, away from the gap it had gone through. All she had to do – so simple and possibly impossible – was to persuade it back to the hole in the hedge and push it through.

Of course she should have brought something with her – a head collar or something – but would a calf be led like that unless it had been trained from birth? Fran was pretty ignorant about cows, she was the first to admit, but she felt this was unlikely.

She climbed up the side of the quarry to join the calf. She couldn't see the hole it had come through but decided if she could push herself through a hedge, she might be able to push a calf, especially if its mother was on the other side.

Bravely, she spoke to it. 'OK, darling, I'm not going to hurt you. I'm just going to join you up with your mother.' She was sure she'd heard the expression 'join you up', or something similar, with regard to horse whispering.

Annoyingly, however, the calf hadn't watched the same television programme and was obviously going to need something more hands-on. She put her arms round the little chap's neck and pulled, hoping to get it to move towards a gap. 'Come on, lovely, Mummy's this way!'

She managed to drag it along a little bit and then fortunately the cow was able to see her calf and butted the hedge. That made a bit of a bigger gap and, with Fran pushing from behind (having forgotten cows could kick), it got through to the other side.

The calf might well have been fairly scratched – as she was herself – but it was with its mother, who stopped bellowing, obviously delighted to be reunited.

Fran became aware of a trickle of blood running down her own face and realised she had to find the gate to the field or go back through the hedge. She was so buoyed by her success she decided to go for broke and return through the hedge. She was grazed and muddy and her coat was torn but who cared? She'd found the quarry and rescued a calf. She almost felt like a proper farmer – at last!

While Fran was washing her hands and face and generally returning herself to looking fairly normal, she realised she really wanted to go back to the care home to tell Amy about the quarry immediately.

She tried to talk herself out of it – she'd seen her that day; it would be nice to have news when she went in next time – but she realised she just had to go.

She wrote a long note for Issi, including a certain amount of boasting about rescuing the calf, and set off back to town.

She passed Roy's car and gave him a brief wave, hoping he hadn't just come from Amy in spite of having seen her earlier in the day. Amy would be exhausted if he had and she'd have to tell her about the quarry tomorrow.

'Hi,' she said to Monica, on reception. 'I'm here again.' She signed in. 'Do you know if Roy's just been in?'

'I don't think so,' said Monica. 'But I've only just started my shift.'

307

'I'll go and see if Amy's awake – that'll tell me if she's just had a visitor.'

Amy was awake, but in bed, her hair in a plait. 'Oh?' she said, surprised. 'You here again? Weren't you here earlier?'

'Yes I was. But I had to come and tell you. I found the quarry!'

'About time too. And how did that come about?'

'I had to reunite a calf with its mother. The calf had gone through the hedge and Flora couldn't follow. I had to go through the hedge myself because I couldn't remember where the gate was.'

'You still don't know the farm very well, do you?'

'I'm learning, Amy!' Fran laughed gently, beginning to accept that nothing she ever did for Amy would produce praise.

'But didn't Roy tell me you were afraid of cows?' Amy went on, frowning a little, as if doubting her memory.

'He might have done, and I do admit I find them a bit unnerving. They're so big. But I did my duty by this one, I'm pleased to say. I couldn't find Tig.'

'Well done, dear,' said Amy, to Fran's huge surprise. 'Now just sit with me for a bit.'

This was also a surprise. Amy never seemed to want visitors to stay long. But Fran was more than happy to sit in the comfy chair, next to the bed, especially as Amy was in the mood to reminisce.

'I think my proudest day was when we won Best in Show, just before the war,' she said. 'Me and my husband had worked so hard to get this bull trained for the ring, and he looked so smart. He was strong, but not too strong for my husband. Proud as punch, he was.'

'Did your husband have to go away in the war, or did he stay and work the land?' Fran asked, delighted to have an opportunity to ask all these things that Amy hadn't talked about before.

'No, farming was a protected occupation. It was our duty to feed the country. Mind' – Amy's accent was becoming more rural now; usually her voice mostly lacked a country burr – 'we were lucky. We thought we'd have to plough our fields to grow cabbages and the like. In fact' – she lowered her voice although Fran was the only other person in the room – 'we always blamed that Gilbert Arlingham for sending the Min of Ag to inspect the land. He worked for them, you see? It was his duty to go round telling people what they should plant.' Amy was obviously outraged by this, even now.

'Goodness!'

'But when the man did come round he said the fields were too steep to plough. Well, we could have saved him the visit. Those fields have never been ploughed, which is why we have all the wild flowers on them.'

'Which is why the milk and cheese is so delicious,' said Fran.

'Exactly. But Gilbert needn't have mentioned us to the Min of Ag. He could have just left us alone. Supposing we had had to plough our fields?'

'It would have been a dreadful shame.'

Amy reached for Fran's hand and they sat in silence for a bit. Fran felt her little hand in hers, thinking of all the hard work it had done over the years. Amy had battled through the winter cold and the summer sun, every day, for all of her adult life.

Fran felt humbled and immensely grateful to have been given a glimpse of what she now understood was a noble and very valuable life. Fran suddenly realised she was crying.

As if sensing her tears, although her eyes were shut, Amy gave Fran's hand a little squeeze. 'I've had such a happy life.'

A little while later, Fran realised that Amy had gone to sleep. She kissed her forehead and tiptoed out of the room.

Chapter Twenty-Three

Fran set off for home feeling uplifted and, on impulse, stopped at the off-licence and bought a bottle of chilled Prosecco and some fancy olives. It had seemed a bit crazy to go back to see Amy for the second time in the day but it had produced a lovely chat and a real point of connection. She felt their relationship had made progress. That was something worth celebrating. And of course she'd found the quarry and rescued a cow. She was on a roll!

She was further delighted to see Antony's car in front of the house. She decided to ignore Roy's car – badly parked as usual. He was just a minor irritant; she wasn't going to let him spoil the moment when she told the others how well she'd done.

'Hi! I'm home!' she called joyfully she went in through the back door. She was surprised to see Issi, Roy and Antony in a row in the kitchen, all staring at her. Tig was looking awkward by the stove.

Fran knew that something was horribly wrong. Panic rose like a huge moth from her stomach. She put her carrier bag on the table before she dropped it. 'What's the matter?'

Antony stepped forward and took her into his arms. 'I'm so, so sorry, darling.'

She wanted to stay enfolded in this warm, safe place feeling loved and secure. But she knew she had to face the real world.

'The old lady's dead,' said Roy.

Fran didn't need Roy's blunt announcement. She had known from the moment she saw them all standing there when she'd got through the door. But neither could she believe it. How was this possible? She'd left Amy an hour ago at most.

'The care home called, just now,' said Issi. 'Someone went in to tuck her up just after you'd left and she'd gone.'

Fran waited for her tears to come but there was nothing, just a ghastly feeling of emptiness.

'Come and sit down,' said Antony. 'Cup of tea? Big drink?'

'Hot chocolate?' suggested Issi. 'For the shock?'

'I bought Prosecco,' said Fran. 'I wanted to celebrate because I'd found the quarry. It was why I went back to visit again although I'd been this afternoon.'

'Oh, love,' said Issi. 'Let's go for the gin and tonic. It's got a bit more punch than fizzy wine. Antony brought it. It's a special artisan gin.' She paused, embarrassed. 'Not that the fact it's fancy gin is going to make you any less sad.'

Fran smiled. 'But it'll make being sad taste better.'

'It might,' said Antony. 'We don't know what it tastes like yet.' He started opening the bottle and cans of chilled tonic.

'I don't know why you're making such a fuss,' said Roy. 'She was a really old lady and she died. Big deal!'

'Roy?' said Issi and Fran, almost in unison. 'Shut up!'

'Pardon me,' he said with a shrug. 'She was my relation too.'

'I'm really going to miss her,' said Tig. 'She was a great boss and a really good farmer.'

Issi moved closer to him and took his arm.

'You must be wondering who your next boss will be,' said Roy. 'Me or her.' He jerked his thumb in Fran's direction.

'You know what?' said Tig, frighteningly calm. 'I'm going to spend a few days thinking about Amy, what she's done for me, what she's done for this farm and I'm not going to think about who she's left the farm to. And I suggest you do the same.'

It was a long speech for Tig and Fran wanted to applaud, but didn't.

'That's all very well for you to say, mate,' said Roy. 'But you're not in the running for a big inheritance.'

'We don't know that,' said Fran. 'Amy may have thought that neither of us were suitable and left everything to Tig.' She smiled as she realised this would be a good result.

'I'd contest the will,' said Roy. 'Tig isn't related.'

'Oh, for God's sake!' said Fran. 'We're hardly related either. I'm going to sit down next door.' She suddenly realised she felt exhausted.

'I'll come with you,' said Antony. He followed her into the sitting room holding two gin and tonics. 'Here,' he said, handing her one. 'I'm going to light the fire.'

Fran took a large gulp of her drink. It was extremely strong although Antony had managed to find some ice to put in it. She sat back and closed her eyes, her mind whirling with thoughts and memories. How could Amy be dead? How could she be so fit and well and animated and then just be gone? She knew another couple of sips and the tears would come. She put her glass on the table next to her.

'Was it just coincidence that you came over? You didn't know Amy was dead?' she asked Antony, watching as he scrunched up newspaper and broke up sticks.

'Coincidence. She must have died minutes after you left her.' The fire was now crackling away and he straightened up. 'I think you need food. And I expect the others need drinks.'

'Ask Issi to come in, will you?' said Fran. 'I think I need her.'

Issi came in without being asked, holding a drink. She flopped down on the sofa next to Fran. 'Roy's gone for fish and chips, which will take a while. I put the oven on and Tig is making us cheese on toast to keep us going.' She sipped her drink. 'Boy, that's strong.'

'Good, isn't it? I reckon I'm three sips away from a good cry,' said Fran.

'It is awfully sad, isn't it?' said Issi, already sounding tearful. 'I mean, we knew it would happen eventually, but so soon?'

'And she was so well this evening. We had a lovely chat. She told me about the feud between her and Antony's family, how she was worried they'd have to plough the fields during the war, when everyone had to, more or less. But these fields were too small and steep.'

'Which kept the pasture pristine. A unique habitat,' said Issi, reminding Fran of her academic background.

Fran sipped her gin. 'You know, today, when I managed to get that cow and its calf together, on the same side of the fence, I felt like a proper farmer.'

'You mean you'd give up your dreams of having a restaurant to be a farmer?'

Fran nodded. 'I think so. The farm is so important. It has to be kept going. And we had the supper club, which was amazing. We could have more of those.'

'Not quite the same though,' said Issi.

Fran sighed. 'What about you? Are you and Tig properly a couple?'

Issi nodded. 'He's the one, if that's what you're asking. But right now our future is a bit uncertain.'

Fran frowned. The gin was beginning to muddle her brain a bit. 'Why?'

'Well, Tig could be thrown out of his house. Thank goodness Mary owns hers. But he'd have to find another job and hope a house went with it. When I've finished my PhD I'd then find work but things would still be tight. He earns very little, really.'

'You know I'd never throw Tig out of his house. If I inherit.'

'Of course I know that, but supposing you don't?'

Fran suddenly realised that her best friend needed the farm more than she did really. She'd be OK one way or another, with Antony, although seeing the farm ruined would nearly kill her. But it was much more important for Issi and Tig. 'Oh God, Issi!'

'We've talked about it, obviously, and we'll work something out. Don't worry, Fran. I know it's not up to you – you can't sort the situation.' She put her hand on her friend's knee. 'We'll get through.'

But still, in spite of the gin, the healing tears wouldn't come. She and Issi drank more gin and ate the cheese on toast while waiting for Roy to come back. Although reluctant to credit Roy with anything, ever, they had to admit that he did appear with fish and chips fairly quickly.

They sat in the sitting room, throwing the fish and chip paper on to the fire. Tig made tea and they talked about Amy.

'She didn't praise much,' said Tig, 'but you knew when she was pleased with you. A nod was enough.'

'I thought she was great,' said Issi, 'but one of those feisty old ladies who are easier if they're someone else's relation.'

'I always got on great with her,' said Roy. 'But I've always had a way with the ladies.'

The two ladies present exchanged glances, not convinced.

'She made it very plain what she thought about me and my family,' said Antony. 'But I respected her for that.'

'I never knew what she felt about me,' said Fran. 'I wanted to please her so much and yet I could never do anything right. Apart from today – oh God, was it only late this afternoon? She did seem pleased I'd found the quarry, although it would have been better if I'd found it sooner.'

'So where is this quarry you're going on about?' asked Roy.

Fran hesitated a moment, but there was no way Roy could use the information to his advantage now. 'Oh, it's up the top field, on the left.'

'Did you know where it was, Tig?' Roy went on.

Tig shook his head. 'If I did, I'd have told Fran straight away. Amy was always very secretive about it. I think she used to hide food up there during the war or something.'

'Well, that makes me feel better about not discovering it until now,' said Fran. 'But it's only important if you make cheese,' she said to Roy.

'There won't be any of that making-cheese malarkey if I get the farm,' he said. 'No money in it.'

'There is! I sell my soft cheese direct to retailers!' Fran had had too much gin to be tactful.

'Still not enough!' Roy went on. 'You can't always sell roof tiles to pay off the bank. You'll have to start taking them off the farmhouse, soon.'

Fran swallowed. She'd hoped Roy hadn't noticed what she'd done with that pile of tiles and hadn't realised he knew about the bank loan. And he was right; she couldn't go on selling off the farm's assets. She'd have to find another way.

'So what's your grand plan, Roy?' said Antony.

Roy's gaze flicked around the room as if he was debating whether to reveal his plan or not. 'There's always money in land,' he said slowly. 'They're not making any more of it. Makes it very valuable.'

'So you'll sell it off, in dribs and drabs?' asked Issi. Gin was inclined to make her argumentative.

Roy nodded slowly. 'There's a bit down the bottom near the road that could be sold off without it affecting the main plot.'

Fran was surprised he knew so much about the farm when he'd appeared to show so little interest in it. And she didn't like the way he said 'plot'.

'So would you keep a bit for yourself, to live on?' asked Antony.

'Ah no. I'd sell the whole lot off. It's how I'd sell it would be the thing. To one big developer, or in bits and pieces.'

Now Fran wanted to cry, but she wasn't going to, not in front of that heartless monster. She yawned instead.

Antony got up. 'You're tired. You need to get to bed. There'll be a lot of things to sort out in the morning.'

Fran got up too, and staggered a little. 'I'll see you out.'

She longed to go home with him, to spend the night in his arms, to let passion sweep away grief and shock and worry. But she knew she couldn't. She couldn't let Roy have any excuse or opportunity to lay claim to the farm.

Antony knew it too. She didn't have to explain. He'd been a calm, strong presence this evening and having him in her life made everything seem a lot better.

They hugged in the dark of the passage before comfort turned to passion. But after kissing for some time Fran pulled away. 'It will be all right, won't it? If Amy leaves the farm to Roy, he can sell it to you?"

Antony didn't say anything for a few moments and then he spoke into her hair. 'Darling, I'd buy it in a heartbeat and it could be yours to do what you like with. But – I hate to tell you this, especially now – going on what Roy's just been saying tonight, and other sources of information I have, Roy's been in meetings with Noblesse Homes.'

'What does that mean?' Fran asked.

He sighed. 'It means he may have got planning permission for the land already. If it goes up for sale as housing land I'd never be able to afford it, even if I sold everything. I've worked it out.'

'Oh God!' Now she wanted to cry, but from fear not from sadness. 'But surely you can't apply for planning permission on land you don't own?'

'Yes you can, I'm afraid. But the land is very steep and there's no infrastructure so a big housing estate would be very expensive to build. But a few executive homes could be possible.'

'I can't believe they'd even consider putting houses on land that managed to get through the war without being ploughed up.' She paused. 'And it's not just me, is it? It's Tig and Issi. They're more bound up in the farm than I am, really. I could make cheese somewhere else, or even open a restaurant. They've only got the farm and the herd is so important to Tig. The cows – they're...' She struggled to find the word. 'They're almost like his relations!'

He laughed gently at her exaggeration. 'Come on, I'm going to put you to bed. You're tired beyond reason and any minute now you're going to be really upset. Bed is the best place for that.'

It was almost funny, Fran thought. She and Antony should have been together, ripping each other's clothes off, falling on to the bed, or the floor, or whatever was nearest, but in fact he shook out her duvet while she got into her pyjamas and brushed her teeth. She felt strangely embarrassed appearing in her flowery brushed-cotton nightwear, which she realised Amy would have called 'winceyette', although he'd seen her in far less.

He treated her with the same matter-of-fact practicality that he had treated the puppies they had helped hand-rear. Somehow his restraint made him even more sexy.

'Come on, tuck up,' he said. He had a book in his hand. 'I found this. It must be one of Amy's.'

'What is it?'

'It's called *The Farm on the Hill* by Alison Uttley. It's about a girl who lives on a farm. Now get in and close your eyes.'

It was lovely to be in her bed, her pillow smelling faintly of the lavender oil she often sprinkled on it.

321

He lay on the bed next to her, his big shiny shoes nearly hanging over the end of it. It was supremely chaste and very sexy.

He began to read. '"Like a traveller to an inn, the darkness came…"'

He had a really beautiful voice. Of course she'd noticed it before but now he was reading aloud to her it sounded even more mellifluous and flowing. She hadn't been read aloud to since she was a child and she loved it. Sadly, she couldn't listen for long before her eyes closed and she slept.

When Fran awoke in the morning her first memory was of Antony reading to her. And then reality hit her. Amy had died. Alone in her bed, tears began to fall. She stayed there until she'd stopped sobbing and then she got downstairs and into the kitchen, to do what she knew would calm her: cook.

She decided to bake brownies for the care home, having to adapt the recipe to cope with gaps in the ingredients. Soon she had the kitchen smelling of vanilla and chocolate.

Then she made an improvised pesto, managing without the main ingredients of pine nuts, basil and Parmesan. She was very satisfied with the result – chives, random seeds, cheddar and a lot of garlic – which she was eating on toast when Issi came into the kitchen.

'You always did cook when you were stressed. But if you eat any more garlic you won't be able to kiss anyone.'

Fran laughed. She was surprised. She'd thought laughing would be something she'd be doing after a few months, not mere hours since she'd heard of Amy's death.

'Well, you know me. I like a world where I have control, at least some of the time.' She walked across to put the kettle on. 'I thought I'd give the brownies to the care home. They've been so good to Amy. I'll brush my teeth really well before I go.'

'Shall I come with you? There'll be a lot to sort out. You won't want to be on your own.'

'That would be really kind. I might break down at any moment. It would be good to have someone there who could finish my sentences if I can't.'

Fran did cry when she arrived at the care home. It seemed like five minutes ago when she'd last been there to see Amy and in fact it was less than twenty-four hours. She and Issi went into the office.

'We are so sad about Amy dying,' said Monica.

'She was such a character,' said another nurse. 'And she seemed so well – completely recovered after her infection. Yet it was as if something told her she could go and she went.'

Fran was very grateful they didn't say 'sorry for your loss', which she felt was an expression best fitted to an American cop drama, and not an actual expression of sympathy.

'We're very glad you've come so soon,' said the woman who was in charge, whose badge said 'Moyra Jenkins'. Fran was grateful to be reminded of her name.

'We'd have had to get in touch with you otherwise,' Moyra went on. 'As you can imagine, Amy left very strict instructions about what was to happen to her after she died. She gave them to us the day after she arrived in the home.'

'Goodness me! She liked to plan ahead,' said Fran.

'She did. And thank you so much for these. Chocolate is always so comforting, I find. Have one?'

While Fran had found the smell of the brownies baking comforting, she didn't want to eat one now. 'No, thank you.'

Issi took one and Moyra went on. 'Firstly, Amy's already gone to the funeral director. She knew which one and already had a word. She wanted a conventional funeral—'

'Oh. I'd fancied a green burial, with a wicker coffin,' said Fran, who had added a horse-drawn hearse leading the cortège through the town to her mental picture.

Moyra shook her head. 'Nothing like that. Maybe you'd better go and see the undertakers?' She patted Fran's hand. 'It's all right, the brownies will be just fine with us.'

324

Fran laughed. 'Thank you for being so good to her. I know she could be difficult but I loved her.'

'She was just fine, and we loved her too.'

Fran felt herself start to cry.

'Come on,' said Issi. 'Undertakers next.'

The undertakers were very kind too, and ushered Issi and Fran into a separate room where they were soon joined by a woman in her early thirties.

'Hi,' she said, holding out her hand. 'I'm Kirstie and I'll be looking after you.'

'Thank you,' said Fran, glad that this attractive young woman didn't fit the funeral director stereotype.

'I have your – what was she – great-aunt?'

'Kind of. I was only a very distant cousin but I was living – am living – on her farm and looking after things.'

'Well, Amy was a wonderful woman,' Kirstie said.

'She was, but how do you know that?' said Issi.

'She left such detailed instructions you won't have to make a single decision – or hardly any. That's why I think she's wonderful,' said Kirstie.

Fran sighed. 'I gathered from the home that we can't have a wicker coffin, horses draped in black crêpe and all that.'

'People lining the street, hats off in respectful silence,' added Issi.

'Us following behind, wearing black veils…'

'I like your thinking,' said Kirstie. 'Sadly, your aunt had other ideas. She's chosen the church, the hymns, the flowers – just one wreath, roses and lilies.' She paused. 'Your option would have been very expensive and your aunt has prepaid.'

'Of course she had. It was very like her,' said Fran, thinking of the care home fees paid for in advance.

'As I said, very thoughtful. However…'

'What?' asked Issi. 'A problem?'

'We might not have time for all the hymns.'

'How many has she chosen?' asked Fran.

'Eight. I think she just went for her favourites. You should just choose three you think people will know,' said Kirstie. 'Or hire a choir.'

'I think we'll just choose hymns from the list,' said Fran.

'Then there's the music leaving the church—'

'Please don't say it's "I've Got a Brand New Combine Harvester",' said Fran.

Kirstie laughed. 'No, no, it's Widor's 'Toccata'. She had it at her wedding, apparently.'

Suddenly Fran was in bits. She remembered the wedding photo of Amy and her husband in a silver frame at the farm. Amy was wearing a long dress and her husband, tall and handsome by her side, wore a suit. There were a lot of little bridesmaids with large wreaths of flowers on their heads and about three grown-up ones, also with elaborate headdresses.

What were the young couple feeling then? she wondered. They'd have been excited, a bit nervous, tired maybe, after days of preparation. But somewhere in their thoughts would have been babies, children who would take over the farm in due course. Not her own widowhood so young, no children, and a bit of a mess when it came to passing on the farm.

Issi looked at her friend, and realised she needed help. 'Quick trip to the pub, I think,' she said briskly. She glanced at her watch. 'The solicitor's not expecting us for an hour. We've got time.'

Chapter Twenty-Four

Issi parked in the pub car park. 'Will Roy be in here, do you think?'

Fran shrugged. 'I don't know.

'It would be more his thing than helping with the care home or the undertakers,' said Issi. 'Come on, let's get you a gin.'

Fran put her hand on Issi's arm. 'It's so kind of you to come with me. But I'm not sure I really want a drink just now.'

'You could just have a coffee or something?' suggested Issi.

'I'm OK, but I just want you to know how much I appreciate your support just now.'

'Don't be daft. I wouldn't leave you to do something like this on your own. You need a chum. Did you tell your mother?'

'I did and she's all set to come down if we need her, but I think I'd rather do without her really. It would be nicer if she came when we knew what was what. She'd only quarrel with Roy.'

'And you and me are here to do that!' said Issi. She looked at her watch. 'We're a bit early for the solicitor but we can wait if he's not ready.'

'Good idea. We can read the ancient magazines; it'll calm me down.'

In the event, they were shown straight in and Fran was annoyed to discover that Roy was already in the solicitor's office.

'I hope it's all right me bringing Issi,' said Fran as soon as the hellos had been said.

'Of course I'll go out if anything confidential is being discussed,' Issi added.

'No worries,' said Roy, sounding displeased. 'We can't find out a damn thing until after the funeral, anyway.'

'Oh!' said Fran, who hadn't taken in that a meeting with the solicitor might have been so momentous. 'Well, that's OK. I brought you these.' She handed over a foil package to Mr Addison. 'Brownies,' she added.

'That's very kind!' said Mr Addison. 'And coffee is on its way.'

He seemed pleased to see both the brownies and Fran and Issi. Fran wondered if Roy had been being difficult. Mr Addison opened up the foil package.

'Can I have one of them?' demanded Roy.

'No,' said Fran and Issi.

Mr Addison put his head on one side. 'That seems a little ungenerous.'

'Oh, go on then,' said Fran, sighing.

'But wait for the coffee!' said Issi.

Luckily for Roy, a young woman came in with a tray of coffee just at that moment.

A cup of tea and two brownies later, Mr Addison made sure everyone was paying attention. 'I'm afraid I'm not in a position to tell you anything now. Mrs Flowers has been very clear and she wishes her will to be read after the funeral.'

'Like in a film!' said Issi.

'Exactly,' Mr Addison agreed. 'She has – had – a sense of the dramatic. She wants everyone gathered together, in this office. She's also said who is to be present.'

'Can I bring Issi? I think I may need some support.'

Mr Addison referred to a list. 'Is this Miss Isobel Sharpe?'

Fran and Issi both nodded.

'In which case, yes.'

'That's very nice of Amy to realise I'd need a friend!' said Fran.

'Actually, I think Miss Sharpe is invited because of her connection with Mr Christopher Brown, the herdsman?'

'That's Tig, yes,' said Issi.

'I don't think I knew what his real name was,' said Fran, surprised and a little embarrassed.

'So who else is coming?' asked Roy.

'Well, you and Francesca here,' said Mr Addison. 'Antony Arlingham—'

'But Amy hated him!' said Roy indignantly.

'Maybe she invited him so she could hate him officially?' suggested Issi, obviously feeling a bit skittish because she was on the official list.

Mr Addison ignored this. 'You probably know that Mrs Flowers' wishes for her funeral were very precise.'

'I suppose I should visit the vicar,' said Fran, a bit overwhelmed by her responsibilities.

'I've telephoned him with the long list of hymns,' said Mr Addison, 'and he's going to discuss with the church choir the ones they sing best. The choir is also going to rope in a few members of a local choir that Mrs Flowers was a member of for years, for added body.'

'I didn't know she'd ever been in a choir,' wailed Fran. 'So many things I didn't know about her and now I'll never find out.'

'Do they have to be paid?' demanded Roy, ignoring Fran's distress.

'Of course! Why should they do it for nothing? Even if it was Amy's choir!' said Fran. 'And to be honest, funerals cost a huge amount anyway so a couple of hundred quid won't make that much difference.'

'I'm sure they'd be very grateful for a contribution, but in the scheme of things, this isn't an extravagant funeral. A very simple coffin and the reception at the village hall, catered for by ladies of the village.'

'If they're offering to do it for nothing we'll make a contribution to the village hall fund,' said Fran quickly. 'As well as pay for the food.'

'You're taking things for granted a bit, aren't you?' said Roy. 'If I inherit, I'm not going to contribute to any choir or village hall.'

'The cost of the funeral is the responsibility of the estate,' said Mr Addison. 'So I'm in charge and most of it has been prepaid.'

'Good,' said Fran. 'I'm sure we can trust you not to be mean.'

'Do we have a date yet?' asked Roy. 'And do we get a choice? I have some business I need to attend to.'

'The vicar is checking availability with the organist and bell ringers,' said Mr Addison.

'Bell ringers? Like a wedding?' asked Fran, confused.

Mr Addison smiled. 'Not like a wedding. Amy wants traditional muffled bells and the years of her age tolled out. Although strictly speaking it would have happened just after her death.'

'Goodness me, she was a one for tradition,' said Issi. 'I admire that. Not ashamed to be old school.'

This made Fran smile. 'I'm not sure Amy would recognise being referred to as "old school", but she certainly was.'

Roy got up. 'Are we done? I've got things to do, people to see.'

'I didn't realise people actually said that in real life,' muttered Fran to Issi.

As Roy strode out, Mr Addison said, 'I think he must have heard that expression on the television.'

Fran looked at Amy's trusted solicitor, knowing he knew what she was burning to know. But she couldn't ask.

'We'd better be going,' she said, looking at Issi. 'We've got a funeral to sort out.'

'Just follow the instructions and all will be well,' said Mr Addison.

'We could have asked him who was going to get the farm. He has the information,' said Issi, later.

Fran shook her head. 'He wouldn't have been able to tell us and it would have been cheating.' She looked at her friend. 'And while we don't know we can hope.'

The next few days were full of seeing people, accepting condolences and baking. The baking was partly for comfort and partly to supply the seemingly endless line of people who came to pay their respects.

Roy took no part in this. He was off, wheeling and dealing, while Fran, assisted by Issi, made tea and served cakes, scones, biscuits or whatever Fran had made when she was up at six in the morning.

Although the visitors were very time-consuming – Fran hardly had time to make cheese – she didn't resent their coming. Every one – or pair – had some little anecdote about Amy that helped build up a picture of what she'd been like before she got too old to work the farm properly.

Issi had gone through all the photographs and put out the ones of Amy, and these were lifted and inspected by the visitors, which was always followed by an 'I remember when...' or 'I recall Amy...' or 'Mrs Flowers once...', depending on how they'd addressed Amy when she was alive.

It was relaxing to sit in the sitting room, with the fire going (not that it was really cold but it was comforting to have it burning away), drinking tea, talking about Amy and sometimes weeping.

She'd been much loved in the area and even her more elderly friends found someone younger to bring them to the farm.

As Fran said to Issi, 'It was like watching a film of Amy's past life. Whoever gets the farm in the end, I wouldn't have missed these days finding out about her.'

Fran had walked up to look at the quarry after one of these sessions, wanting time to process all she had learnt about Amy since her death. She couldn't help feeling sad that she had missed Amy's best days but there was no point in bemoaning things that couldn't be changed, and at least she knew a lot more about her now. Amy had been a feisty, go-ahead woman, who mixed skill with instinct and produced a prize-winning herd. She was a role model and Fran realised Amy always would be one to her, even if she didn't inherit the farm. Amy's strength of character was what had got her through a hard life.

Fran was admiring the wild flowers that filled the field and the hedgerows, frothy white cow parsley at the edges, yellow cowslips in the middle, knowing they were there because of Amy's traditional farming methods, wondering how she ever found time to make wine out of the cowslips, when she heard raised voices floating up from the farm. She ran down to see what was going on.

There was a trailer in the yard with the ramp down. Roy and Tig were facing each other, both looking as if they might throw a punch at any moment. Two other men, who had obviously come with the trailer, looked on, half excited at the prospect of a fight and half confused.

'What is going on?' said Fran, out of breath from her rapid trip down the fields.

Roy faced her. 'Tell Tig he has no bloody right to stop me from selling animals that are mine!'

She turned to Tig.

'He can't take the bull. He was born on this farm and he'll die on it.' Tig's voice wasn't loud but his words had a lot of power.

'I don't understand,' said Fran. 'Roy? You can't sell animals that aren't yours.'

'They're as good as mine!'

'What makes you say that? We don't know whose they are, do we?' Panic struck her. Had Roy already heard that he was going to inherit?

Roy exhaled deeply, as if he was facing very stupid children who needed things spelt out for them. 'I know I'm going to inherit, OK? Now get that bloody bull into the trailer. But carefully – I'm getting a lot of money for him.' He turned on the trailer drivers. 'You can tell a bull from a cow, can't you?'

'Not sure *you* can,' said Tig.

'Listen, mate,' said Roy furiously, 'you can bugger off out of here! You're living on my land in one of my houses. You have absolutely no right to anything. Now if you know what's good for you you'll help these guys get those animals into the trailer!'

'Roy!' Although she felt ready to tear Roy limb from limb she knew it wouldn't help. She tried to keep calm. 'What do you know that none of the rest of us do?'

Roy groaned. He was obviously having a trying morning; things weren't going to plan at all. 'I don't know for a fact. That bloody solicitor wouldn't tell me. But what I do know is—'

Before he could elaborate further, Issi drove up in Tig's car, parked as best she could in the space and got out. 'What's going on?'

336

'This clown' – Tig gestured towards Roy – 'seems to think he can sell Lorenzo and five heifers as if they were his.' He paused, his anger almost visibly throbbing under his measured tones. 'They haven't even sent a big enough trailer.'

'But Roy can't sell the cows, can he?' said Issi. 'He doesn't own them.'

'I do own them, bar the shouting,' said Roy, shouting.

'What makes you say that?' asked Issi. 'Surely no one owns them at the moment.'

Roy swore again. 'Wait here!' he commanded and strode into the house.

'As if we were going to run away and hide,' said Fran. She paused. 'Although I do quite like that option.'

Tig and Issi looked at her as if she wasn't taking the situation seriously enough. She swallowed. She was frightened and it did sometimes make her flippant. She cleared her throat. 'Surely you can't move cattle without loads of paperwork anyway?'

'True. And I've got the paperwork at my house,' said Tig. 'Even if he does own them he can't move them without me agreeing.'

'I think you had better go home,' said Fran to the two men who were getting increasingly uneasy. 'You're not going to be able to take any cattle away today.'

'We're not going unless we're paid,' said one of them. 'In cash. As agreed.'

'Do you think one of us should go and see what Roy is doing?' said Issi, standing as close to Tig as she could.

'No,' said Fran. 'He'll either find what he's looking for or he'll have to come and tell us he hasn't found it.'

A pair of buzzards mewed high in the sky and tugged at Fran's already damaged heart. How would she feel if she had to leave here? More to the point, how would Tig feel?

At last Roy came out of the house with a piece of paper in his hand. He thrust it at Fran. 'Here. Have a read of that.'

It took her a few seconds to realise she was looking at a letter from Amy. It had been sent at the same time as the letter she had received when Amy was looking for someone to leave the farm to. She read it as quickly as she could given the faded ink and Amy's handwriting.

Roy snatched the letter back before she'd quite finished reading it. 'I'll tell you what it says and I'll read this bit aloud:...*but because you are male, and I feel strongly that property should pass down the male line, I will leave the farm to you unless you turn out to be quite unsuitable.*'

No one spoke.

'Well, you are quite unsuitable,' said Issi at last. 'You don't love the farm like Fran does. Amy would be mad to leave it to you. You'd sell your old grandmother, let alone some land in a country you don't even want to live in.'

Roy gave her fake smile. 'Amy never knew that. She was convinced I'd shed my last drop of blood to look after the place. It's mine.'

'But you still can't sell the assets before we know for sure,' said Fran. 'And there's probate to consider.'

'And even if you could,' said Tig, 'I won't give you the paperwork to move these beasts.'

'You'll have to, after the will has been read,' said Roy.

'It doesn't change anything,' said Fran, who was now feeling sick. 'You can't sell the cows now. I suggest you pay off the drivers and learn to be patient. It's not long now until you'll know for certain. Just don't count your chickens – or should I say cows – until they're hatched.'

Then she walked back into the house, her back straight, her guts churning, knowing her days on the farm she had come to really love were numbered.

Chapter Twenty-Five

A week had passed, and it was the morning of the funeral, and in spite of the sadness of the occasion that was to come and the possible – probable even – ghastly outcome to follow, Fran felt oddly positive.

She found Issi in the kitchen, making tea, looking anxious. Fran realised all over again that Issi had far more to lose than she did. Fran would be devastated to lose the farm but she had Antony, who had a house of his own. But Issi and Tig would be really stuck if it all went the wrong way.

'How are you feeling, Is? And what about Tig?'

'You know him; he's not saying much but he's worried. I don't think he's even worried for him – us – it's the cows. They're like family, almost. He knows them all, who their mothers and grand-mothers were.'

Fran put a quick hand on Issi's arm. 'I know Antony will find something for Tig – maybe even start a herd of cows himself. It'll be all right.'

'I know. But it won't be the same.'

Fran smiled. 'You never know. Perhaps Antony will buy the herd and Tig will keep his family.'

'That would be good.' Issi looked curiously at Fran. 'I must say, I was expecting you to be much more gloomy about it all. I mean it's great that you're not, but why?'

'It's the hard cheese. Making it last week with Mary and Erica was so brilliant.' Fran paused. 'Apart from it being so satisfying and interesting, it was healing, us three women, working together, crying sometimes. And then we all walked up to the quarry together and put it in to mature.'

'I'd forgotten when you did that,' said Issi. 'I was doing something with Tig, but that sounds lovely.'

'It was. And it's a sort of two fingers up to Roy. It's there, in the quarry, waiting to mature, and he may never know about it. It should be turned every day for three weeks and if Roy's still here in a year, I'll come back in the dead of night and steal it.'

'And I'll come with you.' Issi took out some bread. 'Do you want toast? I had breakfast with Tig but I wanted to get dressed here with you. I have a selection of suitably gloomy items to choose from.' She cut a slice of bread and put it in the toaster.

'Amy is very old-fashioned, not saying anything like "no black please".'

'She is – was – very old-fashioned in many ways. Wanting to leave the farm to a man, for example. But in other ways she was a trailblazer! Many women would have given up the farm when their husband died, or found another husband to run it for them.' She sighed.

'Did you get your eulogy written?' asked Issi.

Fran suddenly felt less positive. 'Yes. It's very short and simple. I just hope I get it out without breaking down.'

'You don't want Roy—'

'No,' said Fran, just as Roy came into the kitchen.

'Are you girls making coffee?' he asked.

'I think if you're going to inherit it, you should learn your way round this kitchen,' said Fran.

'No point. I won't be keeping it.'

Rather than have Roy cover her kitchen – she felt it was her kitchen – with coffee grounds and mess, she elected to make another cup for him. She realised it wasn't only Amy who was a mass of contradictions.

It had been arranged that Seb and the funeral cars should drive to the outlying farms and villages to pick up people who wanted to go to the funeral but didn't have transport. There had been quite a long list.

When Issi had said to Fran and Antony how kind this was, Fran said, 'Well, this way you and I don't have to travel in a funeral car with Roy. I don't think I could have borne it.'

So Antony was taking Fran, while Issi and Tig were taking Tig's mother Mary. Roy was making his own way, and Fran wondered if Megan was going to drive him so he could drink at the wake. But seeing him in his suit, borrowed from a mate and far too loud for a funeral, stopped her. He looked like a man on his way to the bank after winning the jackpot at roulette. She hoped he wasn't going to win anything but not with any conviction.

Antony and Fran had hardly seen each other recently, so when he came to pick her up to take her to the church, for a few moments they just enjoyed the bliss of being together in silence.

'I just hope I don't make a complete fool of myself and sob uncontrollably,' said Fran after a few minutes.

'That would be fine. No one would mind. Although Amy might think you were making a fuss.'

She laughed gently. 'She would. At least she won't have to accuse Roy of displaying unseemly grief.'

'Unlikely,' said Antony, smiling. 'Although he may surprise us all by breaking down in tears.'

'I wish I could believe that was likely to happen!' Fran smiled back at him, in spite of everything.

Antony glanced at her. 'I will look after you, you know. Afterwards.'

She nodded. 'I know. To be honest I'm more worried about Tig and Issi. They stand to lose more than a job, but their home. And of course, as Issi said to me, the cows are like family members to Tig.'

Antony didn't say anything reassuring, but just put his hand on hers for a second and squeezed it. Without asking, she knew he thought Roy would get the farm. She did too.

The church was completely full. Although they weren't late, Fran and Antony were nearly the last to arrive. People had obviously been aware of Amy's popularity and got there early.

Fran spotted Seb, looking magnificent in a dark suit, surrounded by a cluster of old ladies, sending him adoring glances from time to time. It made her smile inside. It was a very sad occasion, but it was also a day out and a chance to meet up with old friends. Funerals should be enjoyed, she felt.

She was dreading giving the eulogy. The thought of Roy doing it – and in some ways it would have been more appropriate – was too awful to contemplate. He hadn't ever really understood Amy, Fran felt. To be fair, Amy was tricky, but to listen to him spout a series of clichés about 'a wonderful old lady', when she was so much more, was unbearable. He hadn't objected at all when she said she'd do it.

344

It was brilliant having Amy's choir there. They sang the hymns vigorously which meant anyone too overcome to sing didn't have to worry. Fran sometimes could join in but sometimes her throat closed and only tears came.

Eventually, Fran was beckoned forward by the vicar. It was time.

'Chin up, chicken!' Antony whispered and she couldn't help smiling. She knew it was the last thing he'd say usually and meant it to stop her feeling gloomy.

She walked up to the lectern and began.

'I didn't know Amy long, but it didn't take much time to realise what a very admirable woman she was. A role model...'

She got through it without crying, but when the congregation applauded as she walked back to her seat she couldn't stop herself and hid behind Antony's very large, ironed white handkerchief.

'That was a wonderful do, dear,' said an old lady to Fran. 'Worthy of a great woman. How were you related?'

'Distantly, I'm afraid,' said Fran, more afraid than she cared to express. If she were more closely related, what lay ahead of her would have been less daunting.

Antony appeared at her elbow. 'Darling? It's time to go to the solicitor's.'

'To see what's in the will,' Fran explained to her fascinated companion.

'To see who gets the farm, do you mean?' The old lady's eyes opened wide at the prospect of a bit of upset. Then she grew more serious. 'I do hope it's you, dear. You're liked in the community.'

After some goodbyes, which threatened to become protracted, Antony led her away by the elbow.

'I don't think the community around Hill Top really knows me that well,' said Fran, 'but I don't think Roy would contribute much.'

'Apart from some executive housing,' said Antony.

Fran shuddered.

Although they hurried, everyone else seemed to be there already when they arrived in the meeting room at the solicitor's office. Mr Addison was at the head of the table, with Roy on his right. Issi and Tig were sitting together and Fran suspected they were holding hands under the table. Rather to her surprise, Moyra Jenkins, manager of the care home, was also there. Fran and Antony sat down. It wasn't a big room or a particularly big table but Fran couldn't help noticing that only Mr Addison and Antony looked comfortable in their clothes. They were accustomed to wearing suits; no one else was, really.

'Right,' said Mr Addison. 'First of all, may I say what a very successful and appropriate funeral that was, Miss Duke. And a charming eulogy. I felt Mrs Flowers was truly represented by your words.'

'Thank you,' muttered Fran, embarrassed.

'As you all know, Mrs Flowers had her little eccentricities and left very detailed instructions in her will. I am one of the executors and Mrs Jenkins, as manager of the care home, is the other.' He smiled at his co-executor reassuringly. She seemed a bit nervous. 'So, shall we begin?' he asked.

'No one's stopping you,' said Roy.

Silently, Fran echoed his words. She wanted to know what was going to happen to the farm.

Mr Addison looked at the sheets of paper in front of him. 'Mrs Flowers has put a long list of beneficiaries, charities and small bequests first, but I won't read them all out. The first bequest of any significance is for Christopher Brown.'

'Who's that?' asked Roy. 'And why does he get to get anything?'

'That's me,' said Tig. Fran could see his jaw was clenched and a vein pulsed in his neck. He was obviously extremely tense.

'*To Mr Christopher Brown I leave the cottage he currently lives in, the bull and five heifers of his choice. I also leave him the field at the bottom of the farm, by the gate, to start him off.*' Mr Addison frowned. 'She goes on to say, *I know this isn't enough land really, but he should be able to rent some more locally.*'

Tig gulped. 'Thank you very much,' he said quickly, obviously too overcome to say more.

347

'That's amazing,' said Issi. 'We don't have to leave the cottage!' She flung her arms round Tig's neck and kissed him.

'Hang on!' said Roy. 'Is she allowed to break up the property like that? I want to contest the will!'

'Mrs Flowers can do exactly what she likes with her property,' said Mr Addison sternly. 'There are no grounds for contesting her will. Now shall I go on?'

'Be my guest,' said Roy, looking mutinous.

'Right! Now. *To my husband's distant cousin from Australia, Roy Jones—*' The telephone started ringing. 'I am so sorry, I will have to take this.'

'Oh, for God's sake!' said Roy.

Fran was sympathetic and she also wanted to giggle. It was nerves, she knew, but she also knew she mustn't give in to them.

It was hard to tell what Mr Addison's conversation was about, as only one side of it was audible and he was monosyllabic. It seemed ages before he ended the call.

'Sorry about that,' he said.

'It's unprofessional to take personal calls in the middle of a business meeting,' said Roy.

'Indeed,' Mr Addison agreed, 'but that was about some test results for a family member. It was personal, but important.'

'Not acceptable!' said Roy. 'You're holding things up here.'

'Actually, so are you, Roy,' said Fran. She smiled at Mr Addison, who did seem a bit embarrassed, but also pleased. 'I hope the results were good?' she added.

'They were perfect, thank you,' he said. 'Now, getting back to the matter in hand. *To my husband's distant cousin from Australia, Roy Jones, because he's always expressed such a deep love for the farm, I leave—*'

Fran clenched everything, including Antony's hand, which she found in hers although she didn't remember holding it.

'*—the picture of the farm that hangs over the fireplace.*'

Everyone exhaled at the same time. Of course it didn't mean Roy hadn't got the farm, it just meant Amy was keeping everyone on tenterhooks a little longer.

'I don't want a crappy painting!' said Roy disgustedly.

'We all know what you want,' said Tig. 'If you keep quiet you may find out if you're going to get it.'

Mr Addison cleared his throat. 'I'm reading Amy's words now:

'I had a very hard job deciding who to leave the farm to. It's been in my husband's family for many generations, going from father to son or in some instances to a nephew. It's never been left to a woman, although I myself ran it for many years. It has not been easy to decide who should have it now.'

'Couldn't you cut to the chase?' Roy spat out the words. 'I have an important meeting to go to directly after this.'

'You're all right, Roy,' said Tig, the only one who knew his fate. 'The pubs will stay open for hours longer.'

'Please, Roy! Stop interrupting!' said Fran.

'Maybe I should point out that the bulk of this was written shortly after Roy came to England,' said Mr Addison. 'Mrs Flowers made several amendments to her will quite recently.'

'She liked to change her will,' said Mrs Jenkins. 'She called it fine-tuning. Mr Addison was always in and out.'

Fran bit her lip. This probably meant that Roy was definitely going to inherit.

'Perhaps we could press on?' suggested Antony, sounding polite and businesslike in contrast to Roy's impatience.

'You're mentioned, Mr Arlingham,' said Mrs Jenkins, blushing slightly as she addressed Antony.

'Really?' Antony expressed everyone else's amazement. 'But Mrs Flowers had no time for my family. You could even say she hated us.'

'She changed her mind,' said Mrs Jenkins. 'Mr Addison? Why not read out the bit referring to Mr Arlingham?'

Roy was visibly biting his tongue. Fran was less desperate. She felt fairly certain that Roy was going to get the farm and while she wanted to know for sure, she could wait. She was so delighted about Tig's inheritance that her own had become less important to her. At least Tig having the bull and some heifers meant the bloodline of the herd would survive and he and Issi could plan for the future.

'She says…' Mr Addison referred to his papers, obviously looking for the place. *'I have changed my long-held opinion of Mr Arlingham and no longer have any objection if he wishes to marry Francesca.'*

Fran looked at the table and Antony held her hand tightly. 'Well, that's good news, isn't it?' he said.

As Antony and she hadn't discussed marriage, per se, Fran felt desperately embarrassed. But also extremely happy.

'I am trying to be patient,' said Roy, perspiring with the effort of keeping his temper, 'but could we please get on?'

'Maybe we should put the poor man out of his misery,' said Mrs Jenkins.

Something in the way she looked at Roy gave Fran a flicker of hope.

'Very well,' said Mr Addison, 'but I do have to read everything she said. Mrs Flowers was very insistent that I do so.'

Roy made a sound that was a combination of a groan and a sigh.

Mr Addison obviously felt that Roy had suffered enough:

'Over the past weeks I've had an opportunity to get to know the two young relatives I wrote to last year, looking for the right heir to Hill Top Farm. The decision I have made will be considered controversial by many but in order to help me decide which of them should take on the responsibility of my land and my precious herd, I set a little test.'

Everyone sat up and paid even more attention. Fran's heart was beginning to race.

Mr Addison went on. *'I decided that the relative most dedicated to the farm and most interested in its survival would find the quarry in which cheese was traditionally ripened. Sadly, neither one has found this special spot.'*

'But you did!' Issi broke in urgently. 'Fran found the quarry, everyone.'

'Sadly, not before this was written,' said Mr Addison, looking sympathetic and a little sad.

'Please go on,' whispered Fran.

'Very well,' said Mr Addison. *'Therefore I have had to make my decision based on other things. I wish to leave the farm, the remains of the herd and all my effects not previously left to others, to Francesca—'*

Fran didn't hear the rest of the minor details. She felt hot, then cold and then slightly sick.

'I do not believe this!' shouted Roy. 'Give me the will!' He snatched it and frantically scanned the lines of type. Then he threw the will on to the table with an expletive. He strode out of the room, knocking into chairs and the end of the table before he pulled open the door and slammed it hard after he left.

There was a relieved silence and then Issi jumped up from her seat and went round to Fran. 'Well done! This is amazing. I'm so thrilled for you!'

The others joined in the congratulations but Fran just felt numb. This was all she'd been hoping for, ever since Amy had died. She'd been desperate to keep the farm away from Roy, who'd threatened it in every way, from trying to sell the cows to wanting to sell off the land for building. But now she knew it was hers she couldn't feel anything except a vast weight of responsibility.

'Well,' she said eventually, when she realised everyone was looking at her oddly, 'it means I can turn my Cheddar in the quarry every day for a while!'

Everyone laughed and hugged and patted her and said well done. Then it was time to go.

When all the goodbyes and thank yous had been said, Mrs Jenkins put her hand on her arm. 'Amy was very fond of you, you know. She didn't always show her feelings but she trusted you. Even if you hadn't found the quarry, she knew you wanted the best for the farm, and the herd. She knew you wouldn't let her down.'

Fran bit her lip to keep back the tears. 'Thank you,' she croaked. 'Thank you for telling me.'

*

Fran felt obliged to go back to Amy's wake, which was still going strong in the village hall. Partly because there were people she hadn't had a chance to talk to – or rather who hadn't had a chance to talk to her – and partly because she knew everyone was desperate to know what had happened to the farm.

Issi had offered to go with her but Fran knew she and Tig wanted to be on their own. Now, Tig would have his own cows, and with Fran as the owner of Hill Top he would still look after the remaining cows. He and Issi were safe and Fran knew they wanted to go back to their little cottage – properly theirs now – and celebrate.

Antony went back with Fran though. He seemed very pleased with himself too and although there hadn't been a chance to ask him about it, Fran wondered if knowing that Amy no longer disapproved of him had pleased him and that the old enmity between the two farms was finally over.

The hall was still buzzing with conversation. Fran had provided sherry, wine and beer and tongues were loosened; everyone was really enjoying themselves.

'My goodness, there's a lot of food still,' said Fran to Mary, who came up the moment she appeared. 'Have you heard from Tig?'

'Yes! He phoned as soon as he was out of the solicitor's office. Such a relief! But I knew Mrs Flowers would see him right and it was kind of her to give him some land as well.' Mary paused. 'You don't mind about that? It's not a big farm.'

'Not at all. The farm depends on Tig. I'd rather lose all the land than lose Tig.'

Mary laughed, delighted. 'And that friend of yours? Issi? She's a lovely girl, just right for my Tig.' She put a hand on Fran's arm. 'You brought good things to the farm when you came down here.'

Fran was moved. 'Oh, thank you so much. I'm so pleased you feel like that.'

Mary nodded. 'Now, come and eat something. I reckon everyone who came brought a cake with them and only ate one slice, or a plate of sandwiches and only ate a couple.'

'What will happen to all this food?' Fran suddenly felt responsible for this minor food mountain as well as the farm.

'Oh, don't you go worrying about the leftovers. We can see to them,' said Mary. 'So? Are you pleased? About the farm coming to you?'

'I'm delighted – so relieved!' said Fran. 'But I am very surprised.'

Mary shook her head. 'It was just as Amy's old friends expected, dear. She was no fool. She knew who had the interests of the farm at heart. That awful man! Always at the pub! She knew everything. She'd enough visitors to tell her what she couldn't see with her own eyes. Now, shall I make up a nice little picnic for you and Mr Arlingham?'

'Er – that would be very kind.'

'It would indeed, Mrs Brown,' said Antony. 'And as you do seem very well informed you probably know that the bad feeling between Hill Top Farm and Park House Farm is now officially over?'

'I did know that, yes. She told me how kind you'd been to her, taking her all over the farm in one of those fancy motorbikes with four wheels?'

'A quad bike?' said Antony.

'That's it. She loved that, she did, seeing her farm for the last time. Not that she knew it was the last time, of course.'

'I was worried about her seeing what we'd done to the house,' said Fran. 'She had told me she didn't mind but people can feel differently when they actually see it.'

'She didn't have time to fuss about her house,' said Mrs Brown. 'She spent all her energy on the farm. That's what she cared about. And that's why she left it to you, and not Roy. She trusted you and my Tig to look after it for the future.'

When Fran and Antony left a little while later, laden with ice-cream containers full of sandwiches, sausage rolls and slices of cake, Fran said, 'It's a lot of responsibility, isn't it? The farm, I mean. When I came here I was to look after it for a year and make it profitable. I haven't been here more than five minutes really, but even if my hard cheese turns out to be amazing, can cheese on its own keep a farm going these days?'

Antony shifted the bags of food he was carrying so he could take her arm. 'Don't worry. It's been a very long and emotional day. You have the farm and you have me – both with Amy's blessing. Let's go home. To our home!'

Fran smiled up at him, awash with love and relief. 'Such simple words that mean so much.'

Chapter Twenty-Six

Issy came up the next morning for coffee and found Fran outside, staring at the view in the sunshine.

'It is amazingly beautiful, isn't it?' said Fran. While she was truly appreciating the perfection of the morning, gazing out over the valleys, a trail of mist adding an extra layer of beauty and mystery, she was missing Antony terribly. He had left her early and although she was used to him having to go away she wished this morning he could have stayed a bit longer.

'It is beautiful. And now it's all yours!' said Issi.

Fran laughed. 'Well, not quite all. But at least it won't be covered in houses now.'

'I wonder if it would have got planning permission? I mean, if Amy managed to stop it being ploughed up in the war, surely it's too steep for houses?'

Fran shrugged. 'I'm sure we could find out if we had a mind to but maybe it's better not to know?'

Possibly sensing Fran's melancholy, Issi tried to brighten the mood. 'Did Roy come back for his things last night?'

Fran shrugged. 'I don't think so, but it's possible.' She blushed a little.

'You mean you and Antony were having a special cuddle?'

This coy expression made Fran smile and she pushed her friend quite hard.

Issi pushed Fran back. 'Come on, let's make coffee and check on Roy's room. Oh, and I brought the post up. There's masses.'

As they walked through the house to the kitchen, Fran said, 'I expect you and Tig were celebrating, too?'

'Planning, more.' Issi paused. 'He asked me to marry him.'

'Oh, Is! That's amazing, congratulations!'

'Well, when I say he asked me to marry him, what he actually said was: "I suppose we'd better make it official between us, if you're up for it."'

Fran laughed. It was such a Tig way of putting it. 'And did you say you were up for it?'

Issi shrugged. 'Eventually. I made him say it a bit more clearly first though. We haven't told anyone yet. He's going to tell Mary at lunchtime. I'll give my mother a call in a minute. She's going to be so thrilled. The prospect of grandchildren at last.'

'Oh, planning a family already?'

Issi blushed. 'Maybe. I mean, eventually, yes, but not this instant. I'd like to get my PhD first. Now, I'll put the kettle on. Have you had breakfast?'

'I had a bit of toast with Antony but that was hours ago.' Fran leafed through the pile of post, most of which seemed to be letters of condolence.

'I'll make some more toast then. I could do with a second breakfast.'

'Oh, I wonder why!' said Fran, keeping up her teasing for a second before going back to sorting letters. 'Hey! Here's an official-looking one for Roy.'

'Open it then,' said Issi.

'Should I? It's not addressed to me.'

'Did he leave a forwarding address? Or just his dirty washing?' Issi was dismissive of Fran's qualms.

'I don't know.'

Issi sighed impatiently. 'Let's go and see if he's left any sort of forwarding details. If he has, we don't open it, but if he's just scarpered, we do, OK?'

'Why exactly are you so keen to see that letter?'

'Because it's from the planning office! Didn't you see the envelope? You're not really on it this morning, Fran. Although I suppose you've been busy.' She smiled at her vast understatement.

'Let's check Roy's room and then I promise I'll tamper with the post.'

His room looked like a student had got up late for a lecture and just run. The bed was unmade and there were dirty clothes on the floor and on the chair. The wardrobe was empty – possibly he'd never really unpacked.

'If you'd been renting him a room you could have refused to give him his deposit back,' said Issi.

'You're right. I will open the letter. After all, it's the planning office so it must be about my farm.' She gave a little squeak of pleasure. 'My farm. Think of that!'

'Come on. Coffee, toast and that letter.'

Fran sat at the table and slit open the letter with a knife. It was long and closely typed. 'Well, I think it's good news,' she said at last. 'For me, that is, not Roy. Planning has been rejected on most of the site.'

'Can I see?' said Issi, obviously itching to get her hands on the letter. When she'd read all the jargon and provisos, she looked at Fran. 'Interesting. You can have a change of use for most of the farm build-ings.'

'I know. Including my cheese room! Bloody cheek.' Fran reached for the Marmite. 'I must turn the cheese that's in the quarry later. I would have been so sad and fed up if I hadn't been able to do that.'

Issi crunched thoughtfully for a few seconds. 'I have to say, Fran, I thought you'd be jumping for joy a lot more about inheriting the farm.'

'I am jumping for joy,' Fran said flatly, 'in my heart. But I am worried. It's a lot of responsibility and I don't want to let Amy down.'

'But you've been running it for a while now and you'll still have Tig for the cows. He's not going to abandon you. What's different?'

'It hasn't really been paying its way, has it?' said Fran. 'I mean my hard cheese could really take off but will it really earn enough money? I'm hoping there's enough money in Amy's estate to pay off the bank loan but she was running the farm at a loss for years. I'm at least adding value to the milk cheque but – well, I don't really think it's ever going to be enough.'

Issi put her hand on her friend's.

Fran sighed. 'When I said all this to Antony last night, he said something that indicated he didn't think it would make money either. I have to do something else to keep it going. Otherwise, like Roy said, annoyingly, I'll have to keep selling off little bits, like the stone tiles off the outbuildings. Eventually it would just be a farmhouse in a truly magnificent position.'

'Beautifully done up with Antony's money,' suggested Issi.

'I don't want that, Is! I want to pay my way. Antony is truly the most wonderful man, in so many very important ways, but he'd be a bit easier to love if he wasn't so rich.'

'Fran? Are you feeling OK? He's gorgeous, really nice, good and kind and well off, and you're complaining?'

Fran laughed. 'I'm not really complaining. Far from it. I feel incredibly lucky, but I want to pay my way in the relationship. He's giving up a lot to be with me. He's agreed we'll live here, for example, and I know he'd let me spend money on the house – and God knows it does need money. I've no idea what the real state of it is, but I expect it's got a lot wrong with it we're just not aware of. It could be a money pit. I need to make it profitable, not a drain on Antony.'

'I do understand,' said Issi after a few moments' thought. 'Actually...'

'What? You've got an almost visible thought bubble coming out of your head.'

'Ever since I've known you, before this farming lark came up, you've wanted to run a restaurant. Why not run one here?'

Fran bit her lip to help her think. 'Would people come here for a restaurant?'

'They came for the supper club. And I could help with marketing. I think people would love to come up to this gorgeous spot.'

'But only in summer, surely? Would they come all the way up here in winter?'

'I think so! We know for ourselves that the views in winter are just as good – as long as it's not raining and you can see a blessed thing.' She paused. 'And the food will be amazing too. Destination dining! I'm sure it's a thing!'

'And' – suddenly Fran was squeaking with excitement, all melancholy gone – 'thanks to Roy, we could put the restaurant in the barn. If we made one wall glass, our guests could eat and look at the view!'

'You mean because the planners have already agreed to "change of use" they'd agree to it being a restaurant?' asked Issi.

'I hope so! Obviously it's a big project and will cost loads...'

'I suppose we could ask if Antony can be an investor—'

'In what?' said Antony, coming into the kitchen.

Fran's heart leapt with joy. 'What are you doing here?' She jumped up to hug him.

'I cancelled all my meetings and took the day off so I could come back and be with you,' he said, kissing the top of her head. 'I thought you were probably feeling a bit weird about things.'

'I was feeling very wobbly.' She smiled at him. 'I feel better now!' He looked back at her, his love for her shining out, and she knew that while she had his love, she didn't need anything else. But she also had a farm she had to make profitable. She took a breath. 'I think Issi may have found the solution to my problems.'

'Well done, Issi. What was the problem and what is the solution?'

'I need to make the farm profitable. As you well know,' said Fran, rolling her eyes at him.

Issi broke in. 'Fran's going to open a restaurant in the barn. But she may need you to invest in the project.'

'A restaurant? Here?' He thought for a few seconds. 'I once went to a restaurant in Scotland you had to drive miles to. It was full every night it was open, apparently.'

'So you think it might work?' asked Fran.

The expression in his eyes told Fran that he had other things on his mind for Fran apart from restaurants and investments. 'I do. I think you could really make a go of it. You could use it to market your cheese, too.'

'I could really help with that,' Issi said again, for Antony's benefit. 'It's my thing, sort of, apart from my PhD.'

'And,' Fran said, 'Roy has kindly applied for change of use for the barn and got it. Obviously we'd have to reapply to make it a restaurant but this could be the solution.'

'It could. You will need to do something else to get Hill Top back on its feet. And I'll help you in every way I can.'

Fran put her arms round his neck and pulled his head down so she could kiss him again.

'Now, Fran,' he said when she'd finished. 'Let's go and look at this quarry. I feel I should know where it is.'

'Oh, can't I show you later when I turn the cheese? I want to plan my restaurant.'

'Show me now. It's important,' Antony insisted.

'But, Antony—'

Issi laughed. 'I think you should go right now,' she said. 'Antony wants to talk to you in private.'

'It's quite a steep climb,' said Antony. 'It explains why no one found it before.'

'I wouldn't have found it if it hadn't been for the calf getting separated from its mum. I had to really conquer my fear of cows to get them back together. I told Amy. I think she liked it.'

Antony took hold of her hand. 'Come on, let's pull each other up.'

'Do you really want to look at the quarry?' Fran said.

'Not really. I'd rather look at you.'

'Seriously?'

'I've got something I want to talk to you about.'

Fran's heart sank a bit. 'That sounds rather serious.'

'I hope it's good-serious.' Antony stopped and as Fran did too, he put his hand on her cheek. 'It's to do with what Amy said.'

'About what?' Fran looked up at him, this strong man she loved so much.

'I'm not very good at emotional stuff. I'm better in a boardroom. But Amy said she withdrew her objection to us getting together. It meant she wanted us to get married. I want us to, as well.'

'Are you asking me to marry you?' said Fran, thinking how annoying men could be, even while they were being wonderful.

'Yes.' He put his hand in his pocket. 'One of the things I had to do this morning was to collect this. Of course you can change it – you might prefer something more elaborate—'

Smiling, and very happy, Fran put her finger on Antony's lips. 'Why don't you show me?'

He opened the little leather box. Inside was a simple gold ring with a large rectangular diamond.

'My goodness,' said Fran, suddenly short of breath. 'It's the size of a Glacier Mint!'

He laughed and relaxed. 'No it's not! Try it on. Do you like it?'

Seeing the diamond on her finger, simple but enormous, made her heart flutter. It suddenly made everything real. 'I love it,' she said. Then she looked up at him again, suddenly shy and a bit embarrassed. 'But you mustn't ask me to marry you just because you think it was what Amy wanted.'

He kissed her again. 'I'm asking you to marry me because I love you. And before you ask why – I'm sure you're going to ask why – it's because you're beautiful and brave, funny and sexy, determined and full of initiative. And also very slightly afraid of cows.'

Fran gazed up at him. 'Would you still love me if I stopped being afraid of cows?'

'Only the tiniest little bit. Not enough to matter.'

She reached up to kiss him again and as her arms went round his neck she realised how blissfully happy she was. At the start of the year she'd had a farm she didn't own and didn't know what to do with. Now it was really hers, she had plans and it had a future. And she had a man she truly loved by her side.

It was more than anyone deserved and she couldn't possibly have been happier.

Epilogue

Fran was nervous. Although she was looking around at the stragglers from Sunday lunch, all enjoying the warm summer day, having very much savoured their meal (home-reared pork, courtesy of Tig), for once it wasn't the diners whose approval she craved, it was the special guests.

She smiled at herself. All the guests were special, of course, but there were a few among the family and friends who had filled her restaurant that day who were there to be critical.

They weren't restaurant critics either. More than a year had passed since Amy had left Hill Top Farm to her and by now 'Flowers' had already had enough favourable reviews to make sure they were full every time they were open. Fran had a good team behind her and Issi was brilliant on social media. People knew they had to book up well in advance to eat at Hill Top Farm.

From habit, she was looking about her now, even though service had been over for a while, to make sure everything was perfect – and thanks to Seb, it was.

Seb had turned into a great part-time maître d'. As the restaurant was only open at weekends and Bank Holidays this sideline fitted in well with his day job as Antony's driver.

Seb had made sure that every occupied table had jugs of water and he had already taken home some of the elderly locals. There was a group of people who had taken to coming to the restaurant on the farm of their old friend Amy and it was Seb who brought them and took them home. While providing a free taxi service wasn't economic, no one questioned it. The old people got together once a month or so and had a good meal too.

No, it was the group still sitting at the long table in the middle of the restaurant, the table with the best view, that Fran was feeling twitchy about.

It was her fault they were there. She'd invited them. There was her old boss Roger, who had bought all her soft cheese when he tasted it at the farmers' market. There was Erica, who had the market stall, and Mary, Tig's mother, who had both helped her make her first hard cheese just after Amy had died. There was John Radcliffe, boss of the big cheese retailer in Fitzrovia who had told her she had to make hard cheese. Also

Gideon Irving, a food and wine guru, and his wife, Zoe, the famous TV chef.

Also present were Gideon and Zoe's good friends Fenella and Rupert Gainsborough, who were staying with Gideon and Zoe. Their various children were playing together on the specially constructed hay bales, supervised by Issi and Tig. Issi was heavily pregnant, looking radiant and obviously hoping to get a bit of practice in childcare before her own baby was born.

Fran's mother and stepfather were also there, on the same big table. They were embarrassingly proud of their daughter and adored their son-in-law-to-be, who was currently checking everyone had enough coffee, tea, red wine or brandy. June and Jack were there paying special attention to Betsy, the young dog that now belonged to Fran. Antony had given Betsy to her as a birthday present and she had turned out to be a wonderful dog, if possibly a little over-indulged by Fran. Betsy was currently chewing the table leg.

Fran caught Antony's eye and he left the group and came over. He stood behind her, putting his arms round her and pulling her to him. She leant her head against his chest. 'I don't think you can put it off any longer, darling.'

Zoe Irving also came over. She smiled very sympathetically at Fran. 'You must be dreadfully nervous, having to wait all this time to find out about the cheese.'

Fran nodded. It was kind of Zoe to be sympathetic, especially as she was so well known as a TV chef.

'I desperately want it to be good for Amy,' she said. 'I feel it represents all her years of hard work, of keeping the pasture intact, unploughed, original. And the herd, too. Generations of beasts with pedigrees better than anything you'd see on *Who Do You Think You Are?*' She paused. 'They're "original population" you see, so hugely important.'

Tig and Issi came up.

'Tig here has been vital in keeping it all going,' went on Fran to Zoe. 'I couldn't have done any of it without him.'

'So?' said Antony. 'It's the moment of truth. Let's taste the cheese.'

Fifteen minutes later people were still clapping Fran on the back and opening bottles of champagne. The foodie people wanted to buy all she could make, Erica wanted it for the farmers' market and Tig just wanted it in his sandwiches.

'Well done, darling!' said Antony, hugging her. 'I knew you could do it.'

'It's not me, it's the milk, the herd, the farm!' Fran said to the group gathered round her. 'But I am delighted. It means I haven't let Amy down. I was the right person to leave Hill Top Farm to.'

'Even if you are afraid of cows,' added Tig with a grin.

Fran looked at him, wishing she could say she wasn't still a bit unnerved by the huge beasts who were so important to her.

'Only a bit,' she said and sipped her champagne.

UR.